D0729463

The
Magnificent
Marquess

Gail Eastwood

A SIGNET BOOK

SIGNET
Published by the Penguin Group
Penguin Putnam Inc., 375 Hudson Street,
New York, New York 10014, U.S.A.
Penguin Books Ltd, 27 Wrights Lane,
London W8 5TZ, England
Penguin Books Australia Ltd, Ringwood,
Victoria, Australia
Penguin Books (N.Z.) Ltd, 182–190 Wairau Road,
Auckland 10, New Zealand

Penguin Books Ltd, Registered Offices:
Harmondsworth, Middlesex, England

First published by Signet, an imprint of Dutton NAL,
a member of Penguin Putnam Inc.

First Printing, August, 1998
10 9 8 7 6 5 4 3 2 1

To my husband Ralph,
for all the best reasons
(and especially because
"you-know-who" did it . . .)

I love you!

Chapter One

The summons to dinner was heaven-sent, Mariah Parbury decided, despite its quite ordinary delivery through Bennett, her family's purely mortal butler. Even five more minutes spent in the same agonizing fashion as the last forty-five would surely have been too much for anyone to bear.

The problem was not that the new Marquess of Milbourne had dominated all conversation for the past three-quarters of an hour. In Mariah's estimation that was more than justified. His exotic tales of India made her feel as if a brilliant light had burst into the grayness of her life, suddenly revealing just how dull it truly was. The agony had been in watching her family fawn over the man, feigning interest in his stories while in actuality their eyes were glazing over.

No audible sigh of gratitude issued from the company collected in the Parburys' pale blue London drawing room, but a new energy infused the little party as it began to gather itself up into a procession for dinner. Mariah happily abandoned the straight chair that had been her seat and whose carved back had by now left an imprint of every curved line upon her own. However, her sense of relief was cut short by the sight of her sister Cassandra bearing down upon her with a look as purposeful as that of a sheepdog singling out a lamb.

"Mariah, do you not think the marquess is the most *magnificent* gentleman you have ever seen?" Cassie murmured, grasping Mariah's arm and drawing her aside. " 'Tis simply criminal that his conversation should be, well, so *suffocatingly tedious*!"

Mariah looked about warily. "Cassie, hush! What a thing to say! Suppose he should hear you?"

But her caution met only a giggle and a bounce of flaxen curls. Sixteen-year-old Cassie was not known for her good judgment.

"I doubt he can hear anything, with Rorie and Georgie on either side of him and Mama busy telling everyone where they should be!"

Their mother's penetrating tones could mask louder comments than theirs, it was true. Under the cover of her most brilliant smile, Lady Parbury was attempting to correct her son in the doorway as the group prepared to descend the stairs.

"William, since Aurora is the eldest, the marquess must escort her, and you take down your sister Georgina." The baroness nodded benignly as the young gentleman in question moved to comply, but as he passed her she nudged him and added in a disappointed undertone, "You *must* pay attention to these matters, William! You're a grown man."

If only their mother would learn to be less obvious! In many households, the marquess would have escorted Lady Parbury herself, but in this instance the baroness had another quite specific scheme in mind. Mariah sighed.

Their guest was stunningly attractive—Cassie's "magnificent" was perhaps a bit overstated, but Mariah could agree that "handsome" quite failed to do him justice. He was single, reportedly as rich as Croesus, and obviously a prime target for every marriage-minded female in London. In India he had become known as the "Lion of Lampur" and he quite looked the part.

He was a giant of a man—nearly a head taller than William and so broad-shouldered that his coat of claret superfine strained to fit him properly. Unusual golden amber eyes nearly matched the tawny shade of his hair. Mariah imagined that his lazy-lidded gaze could sharpen into a predatory stare upon an instant's provocation. His face showed the patrician lines of his Austrian forebears, with well-defined cheekbones, a straight, narrow nose, and a sculptural curve to his upper lip that she found fascinating.

His skin, while obviously fair, seemed kissed by just enough sun to render it golden, too—as if he himself had been touched by the riches of the exotic land he had so recently quit. He exuded an air of raw animal power that certainly matched his nickname. How Mariah would have loved to ask how he had come by it!

It was exhilarating to meet someone who had led such an exciting life, so different from the endless parade of uneventful days that characterized her own existence, at least as it seemed to her now. How could her family be so uninterested in anything so captivating? Mariah had hung on his every word, thirsty for his knowledge of mysterious places and scarcely able to tear her eyes away from him. She might have made a great cake of herself had there been the remotest chance of anyone noticing her. However, she had been discouraged from asking questions herself and she was not the sort of young woman for whom being noticed was generally a problem.

"'Tis inconceivable how every possible topic leads back to his life in India," Cassie whispered. "If I have to hear one more story about Hindu rituals or gold mining in Lampur, I shall get up on the dining table and scream!" Fortunately for all of London society, Cassie had not yet made her comeout. She was the sort much more likely to be noticed.

"Come along, girls," their mother called back from halfway down the grand stairs. Her voice sounded artificially bright.

Mariah sighed again and gave Cassandra a warning look. "Behave, Cassie, or Mother will never forgive you." *Neither will I,* she added to herself as they descended after the others. Wasn't the evening already in danger of becoming a disaster?

In the dining room, everyone else had taken places at the table by the time the two stragglers trailed in. With its soft green walls and white plasterwork, the room always struck Mariah as rather like a Wedgwood box turned outside in. A massive pier glass and gilded side table to match it occupied the center of one long wall, and the room's heavily ornamented chimneypiece and hearth occupied the other. Over-

head an impressive twenty-four-light chandelier glittered
with dozens of crystal pendants, shining down softly upon a
groaning table loaded with the Parbury's best silver.

Their father stood by his chair at the head of the gleaming
table with his wife at the opposite end. William and the marquess were placed at center on either side, where daughters
of the house could flank them right and left. Another obvious strategy! There were only eight at table for the meal—
just family and the guest of honor. Mariah gave thanks that
at least her mother had refrained from inviting half of the
Beau Monde to join them simply to witness Lord Milbourne's presence there.

His attendance did not strike Mariah as so very remarkable, despite her mother's pride in this accomplishment.
Reinhart Maycott and William had met as students at Harrow, soon after Maycott's first arrival from India. They had
managed to maintain a friendship ever since, bridging the
intervening years and the thousands of miles between England and India that eventually separated them. Maycott, now
Lord Milbourne, had only recently—and quite unexpectedly—come into his grandfather's title. He had returned to
England barely six weeks ago and had been using his time
since then to settle his affairs.

What must it be like to be suddenly thrust back into England after spending most of one's life in a foreign land?
Mariah supposed it might have been lonely, if the marquess
had been anyone else. But of course, the *ton* had embraced
him in an instant—rather, besieged him like bees after
honey. Who could resist the heady combination of high rank
and vast wealth in such a wondrously handsome package?
Perhaps "magnificent" was the proper word for him, after
all.

"Please, do let us *all* sit down," said Lady Parbury, star-
tling Mariah out of her thoughts.

Glancing around guiltily, she realized the others had sat
down. Only she and Lord Milbourne were still standing as
he politely waited for her to take the seat beside her. As she
dropped into it hastily, she caught his image reflected in the
pier glass on the wall opposite them. It *would* so happen that

both of them should have seats facing it! How would she keep from stealing glances at him in it all through the meal? She looked away quickly, mortified, as she realized he was returning her gaze. He looked bemused. If she did not get herself in hand this meal might not be such an improvement over the previous time as she had hoped!

The thought of the meal restored her spirit, at any rate. The table was crowded with twice the usual number of covers, and tantalizing, exotic aromas filled the room. There had been a bit of commotion when the marquess had first arrived, and now Mariah thought she guessed why. Curiosity and delight replaced her self-consciousness.

"It is a bit of a departure from the usual way of doing things, but Lord Milbourne has brought with him tonight a number of dishes prepared by his own cook to supplement our table," her mother announced, confirming the guess. "I'm afraid I must leave it to him to direct us and explain things." The tight smile on Lady Parbury's face concealed what Mariah knew must be considerable chagrin. What a scene there had probably been in the kitchen!

"I thought you might enjoy the opportunity to sample some of the native fare I am accustomed to eating in India," the marquess said. His voice was deep and resonant and touched a chord somewhere inside Mariah, causing a tiny ripple of pleasure to run through her, quite as if he had physically touched her.

Ridiculous! She must stop this. She was responding to him like the worst moonstruck ninny. If that became obvious to their guest, it would be just as embarrassing as if he had overheard the comments whispered behind his back or realized the lack of interest her sisters had in his stories. But Mariah was interested. She sat up a little straighter in her chair.

"What a novel idea, Lord Milbourne!" her father said diplomatically. "I'm certain we should all be delighted to taste what you have brought." Normally taciturn, Lord Parbury commanded everyone's attention when he spoke, since it happened so rarely. He directed a look at Mariah's sisters that could only be interpreted as an order.

Watching the interactions around the table, Mariah witnessed a quickly exchanged smirk that passed between her brother and the marquess. Suspicion blossomed in the back of her mind. Had they planned all of this evening in advance? What devils! Yet, how like William. Perhaps it was cruel to put their mother through such paces, but Mariah could not help thinking that perhaps the lady had earned it. The fuss she was making over the marquess since his elevation to the title and his return to England was a marked contrast to the decided lack of interest she had shown in him in the days when William and plain Mr. Maycott, son of a youngest son, had been friends at school. If this was all intended as a lark, Mariah could appreciate the spirit of the joke. She would have to speak with William later. She glanced at the candlelit tableau reflected in the pier glass and smiled.

"What I have brought you is simply a representative sampling of typical dishes, some from the south of India, some from the north," the marquess was saying. Mariah could mark no sign of the fleeting smirk from moments before—indeed, Lord Milbourne appeared gracious and perfectly sincere.

"In India we might begin the meal with some sweets, but since all this is intended merely as a prelude to the fine dinner your kitchen has created for us, Lord and Lady Parbury, the order in which the dishes are tasted does not really matter. We have here some lamb *biryani*, chicken *tandoori*, and a goat curry, which are commonly eaten among the landowning classes."

As he nodded and pointed to the individual dishes, the footmen on either side of the table removed the gleaming silver covers, releasing waves of deliciously spicy steam. Mariah loved the way the exotic names rolled off his tongue so easily. The sound of them combined with the unfamiliar scents excited her imagination and carried her to far-off places. Cassie, however, brought her crashing back to the reality of the dinner table by making a face at her and mouthing "goat curry?" with an expression clearly combining disbelief with disgust.

Mariah frowned at her severely. What if the marquess happened to notice Cassie's reaction? She prayed that Aurora, seated on the other side of him, was doing her best to catch and hold the man's attention. After all, that was precisely what their mother had in mind.

"There are a number of side dishes and condiments that I suggest you try along with these," Lord Milbourne continued smoothly. "Several chutneys, and rice. There are three types of wheat bread in that silver basket—you'll find them very different, I think, especially the *poori*."

He stopped and looked around the table. Mariah thanked the stars that Cassie wasn't making a face just now! "Who will be the first to try a taste?"

The ensuing moment of silence was painful. Everyone was waiting for someone else to speak first. Mariah could not believe that neither one of her parents leapt into the breach.

"I will try some of the goat curry," she said clearly, causing everyone at the table to look at her. No doubt she had astonished them. She smiled bravely and cast a knowing glance at Cassandra. Then her gaze strayed to the pier glass, where she caught Lord Milbourne with that amused expression on his face again. Resolutely she picked up her spoon and turned to him. "I must assume you recommend it?"

"Yes, of course," he answered, smiling.

"I will try that and then a bit of everything," Mariah said, resolutely ignoring that enchanting smile and feeling quite pleased with herself. She noticed how large and strong his hands looked as he passed the dish to her. She took a heaping spoonful.

Rorie asked for a taste then, as if she was reluctant to let the focus of attention shift, and other voices spoke up after her. Mariah was free to experience the goat curry quite privately. She took a large mouthful and held it on her tongue, thinking to savor this anticipated new taste.

Hellfire! Her mouth was burning up! Tears sprang into her eyes and she barely managed not to spit. Chewing for only a moment and then choking down the food in a great gulp to get it off her tongue, she merely spread the burning sensation down into her throat. Gasping quietly, she reached for her wineglass.

A large, strong hand intercepted hers. "I think you may have taken a bit too much at once," Lord Milbourne said kindly. "Here, let me give you some of the *raita*—it is made from soothing cucumber and yogurt and will help more than wine."

How had he noticed? He released her hand and spooned some of the creamy pale condiment onto her plate, obviously unaware that his touch had set her hand on fire, too. Everyone else was looking again, and Mariah felt like the world's worst fool.

"I should have cautioned you," the marquess said apologetically. "The dishes are very spicy to a palate unused to them. Be sure to take a bite of rice or bread, or one of the cooling condiments, in between very small tastes, to begin." He hesitated, turning his golden gaze upon her as if to make certain she was all right. "I should have been watching you," he added softly.

Mariah was not sure what to make of that remark. She suspected that somehow he must have been watching. At any rate, such concern coming from him nearly took her breath away. "Not at all, sir," she managed to say, not quite completely held spellbound by his eyes. "Apparently I should have been less eager."

The rest of the meal proceeded less eventfully. It seemed that all of the diners except Mariah were taking infinitesimal bites and generally trying to create an impression of enthusiasm without actually having to eat very much of the Indian food. Mariah discovered that she liked it, once she learned the proper approach. After the exotic, almost erotic tastes and textures of those dishes, however, she found the food her mother had so carefully ordered to honor the marquess all tasted very bland indeed.

As for the conversation, it proceeded much as it had before dinner, although Lady Parbury made valiant attempts to direct it into more mundane channels.

"Do you go to Lady Summersley's ball on Friday next, Lord Milbourne?"

"Have you made plans yet to visit your estate in Sussex?"

"You have applied for vouchers for Almack's, have you not? You must have already met the patronesses."

His responses tended to be monosyllabic when he was not discussing India. Mariah attempted to interject a few questions, asking, for instance, about the restrictions that various religious beliefs placed on the Indian diet, but these efforts were so frowned on by her mother, she dutifully lapsed back into the role of frustrated but interested observer.

After the meal the ladies and the men separated, according to the usual custom. Upstairs again in the drawing room, Mariah wished she could be an invisible eavesdropper in the library below, taking in the enlightened conversation she imagined she was missing between Lord Milbourne and her father and brother. Why was it that women were not expected to be interested in the same things that interested men? There was so much that Lord Milbourne could tell her! So much of what she'd read in books and newspaper accounts about the Hindustan seemed too fantastic to believe.

Meanwhile, Lady Parbury paced about and fussed over the fate of her dinner party. "Can you imagine having the gall to bring your own food when invited to dinner? Cook was horribly insulted! What I went through to calm her down, you can hardly imagine. And such food! Why, Lady Eggleston served a curry at her dinner for Lord Bromfield last month and it was nothing like what we ate tonight!"

"More to do with her cook than the curry," Georgina murmured so that only Mariah could hear.

Mariah chuckled. Georgie, the quietest of the four sisters, was her favorite and the one to whom she felt closest. They often shared a similar perspective, even if Georgie did not frequently voice hers. At the moment, Georgie's was a voice of reason in a room singularly lacking in that commodity.

"Mama, do consider," she said calmly, turning to the baroness with a consoling tone. "Indian dishes are becoming all the rage. You are the first to have had an introduction to these truly authentic ones, prepared by the marquess's own Hindustani cook! You will be the envy of everyone when they find out. Lord Milbourne has quite honored you, I think."

Cassie joined in the effort to console their mother. "Just think, Mama. People will seek you out, pestering you for descriptions of what the food was like, so their cooks may attempt to copy it. Our next At Home will be thronged— you'll see!"

As the flustered baroness thought this over, Aurora left her seat and approached Mariah. Her terse "A word with you, sister, if I might?" confirmed that she was not happy, in case Mariah had any doubts.

Was it not enough to have to unruffle their mother without having to soothe Rorie, as well? Mariah walked over to the fireplace, out of earshot of the others.

Rorie followed. "I don't suppose you mean to keep drawing Lord Milbourne's attention, Mariah, but I really must protest. Mama and Papa have made it very clear that as I am the eldest they expect me to make an attempt to fix the man's interest. They think I might have an advantage over at least some of the others setting their caps for him, by virtue of being William's sister."

Mariah was taken aback. "Drawing his interest? Certainly I have not meant to, Rorie! I quite believe that, except for those few moments at dinner, no one was paying any more attention to me than usual, least of all him. Outside of those few moments, I am quite sure that I am perfectly invisible to him. You need not worry."

Aurora did not look entirely convinced, but Mariah was. "Could you possibly think that I, of all people, would try to compete against you?" Golden-haired Rorie, the eldest of the four sisters, was acknowledged to be the family beauty. Mariah was undoubtedly the most unremarkable with her lamentably unruly mouse brown hair and pale gray eyes. "It is only that I find his experiences so interesting. Do you not think so? William told me the marquess's house is filled with priceless treasures he brought back with him from Lampur and other places. Would you not give anything to see them? I would!"

"If Mama has her way, she would have me setting up my

nursery among them," Rorie answered morosely. She shuddered. "They are heathen things, Mariah, made in a savage country. It does not seem proper for you to take such an interest in them. Beware."

Rorie could be amazingly narrow-minded at times. Mariah shrugged off the warning. She returned to her seat, to find their mother looking a good deal more cheerful.

"We had better ring for John and James to come and set up the tables for whist," Lady Parbury said, rallying. "Girls, you do suppose the marquess would play whist?"

"Really, Mama," Mariah answered. "You act as if you think he is a barbarian, and Hindustan the end of civilization. 'Tis no such thing!"

But her mother was not paying attention, already distracted by the need to fuss with one of Rorie's sleeves.

The men rejoined them in a surprisingly short time. The marquess agreed to Lady Parbury's suggestion of whist, although rather reluctantly, Mariah thought. He suggested music as an alternative, but when the baroness did not seem to heed him, he politely let it go.

Mariah knew exactly why her mother had pretended not to hear—Rorie's musical talents did not compare well against those of her younger sisters. Georgie, Mariah, and Cassie must not outshine Aurora on this important evening.

Not surprisingly, the marquess was partnered with Rorie at a table with Lord and Lady Parbury. William and the other three sisters made up the second table.

Mariah played horridly, for her mind was not on the game. She could not keep her attention away from the next table, where Rorie and her mother chattered valiantly in the face of Lord Parbury's usual silence and what Mariah thought was a notable lack of encouragement from the marquess.

Lord, the poor man had to be bored to tears! Well, perhaps not to tears. What *did* men become bored to the point of? The signs were unmistakable, from the foot tapping impatiently beneath the table to the fingers he could not stop from occasionally drumming on the tabletop. If his days were filled with nothing but the new affairs of his inheritance and such inane social travesties as this, how miserable he must be!

She wondered if he missed India—if he felt any homesickness for his life in Lampur. The only time he brightened up was when Lady Parbury asked about the work he was having done on his house in Grosvenor Square. In reply he launched into a spellbinding description of cave temples in western India and various rajas' palaces whose interiors were influencing his renovations.

"Mariah? Your play," said William.

She barely looked at her cards before she selected one to lay down. Surely the marquess would hold their family in the greatest contempt after such a painful evening. What would that do for Rorie's chances? Not that Mariah thought those two would suit, but there was a certain amount of family loyalty and pride involved in her wanting Rorie to have a fair chance. Every other marriage-seeking young lady with a titled background would no doubt be making a play for the poor man.

Cannot you rescue your friend? Mariah wanted to shout at her brother. Short of kicking William under the table, she didn't know how to get her message across.

"Mariah, you've just led trumps," protested Cassie in great annoyance. "You are not paying the slightest attention! Why cannot Georgie be your partner instead of me?"

Why could not Rorie and Mama ask the marquess something intelligent? Mariah's head was full of questions she'd like to ask, but doing so in front of her mother and Rorie would be borrowing trouble. Mama was constantly reminding her that she must hide her addiction to books—that men did not like bluestockings. And Rorie would think Mariah was trying to fix Lord Milbourne's interest, when it was only his knowledge she wanted.

Catching William's eye for a moment, she made a grimacing face and rolled her eyes toward the other table. William tightened his lips and shrugged, almost imperceptibly.

So, he does realize, Mariah thought. There was small

comfort in that—he clearly intended to do nothing. She looked across at Georgina, who frowned at her cards with a tiny wrinkle of concentration between her brows. Georgie was always hard to read—she could be intentionally keeping her mind off the situation, or she could be trying hard to think of some remedy, as Mariah was. Suppose one of them pretended to be taken ill suddenly? No. That might successfully break up the party, but the marquess might think it a reflection upon his food!

Ultimately, it was Lord Milbourne who saved himself. Just when Mariah thought she could stand to see him suffer no more, an urgent message came for the marquess from his household staff, interrupting the card play. She watched him read it, his face darkening with concern.

"Lord and Lady Parbury, please forgive me," he said, folding the note and rising from his chair. "I must depart at once—something has happened that requires my urgent attention. I regret that I must not even stay to finish this hand."

Was it a true emergency, or a conveniently arranged escape? How much of the evening had been a sham? Mariah only knew that he was leaving. He was making his bows to everyone. She was seized with a sudden desperate notion that he must not leave without the knowledge that at least one person in the house had enjoyed his glorious stories.

When he came to her in turn she found herself politely echoing the sentiments of everyone else that whatever the trouble was would not prove too serious.

"That is my hope, as well," he replied soberly, but then he smiled. The brilliant effect lit up his face. "As for you, Miss Parbury, enthusiasm becomes you. Just be cautious of where it leads you!"

Two warnings in the same evening! He meant the dinner, of course, did he not? Now, now was her only chance. "I enjoyed the food you brought. Very much. And also your stories. 'Priests, tapers, temples, swim before my very sight,'" she recited, quoting the first thing that came into her head.

He looked truly astonished. "You are familiar with Alexander Pope? Well, well."

She had not expected him to know the reference. She

hoped fervently that he did not recall the line just before it—
truly too embarrassing! The poem was about lovers, not
India.

"Pray do not get her started," William interrupted. "I'll
walk out with you, old man."

Would that she could be the one to see him out! She might
never have another chance to ask him anything.

"Is it true that they ride on elephants to go hunting?" she
blurted out.

"Hush, Mariah! Let the poor fellow take his leave!"
William was so solicitous of his friend, *now,* of course.

Lady Parbury and Rorie were both sending evil looks in
Mariah's direction, and she wished she could sink through
the floor. Of all the idiotic things to ask, or poems to quote!
If she had not already proven herself the fool at dinner, she
had surely done so now.

Lord Milbourne winked. "Sometimes they do," he said,
before turning to bid good night to Cassie. "It depends upon
what they are hunting." A moment later he was gone.

Chapter Two

The note that liberated Reinhart Karl Maycott, Lord Milbourne, from the agonies of playing whist at the Parburys' was not of his own devising, although he could not help feeling a little grateful for its timing. There was indeed a crisis at his home—one that could cause considerable unease among his neighbors should they learn of it. Ranee, his pet cheetah, had escaped from the confines of the house.

Ren suspected that the cat was no further away than the back garden, but she would find it no challenge to leave the walled enclosure if she so decided. If that happened, the incident could quickly escalate into a true disaster. He could picture the headlines, "Wild beast terrorizes Grosvenor Square!" or worse, "Leopard eludes captors in Hyde Park!"

His greatest concern was that some harm might befall the cat, his companion of five years. Loose in the city streets she might be terrified and forget all her training. He could imagine her crushed under the wheels of a dray, or shot by some citizen perceiving her as a threat. He needed to get home with utmost speed. However, the carriage that had brought him the note could only return him to his house so quickly, and unless he could conjure away the evening traffic in Mayfair, nothing he might do would help his driver Ahmed to speed that process.

What puzzled him was how the cheetah had escaped from the house to begin with. He had made specific arrangements to insure against that risk. This was the second time in as many weeks that something odd had occurred at the house. It made him uneasy.

William, kind soul that he was, had offered to come along

when he learned of Ranee's escape. Ren had searched for a
tactful way to explain that his friend's services would not be
even slightly helpful. Ranee was tame, but if she became
upset her behavior could become unpredictable. His servants were wary of the big cat, and wisely so. All too often
people mistook Ren's efforts to keep them safe as a slight
upon their courage.

Poor William. He had been much concerned that the
evening with his family had damaged their friendship.

"Are we still on speaking terms? I have much to apologize for," he had said as he walked Reinhart through the
entry hall of the Parburys' town house. "I cannot believe
that my father suggested you should visit his tailor! And a
certain amount of ignorant behavior may be expected from
my sisters, but my mother! She was beyond too much. I
would never have pressed you to come if I had realized quite
how awful it was going to be."

Ren had reassured him, pointing out that he had endured
far more difficult evenings. "I cannot shun society forever,
and I did, after all, exact a small amount of retribution. Your
father is correct that I need better tailoring, and your mother
is suffering from a delusion that will be shared by many
other hope-filled mamas during the coming months. Eventually they will accept that I do not intend to marry. Do you
not think I was sufficiently boorish?"

William had chuckled. "It is my impression that such
women never give up, regardless of how you behave. And
what will become of your line if you never marry?"

"Somewhere there's a cousin in a family branch who
stands currently as my heir. He's welcome to it all."

Ren knew his reply surprised his friend. Although
William was sympathetic, at the core he was still as con-
ventional as the rest of his family—except for that one sister, perhaps. Ren had found Mariah Parbury intriguing. She
was not the beauty of the family, but she had lovely eyes,
and she seemed intelligent. He had been going to ask
William about her but had changed his mind—it was more
urgent to get home and deal with the problem of Ranee's escape.

He definitely did *not* wish to become too friendly with any respectable young women! Mariah's interest and enthusiasm for the East was a refreshing rarity among young ladies of her age, that was all. He was curious to know where she had learned what she knew.

As the carriage rounded the corner into Grosvenor Square, he gathered his stick and prepared to leap from the vehicle as soon as it came to a stop. Hajee, a little man with skin the color of coffee, met him at the door of the town house bowing and touching his forehead. They spoke in rapid Hindustani.

"Sahib! I am very sorry to interrupt your evening."

"It was the right thing." Reinhart wasted little time on preliminaries. "How did Ranee get out? Who discovered that she was missing? How long ago?"

He tossed his hat and stick onto the glossy mahogany table in the entry passage as he passed, making straight for the service wing and the door to the garden. In six weeks he had already put his own stamp upon the house, moving many of his ancestors' furnishings into storage. His brisk steps were cushioned by thick Persian and Indian carpets.

"She is in the garden, sahib—Selim found her there." Hajee hastened to keep up with his employer. "She is in the tree and will not come down."

"I doubted she would go towards the square—too much bustle and noise. Thank God she did not take it into her head to visit the stableyard in the mews."

"She went out through the window in the room adjoining hers. Syed found her gone when he brought up her evening meal."

"How the devil could that happen?"

Ren stopped when he reached the door, realizing the need to calm and center himself. Ranee would take her cue from him, and if he seemed upset, she would think there was reason for alarm. Calling on the steely control which had been the hallmark of his diplomatic career, he blocked out the alarming thoughts that pushed at the edges of his mind and focused entirely on the one task of getting Ranee back into the house.

"I will need her lead and my leather gauntlets."

"Here, sahib."

"You are a good man, Hajee."

After seven months aboard ship and six weeks in London, Ren was more amazed than ever that any of his Indian servants had elected to come with him to England. Of the five that had made the journey, Hajee was the only Hindu. That he had the needed items ready to hand was a testimony to his thoughtful efficiency. That he willingly handled articles deemed "unclean" by those of his particular religious persuasion bespoke his loyalty and devotion to duty, something Ren valued in him even more. Hajee was ever performing rituals to cleanse himself—life in London was perilously unclean!

Ren pulled on the gauntlets and stepped out into the dimly lighted garden. Seated on a bench in the paved center court was an Indian youth about fourteen years old, as dusky as the shadows cast by the lantern at his feet. He rose instantly upon seeing Reinhart.

"Sahib, I have kept watch since we found her in the tree," he said, salaaming. "She shows no wish to come down."

"When did a female ever do aught but her own bidding?" The marquess chuckled absently, approaching the tree.

"Why, sahib, they must never do but what their man decrees!" the young Mohammedan replied in round-eyed astonishment.

Ren lifted one eyebrow and gave the boy a sardonic look. "Except for cats and Englishwomen, Selim my lad, and even then, you'd be surprised. Do you not think your mother in the privacy of the *zenana* still contrived to make your father decree exactly what she wished? Think on it."

The marquess looked up among the leafy branches of the tree. Ranee crouched on a stout branch, looking perfectly relaxed, not to mention content to stay there. One long, thin leg hung down casually like the root of a banyan tree.

"Now, my girl, it strikes me that you have not had your dinner," Ren began in a gentle voice. "Can I not persuade you to come down?" Once he was certain he had the cat's attention, he tried a more direct approach. "Ranee, come."

The cheetah's brown eyes could not have more clearly reflected her disinterest. She blinked, and ignored the marquess's further entreaties.

"Perhaps we could lure her down using her food?" Selim asked. "I did not want to try anything until you came, but it is one idea I had."

"That might work," Ren said kindly, "but I do not want to reward her for this bad behavior. I'm wondering if she really does not relish the idea of coming down from the tree. Unlike other leopards, *chitah-baghs* are not great climbers."

The route the cat had taken was obvious. The open second-floor window gave onto the gently sloped roof of the service wing below it. Next to the garden wall at the end of the wing grew the tree that now sheltered Ranee.

"Perhaps we would do better to go inside and lure her back in through the window, the way she came out."

"Yes, Excellency. Perhaps."

In the end, that is how they got the cat back into the house. Filled with a profound sense of relief, Ren ruffled her soft, spotted fur and scratched under her white chin before leading her back into her private chamber. He only hoped that none of his neighbors had noticed the furtive drama taking place in the darkness. He did not care in the least if they saw the Marquess of Milbourne clambering in and out of his own windows or pacing on the roof, but he wished to avoid any controversy that might be raised over his furry companion. It was fortunate that his house was at the end of its row, flanked by another house only on one side. Some small shops and an alley stood on the other side between his house and the corner of North Audley Street.

"Hajee, take a note to order some iron bars for that window," he said, once peace had been restored. Ranee was safely enjoying her dinner in the inner sanctuary of her two-room suite, while Ren stood in the outer room, still grappling with his chaotic emotions.

The chance of losing Ranee had shaken him badly, exposing a vulnerability he had not considered. Clearly, he had become far too fond of the animal! Just because he had raised her himself . . .

He must make an effort to get out more. Perhaps he would give more attention to the flood of invitations that arrived daily despite his refusing most of them. He was not a monk, after all. He could reply to his friend Hayden Carrisforte, and he could begin to spend some time at White's. He had also been meaning to contact some acquaintances who belonged to the Asiatic Society. But in the meantime, he wanted no risk of repeating this night's unsettling drama.

"You will have to enlist Frothwick's help in questioning all the servants, Hajee. I want to know how that window came to be left open!"

On an afternoon some four days later, Mariah Parbury and her sister Cassie could be found working on embroidery samples in the morning room of their house on Great Marlborough Street. Mariah stabbed her needle into her hoop quite viciously and heaved a great sigh each time she did so.

"Really, Mariah. You needn't be so upset," Cassie said. "If you had been allowed to go along with Mama, I would be left here all alone, and how dull that would be!"

"I don't see what difference one more person would have made," Mariah countered. "Above everyone I was the one most eager to see Lord Milbourne's house. It seems a cruel punishment to make me stay home while Rorie and Georgie go with Mama to call on him."

"Perhaps he will not even be there. He has been too busy since the night he dined here to bother to call on us! Too busy, or too rag-mannered."

"Cassie! Mama says a man of his high station is not to be expected to make the usual obligatory visits. That is precisely why she decided to call on him instead. Oh, I do hope Georgie will fix her attention on everything! I know she will try to tell me what it is like, but it just is not the same as seeing for oneself."

Mariah's lament was interrupted by their butler. "Miss Harriet Pritchard to see you, Miss Parbury. Are you at home to her?"

"Harry? Oh, yes, Bennett. Do show her into the drawing room. I will be there directly!" Mariah jumped up and hastily crammed her needlework into the lacquered work-table that stood beside her chair.

"Now aren't you glad that you stayed home?" asked Cassie archly.

Mariah and Harriet Pritchard had become acquainted at the country home of mutual friends during the previous autumn. Plain, pale Mariah had survived her first Season in London, and vivacious, dark-haired Harriet was looking forward to her first one this spring. They had discovered that they shared a common perspective on the world and a similar sense of humor, and had kept up the friendship since then. They had contrived to see much of each other in the past few weeks since their families had arrived in London.

"Mariah! I have been hearing such interesting things," Harry exclaimed as soon as Mariah joined her. The young women hugged and made themselves comfortable on the satin-upholstered settee. The pale blue of Mariah's day dress almost matched the color of the cushioned seat.

"Oh, Harry, you are an angel to come by today. I was feeling particularly blue-deviled. I can always count on you to divert me!"

"Well, I am happy you are still receiving me, after the exalted company you've been entertaining! The town is all abuzz over how the Marquess of Milbourne graced your dinner table with his presence! Any number of hostesses are quite jealous, you may depend upon it."

Mariah laughed. "Yes, we have been receiving cards from them like mad. Apparently we are now perceived as a magic charm that might draw along with us the marquess's marvelous presence—which is fustian, of course! But you should only see the stack of invitations we have received in the last few days! Mama is quite thrilled, of course—she is bent on accepting as many of them as possible."

"Oh, Mariah. I will not even be at half of them, I suppose. You see? You are moving out of my circle already."

"Never, dear friend! Just because you are a baronet's daughter? You are perfectly respectable, Harry." The very thought triggered an idea. "I shall see if you cannot be included in some of these events. Would not your mother allow you to come with me when I go to pay calls? Once you have been introduced, I am certain that is all it would take!"

It was Harry's turn to laugh. "If you could see the crafty look in your eyes just now! You are incorrigible! But of course I would not say no to such an offer."

Mariah sobered suddenly. "This is assuming my own mother is not going to exclude me from too many things on account of my sisters. She is this very hour gone with Rorie and Georgie to call on Lord Milbourne, and she insisted that I stay home with Cassie!" She gave a perfect imitation of her mother's sharp voice. " 'We do not wish to overwhelm the poor man. Three of us is quite a sufficient number to pay our respects.' And I did so particularly want to go!

"The truth is, she does not want anything to dampen Rorie's chances of interesting the man. I think she is afraid if I open my mouth he will take all of us for bluestockings and will run away in disgust."

"That is hardly fair. No wonder you feel blue-deviled!" Harry squeezed Mariah's hand in sympathy. "Is he truly as handsome as everyone says?"

"He is stunning, Harry, although that is not the reason I wanted to go. Cassie called him 'magnificent' and I think she must be right."

Lord Milbourne's image came to mind instantly—indeed, Mariah had been hard-pressed to put it out of her mind since the night of the dinner. She described his stature and his golden eyes and hair in rapturous terms.

"And that is not the reason you wished to call on him?" Clearly Harry found this unlikely.

"Not at all!" Mariah was fiercely indignant. "Why should I care a jot how he looks? William has been telling me all about Lord Milbourne's house. It is filled with precious things he has brought back from India—gold and silver ornaments and chairs all set with jewels, filigree screens carved from ebony wood, sculptures of elephants! The marquess himself told us how he is having the rooms refurbished to look like Indian palaces and temples. I have seen pictures of some of those, with impressive ranks of columns and splendid arches and carvings. I would give anything to see it! Do you not think it sounds sublime?"

"Methinks she doth protest too much," teased Harry softly. In a louder voice she said, "Perhaps they will not find him at home today. You might have another chance to visit."

"No. My mother will say the same thing if they try to go again. It does not occur to her that she is the one likely to scare him away with her obvious schemes to throw Rorie at his head! I keep thinking it would be great fun if he should take a liking to Georgie instead."

Harry made no reply to this remark and Mariah saw that her friend's mind had wandered. With Harry, this often yielded interesting results. Mariah waited patiently and a moment later the girl turned to her, her hazel eyes bright.

"Call your maid and fetch your bonnet and pelisse, Mariah. You and I are going out. I have the perfect idea."

Minutes later, Mariah found herself being hurried along Great Marlborough Street, her mind filled with doubts. The afternoon sun had faded to pearly gray, veiled by thickening clouds.

"Harry, I don't think my mother will like this by half."

"Your mother is too well-bred to say anything in front of the marquess, and once she sees there has been no harm done, she will forgive you completely," Harry responded with perfect confidence. She strode along so purposefully that people on the sidewalks stopped to let the young women and their trailing maids pass.

Mariah noticed a black-faced chimney sweep's boy among the crowd and tightened her grip on her reticule; while her heart ached for the poor little fellow, it was well-known that such boys sometimes picked pockets or cut purse strings to supplement their meager subsistence. The sweeps were working in her neighborhood—she had heard them crying the street when she first awakened that morning. The boy merely tipped his cap respectfully as she and Harry hurried past him.

"That begs the question of whether Mama and my sisters

will even still be there by the time we walk all the way to
Grosvenor Square," Mariah said, a little breathlessly. "As it
is, tongues will wag over my mother's visiting the marquess, even though she says the point is to save him the trouble of calling upon us. I can just imagine what the
gossipmongers will say about you and I joining them there!
We cannot walk all the way across Mayfair without being
noticed by somebody."

They turned a corner and headed west toward Hanover
Square, traversing the twists and turns of narrow streets
doomed to give way for Nash's new Regent Street. In this
section the work had not yet begun. A mischievous damp
breeze played amongst the buildings, fluttering the young
women's skirts and setting their ribbons and bonnet plumes
dancing.

"Do you want to see the inside of his house, or not?"
Harry said with a trace of irritation. "If we arrive there without a carriage and your mother and sisters have left, do you
not think his servants will let us in while a carriage is sent
for? They would not leave us standing on the street! And if
it should chance to rain, that's even better."

"Rain? Oh!" Mariah brightened. "I suppose you are right.
Oh, Harry, you are so ingenious! But I am troubled by what
possible reason we can give to explain our coming to find
them . . ."

"I will think of something by the time we arrive there,
never fear. I will make it appear that you are obliging me.
Surely your mother cannot fault you then!"

The walk to Hanover Square and then along the length of
Brook Street seemed very long. Mariah and Harry admired
the rows of elegant houses, but conversation was sporadic.
Occasionally the two young women had to pause to allow
their lagging maids to catch up. By the time they reached
Grosvenor Square, Mariah was quite certain that her mother
and sisters were long since back at home again, wondering
what had become of her.

The houses facing the square were not uniform, but many
were easily three times the size of the Parburys' comfortable
house in Great Marlborough Street. The grand scale of the

spacious square by itself provided these homes with an aura of majesty scarcely to be equaled in London.

"Which house is his?" Harry demanded, apparently not the least bit awed. Mariah doubted that anything could cow her dauntless friend. She wished she had been born with the same adventurous spirit.

"I believe it is the last one on the north side." She peered ahead, trying to see down to the end of the row. "I do not think I see my family's carriage."

"That's all to the good," Harry said, advancing. "Come on, then." As if she sensed Mariah's hesitation, she added, "Think of those treasures you so want to see!"

Mariah conjured up images of exotic Indian artifacts, the legacy of rajas and an ancient civilization. If she could just keep her mind on her goal, none of these smaller concerns would bother her. She brushed a first raindrop from the sleeve of her pelisse and started forward.

"You were right about the rain, Harry. It seems to be starting." She did not notice the closed carriage that passed them until it drew to a halt just beyond them and an elegantly dressed gentleman climbed out.

By the time Mariah saw who it was, it was too late to call Harry back.

Chapter Three

"Lord Milbourne, you are not at home!" were the first words to pop out of Mariah's mouth. She instantly wished herself to the devil for uttering something so foolishly obvious.

The marquess merely laughed. "Indeed, that is quite true, Miss Parbury. By coincidence I am just now returning. I saw you ladies walking earlier when I chanced to be passing through Hanover Square. This does not promise to be a good afternoon for strolling in the park, if that was your intention," he continued. "It appears to be starting to rain."

"Yes, yes, it appears to be," Mariah said inanely. Something about being near this man stopped the flow of blood to her brain. She managed to gather enough wits to introduce Harry, but that was all.

"We will just have to change our plans," Harry said smoothly, raising both eyebrows significantly and giving Mariah the slightest nudge. "We never thought to bring umbrellas."

"It is much too far to expect you tender ladies to walk back to Great Marlborough Street in the rain. May I place my carriage at your disposal? I am but a few steps from my own door, and my driver will be happy to convey you anywhere."

That was the last thing Mariah wanted. "You are very kind, sir," she said, offering the polite thing. Inside she fought the urge to scream in frustration. Fate obviously did not intend for her to gain access to Lord Milbourne's house. She opened her mouth to say more to him, but the rain began pelting down in earnest and he was holding open the carriage door for them. Blinding inspiration struck her.

"Perhaps we might go to Marshall's Lending Library. It is a lovely place on a rainy afternoon. They have the newest edition of Thomas and William Daniell's *Oriental Scenery,* including the 'Hindoo Excavations.' Have you seen their engravings, Lord Milbourne? I believe they have illustrated some of the very temples you were describing to us the other evening."

She could not read the expression on Lord Milbourne's face, but from the corner of her eye she saw Harry's eyes widen in surprise. As well they might! Mariah doubted she had ever been so forward in her entire life. Why, she might just as well have come right out and invited the marquess to join them. To make matters worse, she had just betrayed exactly the sort of bookish interest her mother had warned her against.

To her mortification, the marquess chuckled. "So is that where you have picked up your vast knowledge of the Hindustan, Miss Parbury?" He held out his hand, so that he might assist her into the carriage.

The thought of placing her gloved hand in his made her hesitate. How well she remembered the quick touch of his hand during dinner. If so little could make her behave like a ninny, what might this do? Obviously, she must hold herself in firmer control. "Oh, I hope I have no pretensions to a vast knowledge, sir," she said, giving her hand and climbing the steps quickly. "A—a vast ignorance, more like."

Never had she felt quite so ignorant as at that moment, when a wave of tingling warmth swept through her from his mere touch. Who knew that such a thing could happen? Despite the two layers of Limerick kid between their palms, his warmth and solid, comfortable strength had come through vividly, setting off an answering response deep inside her. She hoped that he did not notice the catch in her voice or the slight trembling in the hand she snatched away once she was safely inside the carriage door.

He handed Harry up, and then their two maids, who

looked ready to faint at being assisted by a marquess. He closed the door firmly behind them.

A frisson of disappointment ran through Mariah, surprising her. Had she truly hoped that he might join them?

"In what street is Marshall's?" he asked through the window. "I will have Ahmed wait and convey you home once you are finished there. No, do not protest—I insist upon it."

After she answered, he relayed the instructions to his driver. "Good day to you, Miss Parbury. A pleasure, Miss Pritchard."

With a lurch, the carriage started forward. As it pulled away, Mariah saw Lord Milbourne simply standing on the sidewalk, staring after them as the rain came down.

Marshall's was one of the smallest but choicest of the circulating libraries, one which catered less in entertaining novels and rather more in scholarly and historical works. Its front room had fewer cases of jewelry and sundries for sale, presumably as it had a smaller proportion of females among its clientele, and it boasted a large and well-lit reading room along with an intriguing selection of books. Harry and Mariah left their maids waiting in Lord Milbourne's carriage while they went in.

Out of the servants' hearing, the two young women nearly burst with whispered reactions to what had happened.

"Whoever would have guessed that he would happen to come along at just that moment, Harry? Of all the wretched luck. It quite ruined our plan. And of course, it means that Mama and my sisters will not have been able to do more than leave a card."

"Oh, but, Mariah! How gallant he was to give us his carriage! And how handsome he is—just as you said. I am so happy that I was able to meet him!" Harry sighed.

"Lord, do not tell me you are smitten."

"Do you mean to say you are not?"

"Yes—that is to say, I am not." Mariah's denial clearly did not convince Harry. Mariah only wished she was quite convinced herself. The "Lion" was indeed handsome, and charming besides. He seemed to have an extraordinary effect upon her. But he was not for her.

"It is only that we live such ordinary lives, while he has lived such an extraordinary one, full of adventures. He has seen things we should only dream of seeing, Harry! Just days ago I was looking at pictures of places he was actually describing at dinner! He has traveled all over India. Let me show you, if I can find the book."

Oblivious to the frowns their whispers were drawing from several gentlemen patrons standing nearby, Mariah threaded her way to the travel section with Harry in tow.

"He seemed impressed by your knowledge."

"I believe he meant to tease me, Harry. At our dinner I had little opportunity to show anything other than how foolish I was!" She went on to describe her moments of embarrassment along with the folly of her family's behavior during the dinner.

"I should dearly love to apologize to him, but it is not the sort of thing one can say in front of just anyone—wouldn't that give the gossips something to gloat over? It would quite ruin my mother's supposed great success."

"You could ask to have a word with him in private the next time you see him." Harry looked about dubiously, as if checking to see who might hear them now.

"In private? If only I dared! How many things I should like to ask him!" Mariah waved vaguely at the books on the shelves. "I have read most of these travels and descriptions—some of it is simply beyond believing. Snake charmers, and ants that dig for gold! Lord Milbourne would tell me what is really true, I am certain of it. But what I should like most would be to see his house! That would be a little like traveling to India itself, I think."

She turned to the shelves and began to search for the volume of the Daniells' engravings she had recently discovered.

"Do you not think that he will invite the *ton* to see his house when the renovations are finished?"

"William says that he will not. He says that the marquess is having the work done solely for his own pleasure and that he gives not a pin for what Society thinks of it."

Mariah failed to find the book she wanted and was forced

to seek out the library's tall, thin proprietor to ask if the volume had been borrowed. The gaunt fellow looked as if he never consumed anything other than books.

"It has been signed out, miss, but if you wish only to peruse the engravings, I have recently acquired one of the original large editions that came out several years ago. I can put it on one of the reading tables for you."

Nothing could have delighted Mariah more. Soon she and Harry were bent over the large folio volumes, examining the aquatint engravings in all their detail. Waiting servants and passing time were quite forgotten.

The marquess had found himself uncharacteristically struck by indecision as he had stood in the pelting rain where his carriage and the ladies had left him. One part of him had felt impelled to go to Marshall's Lending Library, while another part of him was appalled that he would even consider it.

Miss Parbury's thinly veiled invitation had not seemed coy or deliberate. Ren wanted to believe it had sprung honestly from her own enthusiasm, but the cynic in him suggested that he should not be so naive. An interest in India and his own life there was an obvious route for any enterprising miss to follow if she hoped to gain favor with him. In this case, however, he believed Miss Parbury's interest was genuine. Since that painful evening at the Parburys', William had enlightened him considerably on the subject of his sisters.

The fact was, Ren wanted to see the pictures. He had traveled to many of the same remote places the Daniells had gone and had heard the natives speak about them. Even though their visits had predated his by twenty years or more, in the slow timescape and long memory of India that was no time at all.

Of course, he could go to see the pictures anytime. He could *buy* the pictures; he could pay a call on the Daniells themselves. He had to admit what appealed to him was the idea of looking at the engravings in the company of Miss Parbury and her friend. He suspected that was a singularly bad idea, but in the end, he went. He only stopped at home to check on the workmen, exchange his wet coat and cravat for fresh ones, and check on Ranee while the grooms brought round his recently purchased Tilbury gig. The great-coat he had purchased on first arriving in London would serve to keep him dry enough.

After leaving his wet coat with the attendant at Marshall's, Ren went in search of the ladies. He found them at one of the reading tables near the back of the library and paused for a moment to savor the attractive view they presented as they bent over the large books. Both young women possessed admirable figures, although Miss Parbury's was the more nicely rounded of the two. Their faces were totally obscured by their bonnets but nevertheless the effect was charming as they put their heads close together to exchange whispered comments. They had no idea he was there. It seemed almost too bad to interrupt them.

"Lord Milbourne! How may I help you? It is an honor to have you here, my lord."

The cadaverous proprietor of the library—Mr. Marshall, one presumed—bowed and hovered annoyingly as Miss Parbury and her friend looked up in surprise. Ren favored the man with a pained smile. It still surprised him that everyone in London down to the lowliest shopkeeper seemed to know who he was, whether he had ever set foot in their establishment or not. No doubt they smelled his wealth—such people usually had an unerring instinct. He supposed now he would be expected to pay a guinea or more to become a library subscriber.

"I don't believe I need any help at the moment, thank you," he said, hoping that it was true. He turned to the ladies. "Miss Parbury, Miss Pritchard, I have found you! As you see, I decided to come along, after all. Are these the famous pictures?"

He smiled at Miss Parbury, who seemed to be tongue-tied for the moment. She had turned a most becoming shade of pink. But gamely she nodded and made room for him to join them at the table.

The book was open to a picture of temple ruins near Ban-

galore, looking so like the place that he could feel the searing heat of the Indian sun that poured unmercifully into the
open forecourt. The small figures shown seated there could
have been the same men he'd seen there years later, so similar was the scene. But memory only fleetingly supplanted
his intense awareness of the young women on either side of
him.

He felt like a lion between two little birds, and it was definitely not in the role of a guardian. Their position struck
him as delightfully intimate, as all three leaned over the
books, shoulder to shoulder. He was closest to Miss Parbury
and inhaled a trace of jasmine each time she moved the
slightest bit. That seemed appropriate—no ordinary scent of
lavender or roses for her! He had to be careful how he inclined his head, lest the ribbons and ornaments on the ladies'
bonnets poke him in the eye.

"What do those peculiar sculptures on the columns represent, Lord Milbourne? One looks like a trident, but they do
not worship Neptune nor Poseidon in the Hindustan, do
they?"

He was not certain how to explain their symbolic meaning to a virtuous and probably pious young English miss.
Definitely it was time for him to find some less virtuous
companionship in London, a thing easily done but one he
had so far neglected.

"They are symbols of the gods Vishnu and Shiva," he
said, opting for simplicity. "Followers might leave offerings
at the base of the columns, as well as worshipping within the
temple itself. Strange and exotic, are they not?"

"Indeed they are!"

He was glad that Miss Parbury had found her voice—he
liked the sound. It was low and melodious, pleasant to listen
to. She turned a few pages, stopping at another picture.

"Speaking of exotic, are there really trees that look like
this? The landscape seems an utter fantasy." She sighed. "It
is so difficult to determine what is true, without having been
there. One is totally at the mercy of the artist's honesty."

Could she really be so unaware of how deliciously
provocative she appeared, positioned as she was over the

pages of the book? He found his awareness of her proximity was ripening into something more profound. When she sighed, the sound penetrated deep inside him through some invisible chink in his armor. Blast! Why had he yielded to the temptation to come? In a curiously detached part of his mind, he noted that Miss Pritchard's proximity, while pleasant, did not kindle in him quite the same intensity of response.

"That is what is known as an umbrella tree," he said with studied outward control. "They offer dense shade which can be a blessed relief from the intensity of the sun. Like most things in India, it comes at a cost—the ground beneath them is usually littered with thorns, and after clearing a space in which to sit, one must suffer a small stinging shower of missiles falling down upon one whenever the breeze stirs."

"Heavens! That does not sound at all pleasant. In the picture it looks so delightful."

"Looks can be deceiving," he said solemnly. "That is nowhere more true than in the Hindustan."

Miss Parbury turned thoughtful gray eyes upon him. "Perhaps that is the key to its mysteriousness."

"Perhaps." Gazing into those eyes, he thought that life's greatest mystery was surely the attraction between a man and a woman.

Her sleeve brushed against him as she reached to turn another page; again, he did not think it was intentional, but he was affected all the same.

"Perhaps we might sit down?" he suggested, thinking they would be farther apart. He did not count on the absurd length of his legs, the waywardness of his rebellious knee, or the way, when he offered his quizzing glass to show her a detail, they were suddenly bent close together again, leaning over the picture. It was sweet torture.

Miss Parbury was either entirely oblivious, secretly enjoying it, or purposely ignoring him. She betrayed no reaction. "Did you not say at dinner the other evening that this palace at Madura, and these temples, were influencing your renovations? I can see that they are particularly handsome."

He cleared his throat, which seemed peculiarly constricted. "My tastes are eclectic. I particularly like the mix of Hindu and Mohammedan styles."

"The arches and columns are on such a grand scale!" Miss Pritchard joined in. "I can hardly conceive of adapting them to a London house."

"The trick is to focus on the details, not the grand scheme overall," he began to explain, but he was interrupted.

"Milbourne! Saw your rig outside and didn't figure you would be in the draper's shop." The sandy-haired fashion plate who approached them was Hayden Carrisforte. He had known Ren at Harrow and Hailey Bury College and they had served together in India until Ren had gone to Lampur. Carrisforte had returned to England for health reasons some time after that and had already called on Ren several times since the latter's arrival in London.

"Should have known I'd find you up to your elbows in female pulchritude," the fellow said now with a grin. "I'd no idea Marshall's was the place to come. Leave it to you to discover that!"

Ren hastily introduced the two young ladies to his friend.

"I am utterly charmed, ladies," Carrisforte said, bowing over each of their hands. "Does your brother happen to be William, Miss Parbury? I knew him at Harrow and have seen him about town. And what of you, Miss Pritchard? I do not recall meeting any other Pritchards as yet and would surely remember if they were half as delightful as you."

Carrisforte was pouring it on a bit thick, Ren thought irritably, but Miss Pritchard seemed up to handling it.

"We have only been in London a few weeks, sir. It is my first Season. My father, Sir Barry Pritchard, finds himself in London fairly often, but perhaps your paths have not crossed."

"Well, we shall have to remedy that!" Carrisforte exclaimed. "Milbourne, I demand that you take me with you to call on these delightful ladies, so I may be properly presented. I have in mind an outing next week and I would dearly like to invite them to join us!"

Ren had formed no intentions of calling on either of the young ladies, although he knew he probably should, for courtesy's sake. He flashed a look at his friend. Carris always had a way of putting one on the spot, and clearly that had not changed.

"Do I take it none of you are attending Lady Sibbingham's ball this evening? Half of Mayfair is at home making their preparations for it even now."

"Oh Lord, the ball!" Miss Parbury exclaimed. "What time has it gotten to be? Heavens, our poor maids have been kept waiting this age. I forgot all about everything!"

She leaped up in agitation, causing an upheaval in their little group. In his haste to rise, Ren almost put his chair on Carrisforte's foot, not that the fellow deserved less. Miss Pritchard jumped up as well and Carris offered her his arm.

Ren was normally glad to see his friend, but at the moment he was feeling more than a little annoyed. Whether it was on account of the disruption, the presumption, or the reminder that he had actually accepted the Sibbinghams' invitation, he could not say. He offered his own arm to Miss Parbury, since he really had no choice.

"I had no idea we were here so long!" she sputtered, consulting a small pocket watch she kept in her reticule. "Oh, my mother will be in a taking!" By so occupying herself she neatly avoided taking his arm.

"I will see that you and Miss Pritchard are delivered to your homes immediately," Ren said stiffly. Perhaps Miss Parbury had noticed something, after all. She scurried out the door ahead of him as if he were fire and she had been burned.

Chapter Four

"Perhaps Lord Milbourne changed his mind about attending," Georgina whispered to Mariah that evening during the first break in the dancing at the Sibbinghams' ball. The music had stopped and the throng of elegantly attired guests had spread out into the center of the gilded grand salon, but the sisters were standing at one side of the room where they could survey the glittering legions. "That would show he was wise, don't you think?"

Mariah chuckled. "Wise, but discourteous. He did accept, after all." For her own sake, she heartily wished wisdom would win out. She could hear her mother's distinctive voice somewhere nearby, presently discussing the rash of chimney fires that had recently plagued their neighborhood, but Mariah had already heard an earful from her about the marquess after being delivered home from Marshall's in his coach. Given their own failure to see him that afternoon, the baroness and Rorie had not been at all pleased to discover that Mariah had been with him, and at—of all places—a library!

As she did not know what to make of his actions there, Mariah thought avoiding him was a good idea, apart from her mother's and Rorie's clear instructions. She was not certain if he had actually been behaving improperly at Marshall's, or if her own absurdly heightened awareness of him had only made it seem that way to her. Just the thought of dancing with him made her extremely nervous.

She had managed to enjoy the first part of the ball, having no lack of partners and noting that Harry, too, was having great success. She was very pleased that her friend had

been included among those invited, even if some com-
plained that the event was hardly exclusive. Mr. Carrisforte's comment that "half of London" had been preparing
for it seemed very close to the truth. The flowers and banks
of candles ornamenting the rooms could hardly be seen for
the crowds, but the music was lively and the punch flowed
freely. She had even managed not to think about Lord Milbourne for whole minutes at a time.

"You don't say Mrs. Braddon's chimney started smoking
just two days later?" pealed Lady Parbury in the knot of
ladies behind the two sisters. The entire family had found
themselves quite sought-after since their dinner with the
marquess.

"Don't look now, but apparently the marquess cares more
for punishment than wisdom," Georgie whispered in
Mariah's ear.

Lord Milbourne stood in the doorway framed by a pair of
marble columns as his name was announced, and for a fleeting moment the sense that he cut a very solitary and perhaps,
lonely, figure flashed through Mariah's mind, as it had at the
dinner party. Standing there with his head held high, he was
magnificent indeed. A man of his size would have dominated the room in any event, but instead of evening clothes,
he had chosen to dress in Indian attire, which of course ar-
rested the attention of everyone in the room at once. A gasp
of surprise issued from the crowd as a single sound.

He wore a long, close-fitting scarlet coat that emphasized
the fitness of his splendid physique. It buttoned all the way
down the front from the high collar to the hem at his knees
and was embroidered with gold threat in intricate patterns.
The borders at the edges were set with jewels. Over it a yellow sash with long, fringed ends cinched his waist. Underneath it he wore odd white pantaloons that appeared to wrap
around his legs, just as she had seen in pictures. His tawny
golden hair was mostly covered by a turban fashioned from
cloth of gold and set with more jewels, while on his feet
were embroidered velvet slippers that curled up at the toes.
No true raja could have looked more splendid, she was quite
certain.

"How many seconds do you give him before he is completely mobbed by ambitious mothers and daughters?" came
a voice that was Harry's.

Mariah turned to her friend. "Seconds? I'll give you less
than that for my mother to get there with Rorie."

"Lady Sibbingham's reputation is made, now. People will
be talking for the rest of the week!" Harry made a little face.
"I suppose there is no chance of your getting a private moment with him in all of this!"

"Harry, I think that would be a very bad idea, for a number of reasons. Please forget that we ever mentioned that!"

"I obviously missed out on something," Georgie said,
"but I think I do not want to know."

True to Mariah's prediction, Lady Parbury and Rorie
could be seen in the crowd that had assembled at the end of
the room around the marquess. Wisely, someone signaled
the musicians to begin the next set of dances, thinning the
mob somewhat as young men sought out their promised
partners. Mr. Carrisforte came to claim a dance with Harry,
asking Mariah if she would promise him a later one. Then
Mariah's own partner came to whisk her out into a set for
the sprightly country dance. She saw her brother William
taking a place in another set with a girl who had flaming red
hair.

Mariah knew the dance well enough to go through the figures in her sleep, yet she circled right when she should have
moved left, and lost track of the number of times she had
performed steps that were meant to be repeated only twice.
She was mortified, yet she could not keep her attention from
straying to the marquess. Despite his height, she could only
catch glimpses of him in between the other dancers as the
partners moved in and out. It was little consolation to realize that most of the other young women were having a similar problem.

"I have the feeling the rest of us might just as well go
home," Mariah heard her partner remark to one of the other
young gentlemen in passing. He said it with a good-natured
chuckle but he looked half-serious as he did so.

When the dance ended and the young man returned her to

her place at the side of the room, a small cadre of acquaintances surrounded her.

"Lord Milbourne looks like a prince! Oh, Mariah, did he dress like that when he dined with your family?"

"There is a man very certain of his own consequence! Imagine having the courage to come in such attire, when it is not a costume ball."

Mariah thought the fact that he had come at all showed great courage. If he enjoyed the adulation, surely he would have been out and about in Society a good deal more than he had in the six weeks since his arrival. Yet she could discern no trace of dismay or reluctance on his face now as he conversed with various ladies and bowed as he was introduced to others. She saw only polite interest and his charming, disarming smile.

"Did you see the size of the ruby on his turban?" exclaimed one miss who had obviously braved the crowd around the marquess. "I've never seen so large a gem! And there are pearls and emeralds all over his cuffs and the front placket of his coat. The buttons are made of pearls and gold filigree!"

She sighed dreamily and found an answering echo in the rest of the little group. Mariah thought that his smile far outdazzled any jewels that adorned his person, but she did not say so. Instead she took the opportunity to slip quietly out of the enraptured group and looked about for Georgie or Harry. She suspected that the rest of the evening was going to prove long and trying indeed.

Instead, it was William who found her. "Ren—that is, Milbourne, has asked that you save a dance for him, Mariah," he said, coming up to her. "Take pity on the poor fellow, would you? At least he could have one dance with someone who wasn't looking to put leg shackles on him."

Phrased so inelegantly, the request irritated her. "What makes you so certain I have any dances left that are not spoken for?"

"Oh." Her brother looked crestfallen. "I had not thought of that."

"Anyway, what makes you think he will be allowed a

chance to dance?" She nodded her head toward the small crowd that still surrounded the marquess.

"Oh, that. Milbourne will no doubt take care of that when it suits him. Have no fear. If tactful maneuvering does not get him out of it, he will simply disperse them all with a mighty roar. Not for nothing is he called the Lion of Lampur."

"Heavens! Is he so ferocious?"

William winked. "Do you or do you not have a dance left for him?"

Mariah hesitated. It was not like her to be untruthful, but she did not want to dance with the marquess. Rather, a part of her did not want to. A part of her seemed to be thrilled at the very prospect. She blushed, and William picked up the cue immediately.

"Oh Lord, Mariah, not you, too! I thought you were too sensible to be swooning over him like everyone else. Just dance with the man, and keep your feet on the floor, all right?"

William stalked away, clearly disgusted with her.

"What on earth did you say to him?" asked Harry, arriving moments too late.

"It was what I did not say that caused the trouble," Mariah replied. "It seems I am to dance with Lord Milbourne."

That William knew his friend well was proven only minutes later, as the gathering around the marquess began to melt away magically and he strode out into the dance area with a radiant young brunette, the daughter of his hostess, on his arm. There was a mad rush to form sets, and the next dance began.

"A very diplomatic choice, would you not say?" Mariah's new partner said, obviously following her line of vision. "No matter who Lord Milbourne chose to dance with first, someone would be bound to make something of it."

"Yes, you are right," she answered, surprised by his perceptiveness. He was not a bad-looking fellow, a young officer in the Guards. "I apologize. I should not be neglecting you."

She set herself to pay attention to her own partners for the next several dances and managed to do so with reasonable success, except for the understandable distraction of seeing the marquess partnering her sisters. However, her palms grew moist and her breath seemed to catch in her throat when she eventually returned to her place to find her mother and sisters standing there with Lord Milbourne himself. Lady Parbury looked as if she had died and found herself in heaven.

"Let me see, it must be Miss Mariah's dance next," the marquess intoned in a deep, solemn voice, "as I have now had the honor of dancing with each of her other sisters present tonight."

He looked at Mariah, and she thought she saw a glint of challenge in those golden amber eyes. Had William told him she was reluctant? *Never trust a brother!*

She made a proper curtsy and greeted him. "Good evening to you, Lord Milbourne." *How splendid you look in that beautiful coat. How very large you are. How nervous you make me!*

She simply could not say any of the things that came into her head. Before she could stumble onto something else, Hayden Carrisforte came up to the little group. She had introduced him to her family earlier in the evening.

"My dance, I believe, Miss Parbury?"

There was an audible intake of breath from the people gathered around them. Who would dare to cross the marquess? Surely the man did not realize what he had done. Mariah could not quite believe that two such handsome men both wanted to dance with her at once.

At her hesitation, Carrisforte stopped. "Am I mistaken, then? I thought this was the one I'd spoken for."

Lord Milbourne smiled. "Disadvantage of not using dance cards, eh, old fellow? And here I thought this dance was mine." The two men looked at each other, apparently perfectly amicable, but Mariah still had the feeling of being a bone between two dogs. It was initially flattering, but she decided that she did not like it.

"I believe your friend, Mr. Carrisforte, does have the prior claim, my lord," she told the marquess. From the corner of her eye she could see her mother fanning vigorously, as if she might faint.

"I will yield to Lord Milbourne," said Mr. Carrisforte with a bow. "If you will promise me the next one?"

"Of course."

Mariah wondered if the marquess would say anything, but he only held out his arm to her and nodded as if accepting his due.

"I thought perhaps you might have allowed Mr. Carrisforte his dance with me," she commented reprovingly as they headed out into the center of the room. She could not believe she dared to criticize him.

"I might have, if I thought I had as much chance to be granted a later dance," he replied. He regarded her with a level, steady gaze.

Did he believe that she would have denied him a similar favor? Surely William *must* have said something! She did not think she had betrayed her reluctance by so much as a look. Did a simple dance with her mean so much? Or was it merely the challenge of the thing that appealed to him? She could not fathom it.

As they prepared to take places in the longways set that was forming down the center of the room, Harry caught Mariah's free arm. "My dear," she said, a look of concern etched on her face, "you have not sat out a single dance all evening! Are you not a bit *thirsty, overwarm,* and *fatigued*?"

She darted a sidelong glance at the marquess and Mariah suddenly realized what her friend was up to. Impossible girl! "I am fine," she said, pulling her arm away and making to move on, but Lord Milbourne had caught the hint. She would have to kill Harry later.

Without missing a step or relinquishing her arm, her large companion reset their course away from the other dancers. "You do look fatigued, Miss Parbury, if you will forgive my saying so. Please allow me to get you to some cooler air, and perhaps procure for you a cup of punch. Let us simply sit and talk for these few minutes."

Put that way, it sounded innocent enough. Perhaps less difficult than dancing with him—certainly less physical.

Mariah dismissed the little voice that reminded her of how innocent their activities in the library had been, with what results. Before she could think through the consequences, she and Lord Milbourne were settled with cups of punch on an unoccupied bench in one of the cooler anterooms that opened off the grand salon. It was too late then to consider how her mother or Rorie might view the change in plan or to offer any protest. Instead, Mariah offered an apology.

"I am sorry if you somehow received the impression that I was reluctant to dance with you, Lord Milbourne," she began. "I would have promised you a later opportunity."

In the gentle candlelight of the anteroom, Miss Parbury looked, well, utterly sincere, Ren decided. The pearls at her throat and the pale silver blue of her gown emphasized the soft gray color of her eyes and the fine ivory texture of her skin, but her nose was too short and her jaw too square to allow her a claim to classic beauty. However, sincerity in itself was a beautiful thing, worth testing.

"Perhaps, since we are not dancing now, you would still grant me that honor?" he asked, watching her eyes. Before she looked down at the punch cup in her hands he thought he caught a flicker of—what? Doubt. Hesitation. Confusion.

"Yes. All right," she said, but he thought he'd seen the real truth in her glance.

"If I promise to be the perfect gentleman?"

Ah, that caught her by surprise. Was it a mistake to bring up his folly from that afternoon? "I apologize if I upset you today at Marshall's. I can be the very devil sometimes."

He was gratified when she smiled.

"Is that who was at dinner with us the other evening, then?"

"O-ho, I see I have more to apologize for than merely today's bit of deviltry! Yes, I admit I was not exhibiting my best form when I dined with your family. In fact, I was quite reprehensible."

"I must say in your defense that I have no doubt my brother encouraged you," she said. "And, my mother may have deserved as much. In truth, I have been wishing I might apologize to *you* for my family's behavior that evening. I was embarrassed to the point of pain."

"They were not so bad as all that! I deliberately set out to be overwhelmingly boring. Your mother seems to have fallen into the same absurd infatuation with me as a great many other people, and I thought perhaps to nip it in the bud."

"Well, I did not find you boring in the least," she admitted shyly, looking away. "I could have listened to you for hours! I wish—well, there are just so many things I would love to know. But my mother does not seem to have been cured."

"Yes, I noticed."

He laughed, and she joined in, the sound rich and musical. There was a harmony between them now, as if they had cleared the air. He thought perhaps a seed of friendship had been sown, and that thought pleased him, although mere friendship with a woman seemed a novel idea.

"After listening to me drone on for an entire evening, can you possibly wish to know more?" He drained his cup. "You should think twice before encouraging me."

She clearly did not see any double meaning in his words, which was just as well. He must be careful to keep his baser instincts in check. Perhaps his connoisseur's assessment of her looks was faulty, or perhaps it was a trick of the light, but when she smiled and tilted her head at just the angle as she did now, she looked every bit as lovely as her eldest sister.

She was still defending him. "It was not an entire evening. For one thing, you were called away—I thought it a fortuitous escape. I hope the problem that night was solved?"

He would not speak to her of Ranee. He had built walls around his privacy that he was not willing to breach. "Quick action kept it in hand, I am happy to say. I suspect that is not what you most wanted to know?"

"No, no. That is—" she looked troubled, as if she could not choose a question. "Is it always so hot? In India? That is the impression I receive from all the accounts, even yours."

"India is a subcontinent, huge compared to Britain. There are great differences between one area and another—mountains, seacoast, rivers, plains. It can be very hot, or quite cold, very dry, or very rainy. How can I give one answer?"

"You said very little of what it is like in Lampur, apart from the gold mining." Why gold mining made her smile, he did not know. He had belabored that topic to exhaustion.

"Lampur is hidden in the mountains south of Mysore. The area is remote—the first mapping surveys were done the year I was at Hailey Bury. Soon after my return to Bengal I was sent down to help the survey teams as an interpreter—that is how I first met the raja in Lampur."

She sighed, and he tried to ignore the effect it had on him. "It sounds so exciting, especially to one whose life is as proscribed and dull as mine. I suppose that is one reason I love to read about such things—imagining life through the experiences of others, like yourself. Now I envision waterfalls and ranges of loaf-shaped mountains, right out of the Daniells' engravings."

"And you are not wrong."

She asked him a number of other questions, and he found himself talking about his childhood in northern India, and his more recent years in Lampur. As a younger son not in line to inherit, his father had made India his career, and the same had always been expected of Ren.

"Did you ever face a man-eating tiger?"

Her curiosity struck him as childlike—quicksilver, honest, and innocent. He chuckled. "Yes, I did once, near Sakrigali. It is amazing how much resemblance he had to your mother."

She gave a hoot of laughter and surprise, not at all ladylike. Heads turned in their direction, but he was charmed.

"Oh dear," she said, recovering herself, "is Mama as bad as that? I suppose she is. Please do not say you blame her."

"She is not alone. Half the doting mothers in London look at me with that same speculative gleam in their eyes."

"Oh, heavens. That makes me realize we should be getting back. Have we sat out more than one dance? Oh, I know she will not be pleased."

"And why is that?"

"She would have been pleased to have me dance with you, I've no doubt. But not to sit and talk. Definitely not that. Oh, I am in the suds now—I have done just what she told me not to do." She rose, suddenly flustered, and nearly dropped her empty punch cup. He captured it swiftly and somehow in the process entangled his fingers with hers. He smiled down into her eyes.

"Now why would your mother not wish you to talk with me?" He knew he should release her hand, but he did not.

"Because I—that is, because of Rorie—she is the eldest, and the prettiest . . ."

He had made her blush furiously. He was enjoying the effect he was having on her, but he was also aware of other people in the room, and he was not without mercy. He released her hand just as Hayden Carrisforte found them.

"May I assume this means you are sufficiently rested?" the man asked, looking none too happy and shifting his gaze from one to the other of them. "When I tried again to claim my dance, I was told that you were too fatigued and had gone off to sit somewhere. Your brother is looking for you in the other anterooms even now, and I would be understating the case if I said your mother does not look pleased."

"No, I can imagine," Miss Parbury replied. She hastily snatched up her reticule, which was lying on the bench. After apologizing to Mr. Carrisforte for missing his dance a second time, she marched off toward the salon before either of them could offer their escort.

Chapter Five

" **A** re you not angry? 'Tis hardly fair. She can't make you stay in forever," Harriet Pritchard exclaimed on the second afternoon after the ball. Mariah had just finished explaining the punishment Lady Parbury had chosen to countermand what she had seen as an act of open rebellion.

The two young women were in the garden behind the house on Great Marlborough Street, taking advantage of a few minutes of sunshine that had broken through the afternoon clouds. Mariah thought that if she was not to be allowed to go anywhere, then at least she could get some fresh air. The garden smelled of damp earth and mossy stones, and here the rumble of wheels and clop of hooves from the street was muted, blocked by the house and thick garden walls. She found the trickle of water from the fountain soothing.

Did she need soothing? She had thought that she was not angry, but perhaps she was wrong. "Mama said I have always been the dutiful daughter, the one she could depend upon. She made me feel horribly guilty, Harry, because it is true." She snipped a dead blossom from the daffodils growing around the base of the fountain and dropped it into her basket. The task belonged to the gardener, of course, but Mariah had wanted something to occupy herself out-of-doors.

"When Mama told my father, he said nothing, as you might predict. But he looked at me with a terribly hurt expression, as if I had truly betrayed them. I suppose, in their eyes, I did just that. Rorie is not even speaking to me, and Cassie rolls her eyes and sends me the most overdramatized looks of shock and horror. She was not even at the ball, the little rat! Only Georgie is still my good, kind sister."

"It is all my fault," Harry said apologetically. "I was only thinking of you, and what you had said about wanting a chance to speak with the marquess."

"Well, I had wanted to see his house more than I wanted to speak with him, and now I am effectively a prisoner in my own." Mariah punctuated this statement with a snip of the cutters. After her conversations with the marquess, her desire to see his collections was greater than ever, but so was her despair of ever achieving that aim.

"So much for my great plans to introduce you to a wider circle of people, or any other plans," she continued gloomily, adding to her basket. "If I had known I would be sentenced to stay at home for days, I might have at least done something more deliberate to deserve it. Lord Milbourne whisked me away from the dancing so quickly, I just did not have time to think. My wits seem to go begging when I am near him, that is all. I am guilty of brainlessness, not rebellion."

Harry raised an eyebrow at that admission, but all she said was, "I will think of a way yet to get you into Milbourne House, I promise. I owe you that."

"No, Harry. No more schemes. I think I have gotten into enough trouble, thank you. I do not blame you for what happened—well, not completely." Mariah's honesty was lost on Harry, for that young lady was no longer attending.

"I have the perfect thing," Harry replied several moments later. "If we borrow a set of clothes from one of the maids, you could go in through his servants' entrance below stairs, and pretend you're the sister of one of his maids, looking for her. By the time they hunt around for whoever it is, you could get a good look around and slip out again."

Mariah laughed. "Oh, Harry, that is an impossible plan! It is so full of flaws—I would be sure to be caught."

Harry looked offended. "All right. Sometimes it is the most daring and unexpected plan that works, not the most perfect one. But if I were the one to go in, I know I could make a go of it. I've done worse, and had it turn out rather well . . ."

"My dear friend, you are a natural born actress, which I am not."

"There is that, although you always underestimate yourself," the other young woman conceded thoughtfully. "Suppose we simply called there pretending to be seeking your brother? We would not be able to stay, of course, but you would still get to see something, and it would require a less elaborate scheme . . ."

Mariah shook her head. "No, Harry! But someday you must tell me the tale about when you did worse—you and your family are endlessly intriguing!"

"Not today. Today I must fly—my mother and sister Juliana are awaiting me so we can go shopping—oh, Mariah, I am so sorry you cannot come with us!" Harry paused, and then added encouragingly, "You will be free soon. The Finchleys' ball is Friday, and Mr. Carrisforte has invited us all to his picnic. I am certain your parents cannot mean for you to miss those!"

Mariah took her friend's arm and began to walk with her back into the house.

"Harry, you are certain there's gold at the end of the rainbow, and certain there's glory to be had on the stage. I love you dearly, but I am certain that you had better go home—not only are your mother and sister waiting for you, but the chimney sweeps are doing our chimneys today, and you do not want to be here when the soot and ashes start flying about. I plan to hide in my room and hope the drop sheets keep the soot and mess to a minimum."

Harry wrinkled her nose in distaste. "She is making you stay home with all that going on? That seems monstrous to me."

"There has been a rash of chimney fires in the neighborhood. She is afraid to wait—the rumor is that sparks blowing from one may have lodged in another, and so on. She hired the sweep yesterday morning, first thing."

At the front door Harry gave Mariah a hug. "I will call on you again tomorrow, dear friend, and bring you the latest in the rash of rumors spawned by the ball. But I do think you should consider my idea."

As Bennett closed the door on her irrepressible friend, Mariah looked thoughtfully at the entrance hall of her home, trying to imagine it converted into a Hindu temple. The black-and-white tile floor and Grecian sculptures standing in niches did not lend themselves to the fantasy. She had found the same difficulty in the other rooms where she had tried the exercise—the pastel colors and delicate plasterwork defied her attempts to imagine them into anything remotely like the Daniells' pictures of India. She sighed and headed for her room.

Reading allowed Mariah to block out most of the noise of the chimney sweeper's crew at work that afternoon, but when Bennett warned her that the fireplace in her own room was among those to be done next, she went to her mother's bedchamber, seeking refuge.

The dustcovers were still in place, looking ghostly in the gloom of the late afternoon, but she thought she would just remove the one from the comfortable wing chair, where she might resume her interrupted literary sojourn. She supposed that the darkness in the room was the reason she was well into it, intending to light a candle, before she noticed a small furtive figure standing not in the fireplace, where he might justifiably have belonged, but at her mother's dressing table, where he most definitely did not.

"Here, then, what are you doing?" she exclaimed, although it was a silly thing to say, when she could see perfectly clearly that the boy held her mother's string of amber beads in his hand.

A look of sheer disbelief—not panic, or fear—crossed his face. "Whoa, miss! Where'd *you* come from?" For a moment all they did was stare at one another. Then, as if he realized he needed to say something more, he added, "I was only admirin' these pretty beads, what somebody left out 'ere. They're fine, ain't they?"

His voice sounded entirely too old for the size of his small body. To look at him, she would have guessed he was no older than six or seven, although she knew he must be more unless his master was flaunting the law. He was black with chimney soot and very thin. He placed the beads back on the table and edged away two steps in the direction of the door.

Mariah placed herself between him and that possible means of escape. She battled with her feelings; her mind told her that climbing boys were notorious thieves beyond redemption, while her heart cried out that this was only a child.

"Admiring is one thing," she said. "Stealing is quite another." There were other items of her mother's jewelry spread out on the table, in a way her mother would never have left them. Some of the items had belonged to her grandmother and great-grandmother—they were irreplaceable.

"Look, miss, I've got to get back to work. Iffin Mr. Roberts catches me out o' the chimney, he'll 'ave me hide."

"You might have thought of that before," she said sternly. "Will you empty your pockets, or shall I do it for you?" She took a step closer, ready to spring if he should try to rush past her. He obviously did not see her as much of a threat. "You would be wise to cooperate with me, young man. One scream from me will bring the whole house down on your head, along with the constable."

"Oh, now, there ain't no need to do that." He reached down into one pocket of his ragged, soiled breeches and brought out a small rock and a piece of string.

"Let me see the rest," she ordered. Slowly, one by one, a string of pearls and a pair of amethyst earrings came out, followed by a small silver candle snuffer and an ivory-handled dinner fork. She did not recognize them.

Blue eyes stared out at her defiantly from his smudged black face. "Look, I ain't nipped nothin' from this house yet. S'posin' I put this lot back an' we'd call it quits?"

His temerity amazed her. She thought hard. "What do you do with these after you steal them? You cannot buy food with a pair of diamond earrings."

"Them's amethysts."

"Who taught you the difference? Your master? You will be in more trouble if you don't tell me than if you do." She tried to appear intimidating, although she doubted she could impress this child. "Why should you bear the burden of facing the law if your master is the one behind it all? Do you fancy a life spent in Newgate or the hulks?"

His chin came up and his lips pressed together into a thin line. She decided to change tactics.

"I suppose you consider yourself quite skilled at this sort of thing. Do you steal something from most houses where you clean the chimneys, or is it only certain ones?"

By appealing to his pride, she was able to gradually draw from him an incredible account of his methods and the involvement of his master in a systematic business. Once the sweeper had gained access to a block of houses through one legitimate cleaning job, access to all the other houses was insured, for the boy could climb through attic windows and crawl along rooftops as he pleased. Rags stuffed into a few selected chimney flues explained the rash of "chimney fires" that insured additional business. As she listened, however, an idea began to form in her mind.

"I may be willing to strike a bargain with you. What is your name?"

"Taylor."

She did not know if it was a first or a last name, or even a true name.

"What kind of bargain?"

"A trade, of sorts." The idea she had was daring, and quite possibly more foolhardy than any of Harry's. Still, it struck her as more likely to succeed. "If you agree to help me, I'll agree not to report you. I'll report your master to the magistrates and get you away from him, to save you from the gallows. That is surely where you're headed under his guidance."

"What about the others? If you report 'im, we'll all be out of a job."

"How many of you does he have working for him?"

"Eight."

Eight! That was more than the law allowed, and she did not doubt that some of them were under age, besides. Surely better situations could be provided, even for so many! She was quite convinced that she would be saving their lives. If in the process she could also accomplish her own goal, so much the better.

"You claim there's not a house in London you cannot get into if you choose? I want you to get me into a house in Grosvenor Square."

Harry proved to be right about Mariah's confinement. On the fifth day Lady Parbury relented, just in time for the Finchleys' ball. Mariah suspected that her mother's decision was influenced by the nuisance of continually having to make excuses for her absence as well as by the natural affection deep in her mother's heart. The suspicion bolstered her against the guilt she felt when she pleaded a headache on the afternoon of the ball.

"Why, Mariah, my dear! I am so sorry. Are you quite sure? I thought that you would be so especially happy to finally be out again. And we are going to Lord and Lady Stanfield's for an early dinner first, even Cassie. And I rather thought you were nursing a *tendre* for young Bradshaw, Lord Stanfield's son."

The surprise and contrition in her mother's voice were genuine enough to make Mariah feel very small indeed for deceiving her, but with Lady Parbury things were almost never straightforward. Mariah had evinced a passing interest in Lord Stanfield's son last Season, until he had proven himself rather too frivolous for her taste. She strongly suspected that now her mother was hoping the young man could draw Mariah's supposed interest away from the Marquess of Milbourne.

The news that Cassie would be going along was welcome indeed. If Mariah was ever going to carry out the plan she had arranged with the sweeper's boy, this Friday was the day. With the rest of the family absent, it was much less likely that her own absence would be noted. The Finchleys' ball was a major event, like the Sibbinghams', and she felt very certain that the marquess would attend. William was excused from the Stanfields' as he had plans to dine with Lord Milbourne at their club beforehand. It was perfect. It might be the only time things would ever be quite so perfect. She only hoped the boy, Taylor, would not let her down.

In the bottom of her wardrobe lay a bundle of clothing he had procured for her. She had not been sure she trusted him to keep his end of their bargain, but the fact that he had returned yesterday with the clothes was a good sign. In all fairness, he had expressed doubts that he could trust her in return. They were both operating on faith for now.

Mariah lay on her bed and waited, listening to the sounds of the household. Just before her mother and sisters left, Lady Parbury looked in on her again. Mariah had her maid Jennie bring tea and then left the empty cup outside her door to show that she did not wish to be disturbed. Quickly, she created a sham hump in her bed to make it look as if she were resting there, and took out the clothes the boy had brought her.

A more assorted mix of odd pieces she had never seen. The slightly soiled shirt was large enough to fit her twice over, while the breeches were only a little too big. There was an extremely frayed brown waistcoat with no buttons to fasten the front. She did what she could, making a great fold down the front of the shirt after slipping it over her head and then belting up the breeches using the belt from her rose-colored pelisse. For once she was grateful that she had generous hips!

She donned her plainest pair of worsted stockings and a pair of extremely shabby shoes the lad had informed her would cost his life if they were not returned. To think that they were so prized by someone was a sad statement indeed.

After tucking her hair beneath a cap, she slipped out of her own house easily enough—the servants were all gathered below stairs and in the back service wing. She closed the front door very quietly behind her and hurried through the twilight to the place where she had arranged to meet the boy.

He was waiting for her. "Lor', miss, I thought p'raps you wasn't comin'. Changed yer mind, like." He looked at her closely. "You sure you want to go through wi' this?"

Mariah's heart was pounding in her throat, but she was

not going to come this far only to turn back. What had Harry said about the most daring and unexpected plan? Mariah had never done anything like this in her life. As long as all went well, no one would ever even know. . . . She nodded and gestured that they should set off, for she did not fancy completing the project in total darkness.

They made their way to Grosvenor Square by backstreets and alleys, not at all the route Mariah had followed with Harry the previous week. Taylor knew exactly which narrow ways led through and which mews were cul-de-sacs. Eventually he paused in the brick archway between a small, paved courtyard and a mews full of stables.

"End o' the row, closest to North Audley Street, you said." He waved into the court. "This 'ere's the back o' them shops on North Audley, and that long wall runs along 'is garden." There was a look of disdain on his young face. " 'Tis too easy, by far! Look 'ere."

He moved into the courtyard and pointed out the route with his finger. "First, the wall. Wall to tree. Tree to rooftop, roof to window."

It was easy enough for a monkey, but Mariah was not in the habit of climbing. "How do I get up on the wall?" she asked dubiously.

Taylor rolled his eyes and heaved a great, long-suffering sigh. Mariah was nervous enough that it made her want to laugh.

"Come on, then." He showed her where a stack of crates stood in the shadows close to the wall.

Well, really. That should not be too difficult. Except that the crates looked rather flimsy, and she realized that she weighed considerably more than a mere slip of a boy. She mounted hastily, ignoring the alarming way the pile rocked and teetered as she climbed up. That was when she realized the wall had iron spikes set into the top of it.

"Oh, heavens," she started to say, but Taylor promptly shushed her.

"Use the spikes for grips," he whispered, nimbly ascending the crate pile himself and showing her. "We're just going over." He placed his foot on the rounded wall shoul-

der and hauled himself over the top of the spikes onto a stout
tree branch just beyond. He climbed higher so that she could
do the same.

Thank heavens I needn't go back the same way! she
thought. She should be able to walk out with perfect ease
when she had looked her fill. If she met any servants, she
was planning to pass herself off as a late-quitting member of
the workmen's crew.

From the tree to the roof was easy enough as long as she
did not look down or think about the fact that they were two
stories above the stone pavements of the garden. She did not
drop onto the roof as silently as Taylor; she hoped no one
was in the rooms directly underneath. The slope of the roof
was gentle and getting to the window was not difficult.

"How is it that people never see you crawling about on
their rooftops?" she asked Taylor.

"No one ever looks up," he answered confidently.
"They're always too busy goin' about their own business.
Now, sh-h-h!"

He used a tool to pry the window up for her and before
she could thank him he was gone, back down the roof and
away, muttering something about females who didn't know
how to be quiet.

Mariah's pulse was racing and sweat prickled her skin in
the chill air. Watching Taylor furtively pry open the window
had brought it home to her that she was trespassing, break-
ing the law, something far beyond the mere deception over
which she was already troubled. Staring at the dark opening,
she almost lost her nerve to proceed now that she was alone,
but the thought of trying to reverse her route was too daunt-
ing.

I could have used a hand climbing in this window, she
thought as she squirmed ungracefully over the sill. On the
other side there was a rather large window seat. She stayed
there for a moment, taking stock and allowing her eyes to
adjust, for the room was considerably darker than the dusky
evening outside.

Right away she realized that the room was peculiar, to say
the least. There were no signs of rich treasures from India.

No pictures hung on the moss green damask walls. Instead, the room was sparsely furnished, notably lacking the small useful tables that most rooms offered. Beyond the large window seat it did boast an equally large red velvet sofa and some comfortable-looking upholstered chairs. What appeared to be the major portion of a tree trunk stood at an angle in one corner with a large basin of water on the floor beside it. She began to feel particularly uneasy—she had noted that there was some sort of yellow animal hair all over the cushion of the window seat as well as the sofa.

What kind of an animal could the marquess be keeping? The door to the adjoining room stood open, and Mariah looked anxiously in that direction. A new prickle ran down her spine—one of anxiety. This was definitely not where she wanted to be. Keeping her gaze riveted on the open doorway between the rooms, she edged toward the other door, the closed one she thought might open into a stair hall or passageway.

Just as she reached for the handle, she heard the rumble of a deep voice and the curl of brass moved beneath her fingers. She barely had time to jump back. The door opened. Lord Milbourne stood there with a hunting leopard the size of an Irish greyhound at his side.

Chapter Six

"It would seem that Nuseer was right, Ranee, we do have an intruder," Lord Milbourne said.

Mariah stared.

The cat was a sleek, thin, long-bodied creature clearly built for power and speed. Its coat was spectacular, a golden color spotted all over with black, except for the chin and throat which were white, like the tufted tip of its tail. Dramatic black lines defined its face, running from the inner corners of its eyes down to its mouth.

The marquess looked equally splendid. He was dressed all in white, in simple clothing of a looser yet similar style to that which he had worn to the Sibbinghams' ball. The snowy color set off the bronzed tone of his skin and his golden hair. His head was bare. Draped from his left shoulder to his right hip was curious red cord. He looked every bit as magnificent as he had when bedecked with jewels, and also a little dangerous.

Mariah wondered frantically if there was any hope that he would not recognize her, would not notice the open window. Her plan all along had been to pretend to be part of the crew of workers renovating the house if she ran into anyone. But she had not counted on it being anyone she knew!

"Sorry, milord. Got meself lost," she said, trying to imitate young Taylor's inflections. Maybe in the gathering darkness the marquess would not look at her too closely.

"Lost, is it?" He rubbed his chin in mock thoughtfulness. "Hm, I should say so, especially if you mistook that window for a door." He spoke a curt word to the cat and then crossed the room to close the window. The cat sat down in the door-way.

"I would not try to move," he cautioned Mariah. "Chee-tahs' teeth are sharp and their jaws are powerful. They grab their prey by the throat and cut off the air supply."

Mariah stood frozen in place. At least Lord Milbourne could not see her face from behind her.

"Ranee, is this how you got out last week? I think we have a repeat customer. Perhaps this explains the missing trinkets and silver, too."

Mariah's heart sank at his words. Could Taylor have already come here before her? This was becoming far more complicated than she could ever have imagined!

Before she could determine what she should do, the mar-quess crossed back from the window. As he approached he suddenly seized a handful of waistcoat and shirt at the back of her neck. None too gently he pulled her over to the open door, where the cat sniffed her leg with interest.

"Nuseer! Take charge of our visitor please, while I settle Ranee for the evening."

Oh, no, too late! Just as Mariah was realizing there was naught to do but reveal herself and explain, if she could, now she was being handed over to some stranger! Nuseer was as tall as the marquess and as dark-eyed as a Spaniard, with skin the color of sandalwood and a dramatic black mustache that appeared to be waxed on the ends. He wore a white coat and trousers similar to Lord Milbourne's and a red turban. To Mariah he looked even more intimidating than Lord Milbourne, and more sinister. As the marquess handed her over, a little squeak of fear and protest escaped from her throat.

Slowly Lord Milbourne turned her so that he could see her face. She blushed so fiercely that her skin felt on fire.

"The blazes, what have we here?" The tone of incredulity in his voice was understandable. Still, he did not denounce her in front of his servant.

He released her clothing and made a gesture as if to straighten it, then dropped his hands helplessly at his sides. "Nuseer, perhaps you would escort our visitor to my study,

and send for Hajee, please? I will be there directly. Have tea
sent in. And also something stronger."

As Mariah was marched to Lord Milbourne's study, she
finally saw something of what she had come for. The curv-
ing double marble staircase leading down to the ground
floor came together at a central landing halfway down, and
there in the perfect position to greet every visitor lay a large
tiger skin with the head fully attached, fangs bared. The colors and pattern of the fur were impressive, but she had never
seen teeth like those in all her life, nor had she ever dreamed
that a tiger could be such a size!

At the bottom of the staircase every inch of the stone floor
was covered with overlapping carpets in jewel-like colors
and rich, elegant patterns. On the wall opposite the stairs
hung an embroidery with exquisite floral and geometric designs centered around a tree—the "tree of life," she realized.
A pair of huge stone elephants complete with carved trappings and towers on their backs guarded the doorway to the
front entry hall, but she and her escort did not go that way.
Instead, they turned and passed through a pointed archway
whose graceful shape was echoed by a frame of intricate lat-
ticework.

The passageway beyond still smelled of plaster dust and
varnish, but the renovations undertaken there appeared to be
complete. A series of massive half columns lined both sides,
with doors opening off the passage in between them. The
columns were half-octagons, with strange figures and ani-
mals for their capitals. The effect felt just like walking down
an aisle in one of the cave temples illustrated in the Daniells'
book, and in her momentary delight, she quite forgot the appalling situation in which she now found herself. She
guessed that the columns, which looked so much like ancient stone, were carved from wood and treated with a *faux*
finish.

Nuseer stopped at one of the doors and signaled to her to
enter ahead of him. He had spoken not a word to her, nor did
he after they entered Lord Milbourne's study. She knew he
was not a mute, for he had exchanged some words in a for-

eign tongue she supposed must be Hindustani with a much smaller brown manservant before they had descended the stairs. She selected a chair and sat down; unsmiling, he posted himself by the door like a guard.

This room was furnished quite conventionally, with bookcases, comfortable chairs, and a large desk. The books and papers on the desk were arranged neatly to each side, leaving the center space clear for writing. But a rather unconventional grass mat hung over the window, a collection of curved swords and daggers in jeweled scabbards decorated one wall, and a handsome folding screen of ebony or blackwood carved into filigree stood in one corner. Several fantastic and rather grotesque masks hung upon the wall beside the fireplace, and on a small table stood a most amazing sculpture of a highly ornamented, four-armed figure with a huge stomach and the head of an elephant!

Drawn to examine it more closely, she rose and was standing in front of the remarkable piece when tea arrived with Lord Milbourne right behind it.

"That is Ganesha, the god of wisdom, prudence, forethought and good fortune," said the marquess. "Under your present circumstances, you do well to study him. But perhaps it is a little too late? He is most often consulted *before* undertaking an endeavor."

Was it cruel of him to tease her? Indeed, contrary to her usual nature, she had quite intentionally ignored both wisdom and prudence this time, although she had invested a considerable amount of forethought. There had been a kind of thrill in departing from her normally sensible ways. She supposed she did not deserve luck in return for such defiance!

The other servant she had seen brought in the tea and quickly arranged the contents of the tray on a nearby table. When he finished, he bowed and looked inquiringly at the marquess. Lord Milbourne uttered a few words in the foreign tongue and both servants quickly departed, leaving her alone with him.

Perhaps that was not so shocking. She was not here as herself, after all. He had yet to use her name. Had he not recognized her, after all? Perhaps he had simply forgotten her. He would not be the first gentleman to converse with her and within a week have quite forgotten it. But no—as soon as the door closed behind the servants, he turned to her.

"Well, Miss Parbury. I confess I am not easily shocked, but I admit I am more than a little surprised and confused. I can hardly wait to hear your explanation. But, before you begin, please do have some tea. You look as though you could use a restorative."

She did not appreciate the reminder of her appearance. Standing there before him in ragged, ill-fitting boy's clothing, caught like a common thief, had to be the ultimate humiliation.

"I must compliment you on your fetching ensemble," he said, pouring the tea himself. "It is so fitting to the occasion, for one thing. If I had a wife, I would make certain to take down the name of your modiste."

Now he was roasting her! Apparently she was not already miserable enough. She moved to the tea table and took the cup from him in suffering silence. He poured a glass of brandy for himself.

"Ah-h. One of the smaller but no less happy benefits of the war being over," he said, holding the glass up and taking a deep, appreciative sniff. "Please, do sit. Otherwise I shall feel obliged to remain standing myself. In the company of a *lady,* and all."

She resumed her former seat, biting her lip. What he must think of her now! His tone said it all. How silly of her mother to have worried that she would ruin her sister's chances with her bluestocking ways! She had done a far more thorough job of it now, in a way her mother could never have dreamed of.

"It is one thing, Miss Parbury, for a man such as myself to be completely heedless of what people think of him. But you! Although I have been trying very hard since the moment of discovering you here, I find I cannot begin to imagine what on earth you are doing here, or what you thought you were about. And I am thoroughly confounded at the prospect that this might not be the first time! Please enlighten me."

The same devil that had pushed her to come in the first place must have prompted her then, for she said, "It appears that what I am doing here is sipping tea in your study." Before he could throttle her, she pushed on. "This is not, I confess, what I *expected* I would be doing."

Explaining herself was not going to be easy. She looked up as if she would find strength and help beyond herself and found herself staring at the masks on the wall. *Heathen things,* Rorie had said. She quickly averted her eyes.

"I was quite certain that you would not be at home, Lord Milbourne. Were you not to dine with my brother this evening?"

"I had planned to, but I did not."

He looked at her with a kind of obstinate expectancy. Obviously he was not going to explain himself to her. Under these circumstances, she supposed she had no right to expect so much.

This was not going well. She could not think of a way to explain what had seemed so clear to her before without it sounding thoroughly cork-brained. She sighed, took a deep breath, and let it all out in a rush.

"I only wanted to see for myself all the fabulous things you spoke about—the gifts your raja gave you, the beautiful crafts, the curious artifacts, and the renovations to your house! William said you would never open it for people to come and see it, and I thought it would be almost like visiting the Hindustan itself, to see these things. It became very clear that I would never be given an opportunity. Harry was so full of unlikely schemes, that when I met Taylor, doing this suddenly seemed to make so much sense. I was quite sure you were not going to be at home—are you not planning to attend the Finchleys' ball tonight?"

As an explanation, it was not exactly adequate—that much even she knew. The marquess had been looking very severe, but now she thought, unless she was imagining it, he was struggling to maintain that expression.

"Who, might I ask, is Taylor? For that matter, who is

Harry? I am hard-pressed to believe that anyone might have proposed a more preposterous scheme than this one."

"Taylor is . . . well, Taylor is a boy who got me these clothes!" Truly, she dared not tell him. What if it was Taylor who had broken into the house before? She would have to find him and ask about that. "And Harry is Harriet, my friend Miss Pritchard. Oh, perhaps I should not have told you that!"

To her mixed consternation and relief, he laughed. "Are you so concerned about her reputation, or what I shall think of her? Yet you apparently give no thought to yourself, Miss Parbury." He drained the last drop of brandy from his glass.

"Tell me how the devil you came in through that window! And please, I must know if this is the first time you have attempted this foolishness. It is quite important."

Ren listened as Miss Parbury explained the route by which she had come into his house, thinking all the while that she could never have contrived such a feat by herself. When she insisted that she had never done such a thing before in her life, he believed her; his money was on her accomplice, and he would lay double odds that the boy named Taylor was the one. The absurd collection of clothing she was wearing bespoke street urchins to him, and she was suspiciously unforthcoming about the lad.

He rose and replaced his empty glass on the tea tray. "I will tell you that the night I left your home so precipitously, it was because Ranee had escaped from this house. The same window that you used to enter had been left open, and out she went. You were fortunate that she was with me this evening when you entered—those are her rooms, and you might not have appreciated her welcome. There will soon be bars on that window."

He circled around, studying her. She had stuffed her hair into the boy's cap she still wore, but it was oddly becoming. She was not beautiful, he decided, but had a certain childlike winsomeness that was very appealing. And she looked suitably appalled by what he was telling her.

"Happily, that other night Ranee had not gone far. But all

of my servants have been rigorously questioned, and all deny any knowledge of the window being opened. In combination with the fact that numerous small items have disappeared from the house in recent weeks, you can see why my suspicions are aroused."

He did not mention that there had been peculiarities with his mail, as well. Someone was going to the trouble to spend good money simply to send him blank pieces of paper. It was coming to the point where he never knew what to expect when he slit open an unidentified cover. But he preferred to think that the problems were separate. It was easier to consider the mystery of the open window and the missing articles as a single problem linked to a common house thief.

"I am so sorry," she responded. "You must have been terribly worried about your cat that night."

He brushed her sympathy aside. "I will speak plainly, Miss Parbury. Whoever helped you into my house this evening is a likely suspect for these past trespasses, to my mind. Shall I set the constable onto the boy?"

"Taylor? No! Oh, no. You mustn't do that. I can assure you that he is not your thief." Did he detect a note of relief in her voice? "It was only three days ago that I sought his assistance and brought your home to his notice. You have not had a problem during that interval, have you?"

"No."

"I am certain that he had never been here before that. He was, uh, occupied elsewhere."

Her gray eyes were very expressive—he could see that she was telling him what she believed to be the truth, and that it mattered a great deal to her. He was left with a thousand questions, however, including how she could be so certain she was right.

"How did you come to know this boy? I am astonished that you would seek out help from someone like him. And how did you come to conclude that you would never have a chance to set foot in my house? Your mother and sisters have called here twice since I dined at your home, although it happened that I was not here to receive them either time. I don't doubt that on another day I should be."

"Taylor is a chimney sweep. We met purely by accident. This plan occurred to me only when I became aware that he had, uh, certain skills. I confess I did not leave him much choice about assisting me—I am entirely responsible for my own folly. As for the other, I was not included in the group on either occasion when my mother came calling. It was made clear that I should not expect to be."

She had not been in attendance at any social event since the Sibbinghams' ball. He had wondered at it and said as much now. She seemed more than a little surprised.

"Lord Milbourne, I am astounded that you should have marked my absence, given the way the Beau Monde flocks about you whenever you appear! Astounded, and, I suppose, greatly flattered!"

He had slowly circled around once again, and stopped now directly in front of her. "Have you been ill? Somehow, I do not think so."

She sighed. "No, I was not ill. Since we are speaking plainly, I will simply tell you—my mother wishes to keep me out of your company." She studied the teacup on her lap. "By keeping me at home since the ball she sought to further that end and impress the lesson upon me both at the same time."

She appeared so solemn and at the same time so winsome in those ridiculous clothes, he could not suppress a laugh. "Yet here we are together in such circumstances as would make her hair turn gray. Her method does not seem to have worked very well, does it?"

She glanced up. "You were not supposed to be here."

"You should not be here."

Their glances locked, and for a moment he felt a familiar tugging, in his loins and in his heart, too. The air seemed to grow very warm around them. The longer he stared down into those clear gray windows, the harder it became to think of looking away. Could she see into his soul the way he seemed to be seeing into hers? Other thoughts came into his mind, quite opposite to looking away. This was a dangerous development indeed—one he could not allow.

He broke the contact and turned, seeking a distraction in

the decanter of brandy. As he poured himself a second portion he said, "I take it you were not to attend the Finchleys' ball this evening?"

She rose from her chair, seeming a little distraught. Had she felt the pull, too? He prayed she had enough sense not to come near him.

"My mother is not a despot. She had intended for me to accompany them to dinner with friends and to the ball. I believe she felt I was punished enough to be more careful and would welcome the chance to get out. But I pleaded a headache. I had already set my plans for this evening—it seemed the one perfect opportunity."

She had moved back to the table with the figure of Ganesha and was staring at him. "No one was to be home at my house—not even my youngest sister Cassie. I thought no one would be home here at your house, either. As long as I avoided the servants at both houses, or at least fooled any that I might have run into here, it did seem to me a perfectly workable idea."

"It is ludicrous. I should pack you off into a hackney and send you home this instant," he said, knowing he spoke the truth. But as he noted the dismay in her face, somehow he could not bring himself to do it. She had gone to considerable trouble and risked a great deal all for the sake of simply seeing his house. That she would do so implied an ardent passion for learning and experience that impressed him.

If Nuseer or Hajee suspected what she was, they still did not know who she was, and he knew he could count on their discretion—beyond their loyalty, there was also their limited English and disinclination to mix with his English servants. What he was thinking was safe enough—no one would know. "Before I do so, I suppose there is no harm in giving you a tour."

Chapter Seven

Wide-eyed with wonder, Mariah followed Lord Milbourne through his house, so elated her feet barely touched the floor. Her questions tumbled out one after another, as if she feared she'd lose her chance to ask them if she ever stopped.

"Why does Ganesha have the head of an elephant? Why does he sit in that peculiar position?"

"Do those masks represent demons? Do the Hindus truly worship cows?"

"Why do you wear that cord over your shoulder?"

She could not believe she was talking so much.

The marvel was, the marquess answered every query. His patience, along with his knowledge, seemed inexhaustible. He stopped frequently to explain ideas she would never have known to ask about or to point out details she might never have noticed.

She was amazed to learn that the masks represented "avatars" or incarnations of Vishnu—a monkey, a hawk, and a fish. She was more amazed when he took down a dagger from his wall and showed her how it opened into five blades when struck—truly a lethal weapon! As they walked through rooms full of workmen's scaffolding, rooms splendidly finished and other rooms yet untouched, the marquess opened the mysteries of Hinduism, yoga, meditation, and the Hindustan itself to her.

She discovered that the triple-stranded cord he wore symbolized an introduction to knowledge and the right to study—a privilege reserved by the high-caste Brahmins, but sometimes bestowed on leaders and others as a particular honor. That someone should have so honored him did not surprise her in the least.

What did surprise her was the gentleness she sensed in him. She had expected that anyone who had earned the name "The Lion of Lampur" would be fierce and aggressive. In truth, when she had seen him standing in the doorway with his cheetah beside him, for a moment she had been afraid. William had half-jokingly hinted at a darker side to the man at the Sibbinghams' ball, but now she did not know quite what to think.

Why not ask him about the nickname? She had not held back any other questions, but then, the others had all been safely impersonal. For all the stories he had told at her parents' dinner, at the Sibbinghams' ball and even now, she knew almost nothing of the man himself. And she found that she wanted to know.

The opportunity came when their circuit of the ground-floor rooms brought them to a highly stylized figure of a lion carved in stone in the front entry hall.

"The Buddhist lions are not very representative, artistically," the marquess was saying. "Of course, lions do not live in India or China, and some scholars say that is the reason. I think it is simply because the figures are symbolic, and accuracy was irrelevant."

"What do they symbolize?"

"Protection, defense, the preservation of sacred laws. That is why they were placed in front of Buddhist temples and important buildings."

"But I thought Hinduism was the religion of India."

He shrugged, his eyes fixed on the statue. "There are many religions in India. In some places they exist separately side by side, and in some others, they form strange mixtures that have developed since the ancient times . . ."

She did not want to ponder ancient times just now. "Were you a protector and defender?" she asked softly, admiringly. "Is that why they came to call you the Lion of Lampur?"

If she had not been regarding him so intently, she might have missed the look of pain that flashed across his features. It was gone in an instant, but there was a note of bitterness in his voice as he replied, "Yes, there were times when I performed that role. In Lampur I was fairly successful."

Lampur. Everything seemed always to come back to his time there, or else to his childhood. She realized that he never spoke of the time in between his return to India from school and his sojourn in Lampur. What had sent him there? The shuttered look on his face now warned her that more personal questions would not be welcome. He turned abruptly and led on.

She had expected that his sobriquet would be a source of pride, not pain. Stung and a little mystified, she hurried after him, resolving to ask a few questions of her brother. She attempted to steer the conversation back onto safer ground.

"The work you are having done here is utterly amazing and splendid, Lord Milbourne. In the rooms that are finished I feel as if I have been magically transported to India! I could never have imagined anything so grand."

"I am glad you are not disappointed." He continued walking.

But she was. She realized that through her bumbling, a cold barrier had sprung up between them, where a warm camaraderie had existed before. Now he was not offering comments or stopping to describe how a room would look when the workmen were finished. He was leading the way silently back to his study.

"Will you truly not open the house for people to see all this once it is finished?" she asked. "It seems a shame to deny them such an experience."

"Half of them will only be horrified by all the heathen idols. There will be talk enough when they begin to hear about it, as they inevitably will."

She had to hurry her steps to keep pace with him. "But I thought you did not care what other people think."

"I do not. That is why I do not care to share what I am having done for my own private pleasure."

She did not believe him. He had clearly been enjoying sharing it with her until she had asked too many questions. Now he had wrapped his privacy back around him like impenetrable armor.

If only she had not spoiled their time together! It was clear that the tour was over.

"Of course I apologized for upsetting him and tried to smooth things out," Mariah said the following afternoon in the privacy of Harriet Pritchard's bedchamber.

No longer confined to her house, she had persuaded Georgie to accompany her to call on her friend. Swearing them to secrecy, she had confided the tale of her great adventure to both of them.

Harry was looking at her with an expression of great admiration, almost adoration. "Mariah, that was such a daring thing to do! I can hardly believe it. A brilliant, outstanding performance!"

"Mariah, you were extremely lucky that you were not caught, especially when you returned home," responded ever-practical Georgie. "Suppose one of the servants had heard you slipping back in, or someone on the street had seen you? I cannot begin to imagine the uproar there would have been when we came home." An affectionate hug accompanied these words, which Mariah knew came only out of Georgie's concern for her.

"I was not able to restore the comfortable level of companionship that he and I had enjoyed at the beginning of the tour, but at the end I think perhaps he meant to make amends, after a fashion. He loaned me this!"

Mariah reached into the basket she had brought with her on the pretext of taking some comfits to Harry and pulled out a leather-bound sketchbook. It was filled with scenes of life in India—people engaged in their daily activities.

"He said a friend had made these sketches—are they not wonderful?" She turned the pages, revealing bustling bazaars, roads teeming with pedestrians and bullock carts, pools full of bathers. "It makes the place seem alive."

"I think you have made a special friend," Harry said breathlessly, "if not a conquest. What a shame it must remain secret—but how romantic!"

Mariah thought the notion that she, of all women, might have made any such impression on the marquess was too ludicrous even to address. "Remember, you have sworn not to breathe a word to anyone," she cautioned them again.

"Rest assured! What a scandal, if this ever came out," Georgie said. "Not to mention the wrath of Mama and Rorie," she added with a chuckle. "You must take care that no one at home sees that book, Mariah. I don't think you could convince them a *sketchbook* came from the lending library."

"On the other hand, suppose the marquess had to marry you? To do the honorable thing," Harry speculated. "Imagine being married to him! Oh, Mariah. Don't you think it would be heaven?"

"Harry, I think you are too prone to flights of fancy! I would not want to marry anyone with as little knowledge of them as I have of the marquess."

"He is marvelously handsome, titled, and wealthy—what more could you want to know? You have interests in common, you *like* him . . . Many marriages start with far less."

Mariah giggled. "Mama could not be too upset—at least one of us would have trapped the poor man. Rorie might never speak to me again—would I miss that? Actually, I think Rorie might be relieved. I do not think she has a real interest in him—she is only trying to please Mama and Papa. But I would never feel right in a marriage that was forced on a man by the rules of propriety. Do you not hope someday for a love match?"

Of course they did, all three of them. The conversation moved on to what qualities each one thought made the ideal man, and girlish daydreams of impossible futures. What troubled Mariah was that she could not rid herself of Lord Milbourne's image, and could not quite convince herself that he was not the very ideal that she described.

Lord Milbourne was not much in evidence during the days of social activity that followed. Mariah reentered the whirl with caution, not at all certain how she should behave toward him. His absence simplified matters considerably, yet how hollow her enjoyment seemed without him! She found that she was constantly on the alert for him, watching the entrances of ballrooms and craning her neck at glossy carriages in the street that looked similar to his.

What the frustrated hostesses had in place of him were rumors. Rumor had it that he might attend this rout or that card party, despite the fact that he had or had not accepted the invitations. When he failed to make these appearances, other rumors crept in—Lord Milbourne had been seen with this actress or that opera dancer; Lord Milbourne had been seen with the Earl of Egremont and Viscount Lewisham in White's drinking a toast to the Peshwah of Poona. Tongues clucked, especially when he was rumored to have been seen in Hyde Park in the very early morning hours, racing his horse with—of all things—a cheetah! He was dubbed "a trifle eccentric" but nothing he did was shocking enough to spoil the universal infatuation all of London seemed to have for him.

Each time these rumors went round, Harry's and Georgie's glances slid to Mariah, but fortunately no one marked it. Her secret was safe. Except for a new restlessness of spirit that seemed never to leave her, Mariah's days went back to a semblance of normal routine. At night by the light of a lone candle she would secretly take out Lord Milbourne's sketchbook and gaze at the pictures, but she dreamed more of him than of the Hindustan. She felt certain that she would see him at Mr. Carrisforte's picnic.

In the meantime, she had kept her word to Taylor and had gone to the magistrates in the parish where he lived to file a complaint against his master. She had never set foot in a police office in her life, despite the presence of one on her own street. What a distressing collection of humanity was to be found there! Moved almost to tears and immensely thankful for Harry's loyal company, she had persevered. An investigation had been promised; she would be kept informed of any developments. If her complaint was found to be well-grounded, the boys would be removed from the chimney sweeper Roberts and sent to the workhouse until new placements were found for them. There was nothing more she could do for the moment. Such things took time.

*　　*　　*

The day for Mr. Carrisforte's picnic dawned with a pearly pink sky and a fresh breeze that bespoke a fair day ahead, although few among London's Beau Monde were awake to witness it. By later in the morning, however, the entire Parbury household was in a frenzy of preparation, for all the members of the family had been included in the invitation. Lord Parbury fussed that he had not gone along on a picnic in so long a time, he had forgotten how to dress for one. Lady Parbury soothed and directed him.

The picnic was to be at King's Hill, on the Carrisforte family's estate near Dulwich, some five miles south of London. Mariah realized that the drive there could offer her the chance she had been seeking to ask William questions about the marquess. As the travel arrangements were being settled, she begged that she and Georgie might be the ones to go in the barouche with their brother.

"Wanted to escape Mama's endless instructions to Rorie on how she should set her cap for Milbourne, eh?" William said as he settled himself on the rear-facing seat. "Can't say as I blame you." The driver's whip cracked and they set off with a lurch and a rumble of wheels on cobblestone. The others would follow in the family's traveling coach.

"You do not believe we could simply have wished to bask in your august company?" Mariah teased. "Perhaps you do not give yourself enough credit!" She paused, then admitted, "The truth is, I am curious about the marquess. For all the stories he tells, he says very little about himself. But you have known him all these years. Tell us something of his history. Why did he take up residence in a native state, and why do they call him the Lion of Lampur? He did not go to Lampur directly after he left school, did he?"

"Pesky little sister, allow me to warn you. Do not be bothering the marquess with your curiosity. He is a very private person. When pushed too far, he has been known to retaliate. I remember him at Harrow being extremely patient and tolerant, but he was ferocious if someone crossed over the line."

"I am not bothering him. I am bothering you!"

"Yes, you are." He chuckled. "I suppose that is the better

course, if you insist on having answers. But I do not know everything that happened to him after he returned to India. After we finished at hallowed old Harrow, I went off to Cambridge, and he was given a place in the first class at Hailey Bury—the school had just been started. But he did not complete the program there. He was taught the native languages during his childhood in Bengal and he knew Hindustani, Persian, and Tamil better than many of the instructors. The directors recommended him to be placed in the Company immediately. When I next heard from him some nine months later, he was in Calcutta."

"How long did he stay there? When did he go to Lampur?"

"Hush. I am trying to remember. I was busy leading my own life, you may recall. But you probably don't—you were only, how old? Ten? Yes, a shy and preoccupied ten-year-old, I recollect."

"I don't remember Mariah being shy," said Georgie. "Just quiet and observant."

"You were the shy one, Georgie!"

William cleared his throat. "I remember that Ren was very pleased that they put him to work as a translator almost immediately. He did not have to stay in Calcutta all the time—he was able to travel with delegations of Company officials on business. He sounded content, but then I did not hear anything from him in a long while. I do not know what happened. I had all but given up on ever hearing from him again when his next letter came. He had been there about three years, I think. He was leaving the Company, and planned to seek employment with one of the native rajas. Lampur was one of the places he mentioned."

Mariah looked out at the sun glistening on the river as they crossed Westminster Bridge. Why would a man whose entire life had been directed toward a career with the East India Company give it up after only three years? She supposed that working privately for a raja brought far greater rewards than dutifully plodding along within the Company's structure. Certainly people said that Lord Milbourne's wealth was already vast before he had inherited his grandfather's title and fortune. Yet, he did not strike her as a man motivated by a desire for riches.

"Has he never given you any clue as to why he left the Company?" she asked thoughtfully.

"I believe that politically he had come to see things quite differently from the official Company view, so that may have been part of it. But I do not really know."

"Why is he called the Lion of Lampur?"

"He arbitrated a number of disputes between Lampur and its neighboring states and also negotiated a number of agreements with the Company and our own government, all of which were said to vastly favor and protect Lampur's wealth and interests. As a state it is very small, but apparently its gold deposits are very rich, making it a plum sought by everyone. His skill was as much admired as it was regretted by all the unsuccessful parties. At the time I recall some people felt he was on the wrong side—that he should have been looking out for our country's interests. The name was given him by the Raja of Lampur, but the newspapers picked it up and spread it. You know how they love labels!"

"So, he *was* a protector and preserver," Mariah said to herself, looking off out of the window again.

"What's that?" asked William.

Georgie, sitting beside her, gave her an almost imperceptible nudge.

"What? Oh, nothing. I am just talking to myself." Mariah grinned sheepishly.

"Just remember what I said about him, Mariah, and beware," William admonished. As he looked at her, his eyes narrowed. "You are asking a lot of questions. I can't help wondering what is going on in that active brain of yours."

Chapter Eight

One by one the carriages of the invited guests had come up the drive in front of the Carrisfortes' handsome Georgian manor house. Now the passengers were regrouping for the walk to the hilltop where their picnic was to be served, and Mariah was looking for Harry and the rest of the Pritchards, for Mr. Carrisforte had invited all of them.

"You will need to be careful around William," Georgie warned her. "He is likely to be watching you more closely now that his curiosity has been aroused."

"I am convinced there will be nothing for him to see, Georgie," Mariah responded, keeping her voice low. "There is nothing between the marquess and myself but a single secret and one borrowed book."

If there was more, she hoped he might find some way to signify it. She felt it far more likely that her rash behavior had given him a disgust of her. "Look, there are Harry and Juliana."

Aware of her mother's watchful eye, she repressed the natural urge to halloo loudly and wave her friend over. Unladylike behavior, to be sure. She was determined that today she would prove that she was not a hoyden, contrary to what the marquess no doubt already believed. "Come, Georgie, let us stroll over quietly and join them."

Harry and her sister made a lovely picture standing together in the breeze, Harry with her dark tresses set off by a straw bonnet and Juliana with her light ones set off by pink satin. Mariah felt a momentary pang of envy, regretting her own brown, neither-here-nor-there color hair, framing her face in a fringe of unruly curls that her own bonnet did not hide. She supposed if the entire world were full of beautiful people it would be very boring indeed, but she would not have minded if the designated "beautiful" portion of the population could have included her.

"The house and the park are very handsome, don't you think?" Harry asked as they approached. "I must say I am impressed. Did you notice how fine the view was as we came over the last hill? Someone was saying that the prospect from the hill where we are having the picnic is one of the finest."

"It is unfortunate that Mr. Carrisforte is not in line to inherit any of this," Juliana said, and they all nodded in agreement.

"Apparently he is at least making some progress in his attempts to get back in his family's good graces—they are allowing him to host this picnic," Georgie added.

"I have heard him say that he has a better chance of achieving sainthood than gaining their good opinion," Mariah said. "I think—and for his sake, hope—he must have been joking!"

The walk up the hill was invigorating and pleasant. If any of the young women were disappointed that the noisy, laughing gentlemen went up as a group ahead of them instead of offering to escort them, none said as much. In unmixed company the chatter was less restricted.

"Lord Milbourne is certainly tall, is he not?" commented one of the young ladies in the group. "Look how he towers above the others."

"He is such a fine-looking man. It is a blessing that he came into his grandfather's title—just think of the tragic waste if he had remained buried in the jungles of Hindustan!" said another.

"'Tis a wonder he did not come dressed in native clothing," said the red-haired young woman Mariah had seen dancing with William at the Sibbinghams' ball and a few times since then. "I have heard that he wears it all the time when he is at home."

Was there a hint of criticism in her tone? "I suspect that he finds it infinitely more comfortable than wearing all those tight-fitting layers our fashions require, not to mention high collar points and a cravat fit to choke on," Mariah pointed out reasonably.

"Oh, but he does look splendid in them," came the reply, followed by a lot of girlish tittering.

Mariah had to admit that he did look particularly fine. Leather riding breeches clung to his thighs like second skin, and his dark brown coat fit his broad shoulders flawlessly. His low-crowned hat had a very rakish curl to the brim, or perhaps the rakishness came just from the way he wore it, a product of attitude rather than style. He had barely acknowledged her, but that might have been a precaution against betraying their secret or even a protection against irritating her mother. Was it possible that a fledgling friendship had begun between them, as Harry had suggested? How could she do anything but hope it was so?

The footpath took them past cows grazing in the fields and up through a small copse. From this they emerged into a sunny glade protected from the wind where blankets had been laid out upon the grass and a number of wicker hampers stood ready. Open fields rising to the top of the hill beyond could be seen through the outer ring of trees.

The gentlemen were busily engaged in unpacking something bright and colorful from crates at one side of the clearing. As the young ladies entered the area, they quickly realized the bits of paper and wood were kites. Their host separated himself from the other men and approached them.

"Once we have eaten, I hope you shall find the kites a pleasant diversion. It is one Lord Milbourne and I often enjoyed in India. The breeze up at the top of the hill should be strong enough to support our kites—we shall have a contest!"

"A kite-flying contest? What fun!" came the approving chorus. "But do let us eat something first, after our journeying."

The servants quickly set out a sumptuous repast of cold dishes—chicken and ham, apples and hothouse grapes, breads and several kinds of cheeses. There was enough food to feed three times the number of people in the group, all of it delicious.

William's joking comment, "What, no Indian food?" brought chuckles and knowing looks, for everyone knew the story of Lord Milbourne's dinner with the Parburys. The marquess was a focus of attention for everyone, but particularly for Mariah. She barely knew what she ate, so busy was she with watching him. Would he slip and by some word or sign betray the secret meeting that they had shared? Would she?

At the same time she worried, part of her yearned for a sign that he was not disgusted by her after what she had done. He was being scrupulously polite to everyone and at the same time flawlessly impartial, offering to get more wine for one lady, more chicken for another, pausing to converse with Lady Pritchard and Mariah's mother. He did, of course, direct some conversation toward Mariah and her sisters, but it was perfectly general and impersonal in nature. Somehow, she simply did not feel as grateful for this as she knew she should.

Eventually, the only gentleman still employed with his food was one Lord Hascombe, who by all accounts would keep at it until there was no more to be had. With good-natured teasing, those who intended to fly kites or to watch excused themselves and headed out to the open hillside.

Mariah found a place to stand in the shade of the nearest trees, fully intending only to watch. One by one the gentlemen were seeking out partners among the younger ladies, but she was determined to stick by her resolve to behave in a dignified manner. She doubted that racing about with kites would be considered above reproach, although Harry had already been coaxed out by Mr. Carrisforte himself.

The cavorting gentlemen and their admiring partners made a lovely picture in the sunny green field, with the colorful kite tails fluttering in the cool breeze and the clear sky an arch of blue above them. Mariah shaded her eyes from the sun. She had no difficulty picking out Lord Milbourne's long figure from the rest.

She watched him stop to assist one of the other young

men who had not yet managed to get his kite aloft. Shedding
his coat with the fellow's assistance, the marquess took up
the kite and began to run with it, racing into the wind and
letting out the string just enough at a time to let it climb.
With the wind billowing his shirtsleeves and the sun glint-
ing on the satin stripes of his snugly fitted waistcoat, he
looked more splendid than any man she'd ever seen. He ran
with the smooth, athletic ease of a cat—she thought the
other men bounced about like goats in comparison. The idea
of telling that to William brought a smile to her face.

She sobered quickly when the marquess retrieved his coat
and, slinging it over his shoulder in a way that would have
caused his tailor and valet apoplexy—not to mention a few
mothers and chaperones—walked down to where she stood.

"I can see it in your eyes that you are yearning to fly kites,
Miss Parbury," he said with a most engaging smile.

"Fibber! You could not see my eyes from out there." She
could not help smiling back.

"*Au contraire,* my dear," he said very softly. "I can see
your eyes even when you are not present . . ."

"Saucebox! Such fustian!" It was ridiculous, yet she felt
flattered anyway. Was this exactly the sign she had been
hoping for, or was he only teasing her?

"*Alis volat propiis,*" he quoted. "Of all the ladies here I
would expect this activity would most appeal to you."

"'She flies with her own wings,'" Mariah translated,
slanting a puzzled look at him.

He laughed. "Yes, I thought you would know Latin, little
bluestocking. I think you do not know yourself half so well.
Never mind. Would you honor me by accepting the role of
my kite-flying assistant?"

"Do you think it would be wise?"

"I think if I ignore you it would raise more speculation
and attention than if I prevail upon a pretty woman like any
normal red-blooded male."

Did he truly find her pretty? Again he confounded her.
She had not expected to find him flirtatious and full of compliments, and she could not tell if he was sincere. But perhaps that did not matter.

He hung his coat on a tree branch and reached for her hand. "Come. There is a contest to be won. Here is a chance to run and laugh and be free, for a little while, at least."

Mariah found she could not resist such an invitation.

Ren thought Miss Parbury had the most expressive eyes of anyone he had ever met. In them he saw everything—her hesitation, her disbelief, but underneath all, her yearning. Since that first night at the Parburys' dinner he had come to realize that it was more than a yearning for knowledge—it was a yearning for freedom. She was a kindred spirit, a fellow prisoner like himself, trapped by circumstances beyond her control, if she only knew it. She was also a seeker, not yet awake to the fact that what she sought most she held within herself.

He led her out into the field as if he had invited her to dance, only dropping her hand when they reached the pile of remaining kites. "Which one do you choose? Your blessing will undoubtedly give us an edge over our competition," he said, watching her. He liked the way her hair formed a soft light brown halo around her face.

"The blue one. Blue is the color of the sky, and look, it has a green tail. Blue and green, the sky and the treetops. Surely that is auspicious!"

"Surely it is." He laughed with her, thinking how he liked the musical sound of her pleasure. "The gods of the wind must be appeased, after all."

He was joking, but a serious look suddenly came into her face. "Lord Milbourne, I have heard a rumor saying that the Hindu idols have become your gods—that you became a Hindu living in Lampur. I must ask you—is it true?"

"Does the idea upset you?" He paused, but then he realized that he wanted her to know the truth. "The answer is no. Have you not learned yet that people will say anything when they do not understand a thing?"

He fumbled with the kite string, trying to untangle it from its brothers in the pile. "I would defend the Hindus' right to worship in their way, even to the death. I have learned much about their religion and I respect it. I even understand some basic truths about it that many Hindus do not realize. This does not mean I have converted, but people are ignorant, and many will purposely misinterpret things if it suits them. My views offend some people. I have been surprised by how quiet my critics have been since I arrived in London. I predict that the honeymoon will not last."

"Who are your critics?"

"To start, a number of gentlemen within the Company wish me to the devil, I've no doubt—especially the man who sponsored my seat at Hailey Bury College. I could go on from there."

Finally he had the string free. He handed her the wooden spinner on which it was wound, and picked up the kite by the knotted string just under its frame. The breeze tugged at it, and he laughed, determined that the topic they were discussing should be closed.

"You see? The wind can hardly wait to have it. Let us take it higher up on the hill."

The breeze was tugging at her bonnet, too, and had put roses in her cheeks. He wished the bonnet to blazes. He should have liked to see her running free, her hair and her soul unbound. He smiled at the image he pictured. She was enchanting. He should be careful.

They climbed to a higher point on the hill, where he declared them ready to launch. He extended his arm and held the kite up like a falcon ready to fly.

"I will not have to run far to get this up," he said. "You must let the string out quickly, but the trick is to keep tension on the string. Are you ready?"

She nodded and he began to move. The spinner flew in her fingers. In moments he had only the kite string slipping between his own fingers as the kite rose higher and higher. He nodded to her in approval and she beamed in response.

"The challenge is to see whose kite will fly the highest," Mr. Carrisforte announced, shouting so that all on the hillside could hear him. A half-dozen kites were in the air at various levels, sailing with varying degrees of stability. They might have been giant flowers on the slenderest of stems, nodding in a sun-splashed spectacle of color, or great birds swooping and diving in the wind.

Maintaining tension on the string, Ren moved back, close to Miss Parbury. "Watch," he said. "Carrisforte will add another challenge, I guarantee it. Competition is his lifeblood."

When she silently offered the spinner to him, he shook his head. He was enjoying the effort of coordinating their movements and the sense of a physical link between them, no matter that it was only a slender string that bucked and tugged. Miss Parbury's eyes were on the sky above them, her lips slightly parted in a half-smile of what he hoped was delight. Her breathing was slightly labored from the effort of keeping up and climbing the hill. He was suddenly assailed by the most distracting urge to kiss her.

"Oh, I think you are right," she exclaimed just as suddenly. "What is he doing now?" She pointed to Carrisforte's kite, whose string had crossed Lord Beaumont's, at that moment one of the highest. With Miss Pritchard cheering behind him, their host had repositioned himself on the hillside to ensure a battle.

"Ah. I suspect Lord Beaumont may be doomed to lose his contender. Kite-dueling is a popular sport much practiced in northern India. Carrisforte will try to cut through Beaumont's kite string with his own. His lordship may try to maneuver his away, but Carris is an expert."

They proceeded to watch as Carrisforte continually worked to keep his kite string engaged with his opponent's and in just sufficient motion to rub it.

"What the Beau needs to do is duck and dodge. If he can prevent Carris from rubbing the same spot for long, he has a prayer that Carris will fray his own string first," Ren explained. "And of course, there is always that other unpredictable element—luck. Some strings just break sooner than others."

Of course, anything with an uncertain outcome was bound to inspire the laying of odds. A quick round of wagering had sprung up among the gentlemen as soon as they realized what was happening. Taking advantage of the distraction they presented, Ren surreptitiously jerked the kite string between his own fingers, sending his and Miss Parbury's kite diving perilously.

"Oh, Miss Parbury! Look out! We must have hit a rogue current. Come on!" He set off at a run, pulling in string and knowing she would have no choice but to follow. He had much better control over the kite than it appeared, thanks to much practice under the Indian sun. Circling round one side, he was making for the other side of the hill.

Miss Parbury was winding string furiously as she ran, with no hand free to straighten her bonnet. She began to laugh, apparently aware of the hopelessness of setting herself to rights.

"Oh, look, there it goes," he called encouragingly as he let the kite begin to soar upward again. But he must have been distracted by looking back at the delightful picture she presented, for a moment later it dived again, quite unbidden by him. With a sickening crash, it landed in a patch of shrubbery a short distance ahead of them, most certainly out of sight of the rest of their party. He could not have planned a more satisfactory result.

"Drat and confound it all!" he said, pretending he meant it. "Well, we must try to salvage the wreck." He turned to her with an apologetic look. "No prize for us." But he was thinking of winning a different prize, now.

"I suppose you are right," she said, gamely winding string. She tugged as the string caught on brambles a little in front of them, and he moved ahead to free it.

This side of the hill was wilder, with rocky gullies and bushes amidst smaller patches of grass. He reached in among the briars to free the string and waited for her.

"I do not think we can make our way through this," he said as she came up. "Mayhap we'll have to cut the string and begin again on the other side, or go ahead to retrieve the remains of our poor missile and work our way back."

He took the spinner from her fingers and, placing it on the ground, claimed her hand. "The going is much rougher here—allow me to assist you."

He suspected that she could manage perfectly well—she who had climbed a wall, a tree, and a roof to get into his house. But she did not protest. Moreover, she did not pull her hand away. He took that as an encouraging sign.

They made their way around the patch of briars, heading for the shrubs that had claimed their kite. At the edge of a rocky gully she hesitated, obviously studying the rocks to choose her footing. "There's a better way to do this," he said, and without so much as asking permission he slipped his arms under hers and swung her neatly across.

"Oh!" She looked startled, but not alarmed.

He got across in barely two strides of his own long legs and landed himself so close to her he could hear her quick intake of breath as she took a step back. *Not yet,* he told himself, and settled for a long, intent look into her eyes. He would have liked to nuzzle behind her ear, seeking the source of that sweet scent of jasmine she wore. Bonnets were the devil's invention, he was quite certain. At least hers was loosened and slightly askew from running.

He said nothing, only took her hand again and made for the shrubbery that had captured their kite. It was in plain sight, caught between some high branches with its long tail dangling.

"How will we ever reach it?" she asked.

"You've had some recent experience climbing in trees," he replied, perfectly straight-faced.

"Not in these clothes!" She was aghast until she realized he was teasing her.

"You could stand on my shoulders like an acrobat at Astley's?"

"No!"

"All right, I'm thinking." And he was, just not about retrieving kites. He moved closer, leaving a scant and highly improper few inches between them. *Now? Yes, now.* No one had followed them, no one could see them. "I'm thinking I should help you with your bonnet."

Instinctively, she reached one hand up to feel it. He caught the hand and kissed it. Surely she must know what was coming.

"Here," he said, untying the ribbons. "We must start over." With relish he removed the offending bonnet, but he could not keep his hand from the soft cloud of hair he found beneath. Somehow, from her hair his hand found its way to her cheek, and from that gentle caress slid down to cup her jaw.

She looked at him with huge eyes, but not a murmur of protest. Emboldened, he angled her head and brushed the lightest butterfly of a kiss across her lips.

Chapter Nine

His pulse was thundering. The kiss wasn't even close to enough, yet already he knew it was too much. The power in that slight touch had slammed into him like the sudden unleashing of a monsoon storm. His choice was to leave off, now, or to take her into his arms, into his heart, and to heights of experience she likely had never dreamed of. He had not the right. He had made a huge mistake.

Shaken, he stepped back, and held up her bonnet with hands that were less steady than they should have been. "Here now, let us see if we can get this right." His voice was husky.

She was staring at him, her gray eyes reflecting—what? Astonishment, amazement . . . perhaps a hint of dismay?

"I must apologize," he said quickly. "I promise we will keep our experiments to straightening bonnets and rescuing kites." That was all he had meant it to be—an experiment, and a small one at that. He sounded calmer than he felt.

Still she said nothing.

"Will you forgive me?" He needed a response—any kind of response. If she slapped him, or turned on her heel to stalk away, or burst into tears—well, no, he hoped not that, for how would they explain—but almost any response at all would be better than this silent staring. Had he so shocked her? Or could it be that she had been rocked with the same force that had hit him? For both their sakes, he hoped not.

"You have a singular way of fixing ladies' bonnets, Lord Milbourne," she said finally.

He settled hers into place, his fingers brushing the softness of her hair and lingering as if of their own will. He forced them to move to the ribbons and to tie a bow under her chin. He studied the results critically, and in the process searched her eyes again.

No, there were no traces of moisture collected and held back, no sparks of anger. He had puzzled her, it seemed. If she only knew how much more he had puzzled himself! But now was not the time for reflection—if they did not return immediately, kite in hand, there would be questions, innuendoes, at the very least questioning looks. He would not subject her to that.

"You are respectable again, madam," he said with a smile meant to reassure her. "Let us recapture our errant kite and return to the others at a more sedate pace, so as not to dislodge your silk and feathers again."

"How will you get the kite?"

"If I can find a suitable branch, I may be able to snag the end of the tail, and thus pull it within reach. If not, it looks as if the task may cast me into the briars quite literally." *I believe that figuratively I am already there.* "No doubt it would serve me right."

The effort to rescue the kite from the brambles and shrubbery did wonders to restor Reinhart's composure although at the expense of his fine cambric shirt. A huge rent in the left sleeve earned him far more sympathy and attention than he either wanted or deserved from the ladies and a good deal of teasing from the other men. Carrisforte had, not surprisingly, triumphed over his guests in the matter of kite-flying; Ren suspected that he himself was the only one with enough expertise to have offered his friend a true contest. If anyone had thought his brief disappearance with Mariah Parbury improper, they apparently possessed the good judgment not to mention it.

His thoughts focused upon Miss Parbury for much of his drive home. She had the most extraordinary effect on him. Being with her transformed him into a creature of mindless impulse he hardly recognized. He still had not come to terms with his actions the evening she had sneaked into his house like a thief. That he had allowed her to stay, had even given her a tour of his apartments, had been unthinkably foolish, well beyond highly improper. If any hint of it ever came out, they would both be doomed to face the parson together.

That he had loaned her the sketchbook he prized above almost anything was another impossible puzzle. Not only was it irreplaceable and of great value to him, it was evidence of their secret encounter. He knew he would be wise to get it back from her as soon as possible. Yet wisdom and his actions when in the vicinity of Miss Parbury did not seem to go together.

That he had proved this very afternoon. Like a schoolboy prankster, he had laid a plot to get her off alone in the bushes, all to simply gratify his base desire for a kiss! He should have known better—he had sensed his attraction to her that evening in his study. He was no celibate—he should have recognized it for what it was.

And what was that? Not simple lust—he knew what that felt like. This felt different, deeper and infinitely more dangerous. He could not allow himself to become more entangled with her. He must not.

As was his wont, he drove his gig around to the stables behind his house rather than leaving it out front for Ahmed or Selim to tend to. He did not care if such minor infractions of proper behavior caused his neighbors to gossip. If anything, he took a perverse pleasure in defying the definitions of good *ton*.

He had not asked to be the Marquess of Milbourne, nor had he ever expected to be. At the time of his own father's death, the succession had still looked perfectly secure—his uncle, the older brother, was the rightful heir and had two hale and hearty sons—the proverbial heir and a spare. But while Ren had thrived in pestilence-plagued India, the younger of his cousins had died in the Peninsula, and both his uncle and his other cousin, still unmarried, had succumbed to illness last year at the Derbyshire estate.

It might be a long time before he could bring himself to visit there. It still seemed like a rather cruel joke, on top of the bitter irony, that he should wind up deprived of every soul of family he had ever known and be handed a role and responsibility he'd never wanted in their place.

Well, he would perform it in his own way. In a refractory state of mind, he entered the house through the garden and headed for his room, knowing that Hajee and Nuseer would appear there within minutes if not seconds of his arrival. They would shake their heads indeed over the state of his apparel—from his torn shirt and wrinkled coat anyone might assume he had taken part in a prizefight rather than a picnic.

Later, bathed and attired in clothing that was more comfortable than proper, he went to Ranee's rooms. The big cat chirruped a greeting from the oversized window seat when he entered.

He sat on the edge of the cushion, rubbing the cheetah around her ears and under her chin. He looked out the window as she had been doing, listening to the sounds of the city as day drew to a close. How different bustling London sounded from Lampur or even Calcutta—no voices called Mohammedans to prayer, no gongs beat in far-off temples. But at least a few things were the same.

"Watching for birds, eh, Highness? Any activity out there this evening?"

At twilight or any other time, the roof of the service wing attracted sparrows and doves more often than housebreakers. This was a fortunate occurrence, since the window still boasted no iron bars. Surprised and annoyed by the delayed delivery of those commonly needed items, Ren had gone himself just two days before to look into the problem. The order had been mysteriously canceled.

It could have been an honest mistake, but apparently it was not. The owner of the iron monger's shop insisted that he had received a written order canceling the purchase. Naturally, he had not kept the note, and did not know how it had been delivered. Ren had added the incident to the growing list of small but unsettling occurrences that were definitely not helping him to make the adjustment to his new life.

There had been too many incidents, now, to be dismissed as merely unlucky coincidence. And even more troubling, they seemed to be increasing in seriousness. Blank notes in the mail were annoying but harmless, the theft of small items from the house was essentially undamaging—even the cancellation of the order for the window bars was more frustrating and mystifying than hurtful. Who was so intimately acquainted with his affairs? But Ranee's escape could have escalated into an incident where harm was done, and the most recent event of all disturbed him greatly.

"If only you could talk, my girl," he said to the spotted cat. "You could probably tell me who opened your window so that you could slip out."

His servants had all been questioned about the window incident at that time. He had had to call them all in one by one and question them himself after this latest event. A very valuable dagger—the rare one with five separating blades—had disappeared from the collection on his study wall two days ago. He suspected that whoever had taken it did not know the dagger's secret, and such ignorance increased the lethal danger of either possessing or using the weapon, well, fivefold, he supposed.

The servants had been unhappy about being questioned, especially so soon after the last time. If he was not careful, his recently hired staff would all leave him, and he would have to begin the hiring process all over again. A London house of this size could not be run by a staff of five, English or Indian, even if they were more loyal and capable than his. If keeping his life in turmoil was the ultimate aim of whoever was behind this campaign, that person might very well succeed . . . unless Ren could discover who it was and put a stop to it all.

Hayden Carrisforte came to see him the following afternoon. Ren had asked him to call, on the theory that two heads were better than one. It was time to confide in someone, and Carris was the most likely choice, for Ren knew his measure. They had survived a good deal more than Harrow, Hailey Bury, and kite dueling in India together.

"I am hard-pressed to imagine what trouble you could be suffering these days, my friend, beyond a surfeit of pretty women," Carris teased him as they walked through the columned passageway to Ren's study. "That is one problem

I would be most happy to help you with. Let me see, among the entire town, perhaps you might leave to me a few dozen of the less highly ranked ladies? That would include three out of four lovely Parbury daughters, and the delightful Miss Harriet Pritchard along with her sister . . . although if I am not mistaken, I'm beginning to sniff a surprising little bit of partiality toward a certain Miss Parbury on your part?"

Ren was not about to answer that. "I thought the wind was blowing a bit differently in regards to Harriet Pritchard and yourself, old man. You seemed to be showing a little partiality in that regard."

"I do enjoy her company, it's true," Carris began, and then stopped abruptly as Ren opened the study door.

Ren had brought Ranee down to keep him company while he went over accounts at his desk; she was lying quite comfortably on the blue-and-white Indian cotton rug in front of the hearth as he and Carrisforte entered.

Carris hung back in the doorway. "So, the rumors I've heard are true. You did bring a hunting leopard back with you! You've been hiding her from me." He eyed Ranee warily. "I assume she's tame enough around strangers? I mean, I always thought you and I were friends . . ."

Ren laughed. "You have no need to worry. Ranee will probably ignore you. You may feel free to give her the same treatment if you prefer, although I do think it a fine thing when one's friends become friends."

"Ranee? A majestic name for a cheetah. As I recall, it was more commonly applied to tigers, not to mention the reigning raja's wife. But then, I suppose here in London yours hasn't much competition, so who's to quibble over her royal status. Certainly not I." Carris edged into the room, managing a nervous smile.

"Come, take a chair," bid Ren. "If I know you, you will not think it too early in the day to sample my excellent stock of French brandy, and I consider that a small reward in return for your time."

He made his friend comfortable and proceeded to outline to him all the happenings of the past weeks since he had settled into the house. Carrisforte's face reflected a growing sense of indignation.

"I say! And you have questioned all your servants, and are satisfied with their answers? Such doings! I am surprised to see you so unruffled by it all—but no, I suppose I should not be. I am sure you are right to be concerned, however. Someone certainly seems to have intimate knowledge of your daily activities—most unsettling. Certainly unacceptable."

He drained the last drop from his brandy glass, looking wistfully after it. "Damn but that is a fine brandy." Using his fingertips, he pushed the glass back onto Ren's desk. "What we need is a plan of attack. Had you anything in mind, or is this to be a strategy design session?"

Ranee yawned, as if she found the very thought excessively boring. She stretched, the muscles rippling along her lean frame, and then got up, sauntering over to Carrisforte's chair, where she proceeded to sniff and inspect his leg quite thoroughly.

Carris clutched his chair arms and moved not a hair. Even his mouth barely opened to form the words as he asked, "What is she doing?"

Ren chuckled. "Relax. She is only curious. Cheetahs do not have an acute sense of smell, but she still is learning who you are and where you've been today. She will be satisfied in a moment and will leave you in peace."

Ranee finished her inspection but chose to sit down only inches away from Carrisforte, which did not exactly make him feel more at ease. Ren decided the best course would be to return the cat to her rooms, so that he and Carrisforte could talk without distraction. When he returned from taking her upstairs, Carris was standing by the wall with the display of weapons, apparently studying them and the space where the missing dagger had hung.

"Have you ruled out the possibility that the thefts are the work of a repeat housebreaker? I have heard of cases where once the thief becomes familiar with the contents of a house, he just continues to help himself as need arises, on a regular basis until he is caught or his route of entry is closed off. The thefts seem to me a less personal sort of strike against you than the other events, if that makes any sense. Perhaps they are not related."

"Yes, I have considered that," Ren replied, almost relieved to hear someone else voice thoughts so similar to his own. "Perhaps a simultaneous attack on two fronts would be helpful. I have thought I might post guards at night, to see if the thief can be caught."

I am also going to confront one errant chimney sweeper's boy, he added to himself. Despite Mariah Parbury's certainty that her young accomplice was innocent, he was not convinced of it. He would send a note to Miss Parbury insisting that she tell him how to find the boy.

"Perhaps you might entrap the other offender by setting up some more orders for goods, to see if they are also canceled behind your back. If you alert the shopkeepers of the possibility, perhaps they will help you by keeping any notes they receive or paying attention to how the message is delivered."

"That could become quite expensive," Ren said with a wry chuckle. "Will you pay my bills if none of the orders are canceled?"

Carris laughed outright. "Why certainly, if you will pay off all my other debts. I've no doubt you can afford it better than I can!"

"Never mind. At least it is a workable plan. I do need to order a new shirt. Picnics are very hard on one's clothes."

Mariah received Lord Milbourne's note that same afternoon. She had just come in from a shopping expedition with her mother and sisters, all of them flushed and a little giddy with their successes. As they congratulated one another on their finds and untied their bonnet ribbons, Bennett approached Mariah stiffly with the note on a silver tray.

"This came for you while you were out, Miss Mariah," he said, his expression as inscrutable as always.

Lady Parbury's was much easier to interpret. "Oh? How nice, my dear! Who do you suppose it is from?"

Mariah picked up the note, carefully placing her thumb

over the telltale "M" superimposed on the design in the sealing wax. She had a very good idea who it was from. Why would he be sending her a note?

"I think it must be from Harriet. I will read it in my room," she said. How easily the lie slipped out! She who had always been so honest was becoming quite expert at deception. What a tangled web she and the marquess had made! Before anyone could comment, she quickly headed up the stairs.

In her room she tossed her bonnet and the note onto her bed. It was unconscionably risky for him to write to her, she thought as she removed her gloves and unbuttoned her dove gray pelisse. They had even more secrets to protect now than before. Hadn't he realized her family might ask questions? He had placed her in an awkward position, yet deep down her heart beat a trifle faster.

Thinking things over, she had realized that both she and the kite had been skillfully manipulated—and not by any "rogue current"! The only "rogue" either she or the kite had encountered yesterday afternoon had been the marquess, not the wind.

Questions had plagued her for much of the night. Why had he done it? What had it meant? He had gone to so much trouble for such a slight thing, and then he had backed off as if she had stung him. Had she done something wrong? She did not believe so—the kiss had been so brief, there had not been time enough for her to do anything, either right or wrong.

She had not told anyone—not Georgie, not Harry—although there had been little opportunity. She did not intend to tell them. Some secrets could not be shared. It was not because she was ashamed, for she was not. She was disappointed, and she was not sure what that said about her character. That feather-touch of a kiss had set her heart racing and made her light-headed, but still it had barely been a kiss at all. What would a true kiss from him be like? Trying to imagine it caused her pulse to pound and a restless feeling to move through her. She wondered if she would ever find out.

She laid the pelisse over the back of the chair near the window and reached down to unlace her half boots. How grateful she was for a room of her own and the privacy to think! Waiting her turn for Jennie's help to dress for dinner was a small price to pay for such a privilege, even if it had only been granted because she and Cassie had fought so much. Lord Milbourne was a man who must understand that need—had he not given his cheetah an entire suite of rooms? In her rumpled day dress and stocking feet, she flopped onto the bed and took up the note, turning it over in her hands.

Few had failed to notice that the marquess had chosen her as his kite partner yesterday. On the way home from the picnic Lady Parbury had said, "For whatever reason, it seems to me the marquess has begun to show some favor to you, Mariah, above at least some of the other girls."

It would not do to admit that Rorie was one of those, but the fact hung there, as plain unstated as otherwise. Mariah was fairly certain that she owed today's purchase of the beautiful rose-colored satin for a ball gown and new evening gloves of the softest, thinnest, most expensive kid imaginable to Lady Parbury's realization that she might need to alter her matchmaking plans.

Mariah could well imagine the fantasies her mother would weave if she only knew the true author of the note. It was just as well she should never know. Unlike her mother, Mariah harbored no illusions about her chances with the marquess. Rorie, at least, was an acknowledged beauty, but daughters of barons did not marry three ranks above them without fabulous faces or equally fabulous fortunes. Mariah possessed neither, and this marquess had no need of funds, in any case.

She slipped her thumb under the edge of the heavy, cream-colored paper and broke the seal. Smoothing out the single sheet, she confirmed the signature and eyed his handwriting curiously. It was strong and masculine yet neat and well-formed, reminding her that he had been trained to be a clerk and writer for the East India Company. She ran her fingertips over the pages, touching his words.

Dear Miss Parbury, [he began]
Thievery continues to be a problem in my home. It is of the utmost importance to my investigation that I speak with your young chimney sweep, as soon as possible. I must prevail upon you to contact him and arrange a meeting between him and myself.

Y'r obed't serv't,—Milbourne—

Well! Surely no greater ninny than she breathed on the planet. It was a perfect business letter. Not a congenial word in it apart from the "dear" at the beginning, and she doubted even that would have been there if convention did not require it. He was so indifferent to convention, she was surprised that he had bothered. There was not a single reference to the previous day's events, nor anything personal, in fact.

She might have excused that as his way of protecting their secrets, but the contents of the note were just as revealing and condemning as if he had gone ahead and made such other references. She could not show it to a soul. She would have to lie to her family to cover up what it was. What on earth could she say to them at dinner?

Thoroughly irritated, she read the letter over again. He still thought Taylor was guilty of robbing him, after all her assurances. He did not say so, but the thought was clear behind his request. He did not believe her. Well, she would show him! She slid off the bed and, sitting down at her writing table, took out ink and paper to pen a reply.

Chapter Ten

Two days later Mariah stood in Harriet Pritchard's bedroom, trying to tuck the telltale ends of her hair under the edge of a dark brown poke bonnet that had belonged to a maid in Harry's second oldest sister's employ.

"My dull, straightforward life is becoming complicated indeed these days, Harry," she said. "I am sorry that it is spilling over so much into yours. You know I do appreciate your help."

She had seen no alternative but to send her reply to Lord Milbourne by way of a note to Harry, and she had further prevailed upon her friend for help in carrying out the proposal she suggested to the marquess.

"You know very well that I thrive on intrigue!" Harry answered. "And Merissa is very understanding about these sorts of things, after what she went through to marry her Frenchman. We are so lucky that her maid has gone to visit relatives."

As she spoke, Harry shook out the folds of a lightweight gray cloak that she then held ready for Mariah.

"Everyone knows Mariah Parbury would never be seen in such unfashionable clothes." She chuckled. "As for the marquess, people may wonder how he could be seen with such a dowd—that is, if anyone even sees you—but everyone knows he is eccentric! Have no fear."

Have no fear. That was an easy thing for her fearless friend to advise. Not so easy for Mariah to practice. She found that living a life filled with subterfuge was wearing.

"You are certain your footman is available to accompany

us? Once your 'maid' goes off with the marquess, I would not want you to be left unescorted," Mariah said anxiously.

"He is coming! Do not worry so," Harry replied with a touch of impatience. "Are we meeting Lord Milbourne inside or outside of the museum?"

"*We* are not meeting him, Harry. *I* will be meeting him outside—I pray that he will already be there waiting with a hackney when we get there in ours. It will be a quick thing for me to transfer from one to the other."

Mariah had chosen the British Museum as a meeting place because it was not too far distant from her intended destination. She had had to file her complaint against the chimney sweeper Roberts with the magistrate at the Queen Square police office, and that was where she needed to take Lord Milbourne to learn the current whereabouts of young Taylor. Setting up a meeting between them was not as simple as the marquess might command.

Great Russell Street was full of traffic, but a lone hackney was waiting in front of the grand museum, stationary among all the vehicles that came and went. Sensibly, Harry sent the footman to confirm that Lord Milbourne was waiting in that ancient and somewhat undersized Berline before she would allow Mariah to go forth. Moments later, Mariah found herself handed up and settled opposite the marquess inside the other coach.

The incongruity of his elegance and the shabbiness of the hackney struck her immediately. He looked more impeccable than ever, as if his valet had been taking ever-increasing pains with his appearance. His cravat was perfect, his double caped greatcoat without a wrinkle. She could see the flounce on the hem of her plain muslin dress reflected in the shine on his boots.

Those boots were much closer to her than they ought to be. He was such a large man, he seemed to fill the space, making the interior of the carriage feel very confining and intimate. His long legs clearly did not have enough room, and she realized that his knees would be bumping against the side of hers continually if she did not hitch over a bit to one side of the seat. His fashionable beaver hat rested on the worn leather squab beside him, and she noticed that his head was inclined slightly to avoid brushing against the roof the compartment.

He was studying her with that bemused expression she still remembered vividly from the dinner party almost three weeks ago. "You make an extremely charming maid, Miss Parbury," he said. "Apparently insipid pastels do not become you nearly so well as earthy colors."

She blushed as the carriage began to move. Apparently he was going to be a devil today. "After all I have been forced to go through, it is unkind of you to tease me." She made the mistake of looking up and found his golden gaze upon her. She was not sure why she found that so unsettling. So much safer to look out of the window!

"Why would you assume that I am teasing?"

She decided to ignore his remark. "Thank you, at least, for going along with my plan," she said. "I am not in the habit of inviting men to take me out, but you did not leave me much choice—my receipt of your note stirred up everyone's curiosity. I am blessed to have such a willing accomplice as Harriet, who must now spend some hours at the British Museum before she can go home, to cover my absence. However, this did seem the best way to achieve two things at once—three, actually."

"Those being?"

"Well, to satisfy my family about your note without exposing us, obtain an escort to accompany me to the magistrate's office, and, I hope, to satisfy you about Taylor's innocence."

She glanced at him and saw the feigned look of wounded virtue he assumed. "I merely wish to speak with him. Did I accuse him of anything?"

"No, but you certainly implied it." The carriage came to an abrupt halt, forcing her to fumble for the handgrip by the window.

He merely raised an eyebrow. "You sound more than a little annoyed with me."

She was not used to such blunt speaking outside of her

own family, but she was not going to tell more lies. "Yes, I am. Or I was. Whatever possessed you to send round a note? Or to require this meeting? I told you before that Taylor has not been stealing from your house. It is lowering, I suppose, that you do not believe me."

That much was true, if a trifle incomplete. She had come to admit, sometime between midnight and two in the morning, that she was also annoyed with herself for having hoped his note would be something different, and annoyed with him because it had not been. What a foolish state of affairs, all because of a kiss that had hardly been a kiss! She supposed she was annoyed about that, too.

The carriage began to move again, bouncing over several bumps that fully revealed the inadequacy of the vehicle's springs, or the jarvey's lack of mercy for his passengers.

"I believe in your sincerity, Miss Parbury," Lord Milbourne replied, pronouncing the words carefully and continuing his steady regard of her. "However, I am open to the possibility that you might be mistaken about the boy, or that your faith is simply misplaced. It bears investigation, that is all. I do not doubt but that you would do the same in my place."

Mariah definitely doubted that, but heavens! Was she actually going to argue with the marquess? He seemed much too near, and too imposing. She found his sheer physical presence remarkably distracting. How did he manage to disturb her so just by sitting there? She knew she could not blame all of her discomfort on the jostling of the carriage.

"I do apologize for sending you the note," he said smoothly, saving her the necessity of responding. "It was indeed ill-considered—in fact, it was not considered at all. I was thinking only of my own problems, and not of the consequences of my actions. Can you forgive me?"

How could she not, when he smiled at her in just that way? She could well imagine why, as William had said, the Lion of Lampur won every negotiation that he entered into. Such a smile could melt ice.

She nodded, finding a sudden sympathy for him. "Have you so many problems? I imagine it must be difficult, to leave your old life behind you and to take up the reins of such a new one unexpectedly."

She thought she saw surprise in his eyes before he turned away. Was he so unused to finding a sympathetic ear? "Someone seems to have taken it into his or her head to make it more so," he said, staring out the window now instead of at her. "Let me just say there have been some odd happenings, besides the disappearance of items from the house. I am determined to put a stop to it. It has gone too far."

There was no look of amusement on his face now. Mariah was reminded of William's words on the day of the picnic. This man could be dangerous if pushed too far. Had he other enemies, then, besides some random house thief? She prayed that her faith in Taylor was justified. Quite suddenly she did not know what to say.

The awkward moment passed as the carriage made a sudden turn and hit a bump at the same time, throwing her and the marquess sideways.

"Goodness!" she exclaimed. "I believe we must have the worst jarvey in London driving our coach."

He laughed. "I have half a mind to get out and walk the rest of the way—I never thought the trip to Queen Square could take so long. Or be so painful!" he added ruefully. "But I fear I owe you another apology, for that is my own coachman Ahmed on the box. He is not at his best dealing with narrow streets or such a quantity of traffic."

She stared at him, astounded. Why on earth would a man in his position employ a coachman who was less than a crack hand with the ribbons? She had to ask.

Lord Milbourne's first reply was a chuckle. "I suppose it does seem odd, viewed that way. Ahmed is much more to me than merely a coachman. He is more a bodyguard than a driver—it is hard to explain. In India the duties of servants do not always divide up in the same ways they do here. Here in London I generally have no need of a bodyguard, although today I thought it prudent to have him along since we are placing ourselves amongst rough company. It was simple to make an arrangement with the regular driver. Under

less challenging conditions Ahmed's skills are adequate—
you found no fault the day he drove you and Miss Pritchard
to Marshall's Library, I trust?"

"No, indeed. I must admit I scarcely paid any attention."
*I was too overwhelmed by our chance meeting on the side-
walk.* Thinking of that day, she blushed and then was thankful that he did not appear to notice.

"I have five servants who came with me from India, Miss
Parbury. I feel my responsibility towards them acutely. It
goes well beyond bed, board, and employment, for they
gave up everything to come with me. I believe a man needs
dignity and self-respect to live, hence Ahmed bears the exalted title of coachman, even as he continues to learn the
skills. They will all adapt to living here, but it takes time.
Ahmed's brother Selim will adapt the fastest. He is young."

Mariah was impressed. Who would have guessed that he
possessed such concern for the needs of others? The last
trace of her annoyance with him seemed to evaporate in the
warmth of such a revelation, and renewed admiration took
its place. He was a most remarkable man.

Ahmed finally delivered them to Queen Square a few
minutes later. Ren watched Miss Parbury's face while they
waited in the police office, conversing sporadically and observing the surrounding parade of humanity.

"Who accompanied you here the first time you made this
trip, Miss Parbury?" he asked.

"Oh, Harriet came with me," she said quite offhandedly.

"To a police office? What on earth were you thinking?"
He spoke louder than he meant to, but the very idea was ludicrous. "Do you mean to say you did not have a man with
you?"

"Oh, yes, we had her footman. Harry persuaded her family to let her take one with us without raising any questions
at all, whereas I would not have been able to do so."

"I see. So your family knows nothing of your involvement with Taylor and what you are trying to do for him."

He had to admire her spirit. Most of the other gently born
English females of his acquaintance would have balked at

coming to such a place, although they might visit Bedlam or the Lambeth Asylum—he supposed crime was less fashionable than insanity or destitution!

"I must say I do not know how the officials and magistrates can face it day after day," she commented. "The place is so depressing. So many people, with so many problems!"

"Why did you go to so much trouble for a chimney sweeper's boy?"

"How could I not? His master was making them thieve. What sort of future would he or the others have?" She raised her chin and met his gaze. "Why do you care so much about your servants? When you meet Taylor, I think you will understand."

Even if they were never to meet the boy today, Ren was finding the visit illuminating. She was strong, this young woman—she held her head up at the same time her eyes betrayed the intensity of her feelings. As they waited and listened to the cases and complaints that preceded them, he saw sorrow, sympathy, and occasionally horror, but not once did he see revulsion in her pale face. Her wholesome presence seemed like an island in the sea of vice around them. He would have liked nothing better than to scoop her into his arms and take her out of there.

"How old is Selim?" she asked at one point. Apparently his comment about his servants had made some impression on her.

"Fourteen, I believe."

She smiled. "What title does he have?"

Ren chuckled. "He is the most fortunate of all—he has many. At times he is variously footman, page, tiger, or even cook's helper. I may soon be adding another title: *durwan*, or guard. I hate to think of it as encouraging him to spy, but I can use an extra set of sharp ears and eyes around the house."

"Are you satisfied that none of your own servants are behind the trouble you're having?"

"I am not satisfied of anything anymore, Miss Parbury."

She did not need to know that he attributed part of that state of affairs directly to her. For the two nights since Car-

risforte's picnic he had slept wretchedly for thinking of her
and the kiss he had stopped before it had really begun. He
had been unquestionably right to stop it, although he had
been thoroughly miserable as a result.

His damnable attraction to her was turning into a crav-
ing. He had cursed when her note in reply to his had arrived, requesting that he accompany her to seek out the
boy. He had hoped to avoid her for some time so these
feelings could pass. But her proposal had made so much
sense, he could not refuse. He needed to see the boy. Riding in the hackney with her, pretending he felt nothing, had
been sweet torture.

The magistrate's green baize desktop at Queen Square
proved not to be the end of their afternoon's journey. After
an interminable wait they learned that the chimney
sweeper had indeed already been found in violation of the
laws, with six boys he had bought outright from destitute
parents, and two who had been legally placed with him by
the parish. The case had received unusually swift action.
All eight boys had been remanded to the local workhouse
until they could be placed in charity schools or new ap-
prenticeships were found for them. There was nothing for
it but to climb back into the hackney and allow Ahmed to
convey them to the workhouse, which was situated only a
few blocks away.

In that dismal place, Ren and Miss Parbury were forced to
wait again, and again he watched her. He could not seem to
stop himself, but she appeared to be unaware of his regard.
Even here, her mind was clearly focused on the business at
hand. It was just as well, he reflected, since his mind was
not. He saw uncertainty in her face for the first time only
when they were told the boy might not be there.

"How can he not be here?" she whispered, turning to him
in appeal. "Is a boy so easy to lose? They have a responsibility to keep track of their inmates, do they not?"

"Yes, and yes," he answered, reaching over to place his
hand on the fists she held tightly clenched in her lap. "A boy
is easy to lose if that is what the boy wants, particularly a
boy who is used to going his own way. They have a respon-

sibility here, it is true, but saddled with so many, how can they possibly look out for the strays?"

He saw the moisture begin to well in her eyes. "Do not give in to distress—not yet," he said softly. "We will wait. Perhaps they will find him."

It concerned him that she evidently cared about the boy so much. *If the wretch turns up and my questioning draws a confession from him, she may be even more upset by her lost illusions than if they have lost him,* Ren thought. Still, she needed to know the truth, almost as much as he did. And certainly it was too late to alter their course. Why did it bother him to suddenly feel as if he were the villain of the piece?

A few minutes passed in silence. He had made a thorough study of the shadows and stains on the floorboards and had begun a similar study of the dingy walls when a scuffling commotion in the passageway outside the room signaled someone's unwilling arrival. Miss Parbury leaped up just as he turned his head to look at her, requiring him to rise to his feet as well.

The master, or warden, with whom they had previously spoken reentered, followed by a large fellow with a long staff who was pushing a small lad in front of him.

"Taylor!" Miss Parbury exclaimed, holding out her hand. Whether it was in greeting or supplication, Ren could not tell. A touch of pink colored the cheeks that had been so pale earlier, and her lips were slightly parted in her moment of concern. A rather endearing small pucker creased her forehead.

"We found 'im, miss. Hidin' under a table in the men's common room, 'e was."

Taylor pulled his shoulder away from the hand of the man who was pushing him and appeared to straighten himself up. Ren was amazed that one so small and ragged could muster such a semblance of dignity.

"Beg pardon, miss," the urchin said, addressing Miss Parbury and ignoring the men.

"'Ere, wait till you're spoken to," growled one of them, but the boy continued.

"I figured it was another one of them constables or Sessions men that keep comin' after me with questions. Ain't I told them everythin' enough times over?"

"Last time we couldn't find him, he'd crawled up the chimney in the old nurse's room," grumbled the first man. "Sometimes he just ain't here a-tall. Place is meant to hold two hundred an' we've got twice that number. Can't watch 'em all."

"That's all right, Taylor," said Miss Parbury. She seemed to have regained perfect control of herself. "Would you gentlemen allow us to have a few words with him in private?"

The two looked hesitant and Ren wondered if he would have to hand over a few inducements from his pocket, but it was not necessary. Who could resist a lady as lovely as Miss Parbury when she sent such a sweet look of appeal in one's direction? He doubted he could have. The men left them.

"Aside from all the questioners, are they treating you all right here, Taylor?" she asked. "I must say, you look very different with a clean face!"

The boy shrugged.

Ren decided he should try. "I understand you've slipped out a few times?"

Instead of answering, the boy looked at Miss Parbury. She was his protector, there was no question.

Ren said, "It's all right to answer—I was simply curious about why."

She nodded, and only then did the boy respond.

"They feed us regular, only it ain't enough, and it's mostly gruel. There's eight of us sent over here from Master Roberts—I been slippin' out to fetch us some extras when I can."

She lifted an eyebrow at Ren as if to say, *I told you so.* But the way he saw it, the boy had just admitted to going out for the express purpose of stealing.

"What kind of extras? How do you get them?"

The boy rolled his eyes as if he could not believe the stupidity of some people. "It's likely an apple or two off some old seller's cart, or a meat pasty nabbed when the man ain't lookin'. Things like that, whats we're used to. We always took care of ourselves."

"Do you ever buy them?"

Taylor scoffed. He was obviously coming to the quick conclusion that Ren was daft. "What with, *yer honor, sir?*"

"With ready coin, if you stole something else and then sold it."

Miss Parbury's sudden shift in expression proved she had realized suddenly where his line of questions was leading. She hastened to intervene.

"Taylor, please allow me to introduce you to the Marquess of Milbourne. He lives in a certain house on the north side of Grosvenor Square."

The boy's expression betrayed only the slightest change. "Not the one—?" He cut himself off, looking first at Miss Parbury and then at Ren in apparent disbelief.

"I'm afraid his lordship caught me that night I went into his house, Taylor, but it is all right. We are, we have become—friends."

Ren could not miss the hesitation in her voice on the last words, as if she were not certain she could make the claim. Is that what they were, then? It was an intriguing notion.

"I will tell you straight-out," she continued, "that someone has been stealing from his house."

"Coo! Well, I don't wonder," said the boy, cool as ice. "You and me saw, miss—'is house is so easy to get into, hit's a walk in the park—an open invitation!"

It was Ren's turn to raise his eyebrows. "Taylor," he said darkly, "Miss Parbury explained to me that you helped her to get in that night. If you have made any repeat trips since then, you may be sure I will find out. You might make it easier on yourself if you just tell me."

That approach worked marvelously well. The boy folded his arms across his small chest and pressed his lips together into a thin line. Stubborn fellow!

Miss Parbury cut in with a soft, persuasive voice. "Taylor, your information could help Lord Milbourne to focus his attention on finding the true thief. Won't you help us?"

For a moment it looked as if the boy would say nothing

more. Ren had met pigheaded obstinacy before; he had no
intention of being defeated by this urchin's refusal to respond. But before he could change his tactics, the boy apparently reconsidered his own position.

"I wouldn't need to run down to Grosvenor Square to
crack a fine crib, if I'd a mind to," he declared with a marvelous tone of injured pride in his voice. "There's plenty
enough in Russell Square, or Bedford or Bloomsbury. Any-
ways, since they put us all 'ere, we're too far away. So if
yer thinkin' I done it, you'd best think again. I'm not your
man."

You are not anybody's man, Ren thought with a sudden,
surprising surge of sympathy. *I doubt you are a day over ten
years old.* What an amazingly prickly package of independence this child was! And Miss Parbury was right—without
the change she was trying to work in his life this boy was
headed straight to the gallows.

She was looking at Ren with that same I-told-you-so look
she had shown him before, smiling as if she could tell his
feelings had softened. Damn woman! Since when had the
Lion of Lampur become so transparent?

"Did you ever take anything from my house before the
parish sent you here?"

"Guv'nor, I ain't never set a foot in your house at all. Figured, for one thing, it might be too easy to track back to me,
if *she* knew about it, or on t'other hand, maybe she'd pull the
blame for it."

"That would have bothered you, if she had been blamed?"

"Maybe."

Ren could not suppress a smile. Here they were, a marquess and a street thief, both harboring a soft spot for the
same woman, and both trying their hardest to hide it. Who
would have believed he would feel a kinship with the lad?
Did Miss Parbury know everything? The only problem was,
he still was not certain he believed the boy.

He looked at Miss Parbury, and suddenly an idea struck
him.

"What if I offered you a way to prove what you say—
would you take me up on it?"

Instant suspicion entered the boy's face. Truly, he was old beyond his years. He reminded Ren of so many children who lived by their wits in the streets of Calcutta.

"What would I have to do?"

Chapter Eleven

It was arranged that Taylor would be brought to Milbourne House on the following afternoon. While the marquess was arranging it with the workhouse overseer, Mariah took the opportunity to speak to the boy.

"The marquess is a fair man, Taylor. If he says he has a test, I'm certain you have nothing to fear and everything to gain by it, especially if it means winning his trust. Promise me that you will keep the appointment?"

"Is he really a marquess?"

"Yes, he really is. A remarkable man, a powerful one to have for a friend. He might be able to do a great deal to help you," she added thoughtfully.

"All right. I'll be there."

She lowered her voice. "I am going to try to arrange matters so that I can be there, also."

It was not that she did not trust the marquess herself, was it? She was sure his test must be a fair one, although she could not imagine what he had in mind. He had said only that the boy must come to his house. Perhaps there was a part of her that wanted to hear his apology when Taylor proved his innocence. She definitely did need to return Lord Milbourne's sketchbook. But she had to acknowledge that her spirits lifted simply at the prospect of an excuse to be with him. Just how she would manage that could be worked out later.

"I would like to ask you to do something else for me, Taylor—to help him. May I?" Another idea had formed in the back of her mind when she had heard Lord Milbourne's plans for Selim.

"Depends. What is it?" At least the lad looked at her with less suspicion than he had shown to the marquess.

"Someone has been doing more than stealing from him. I'm not sure what exactly. But it seems he may have some enemies. As you go about in the city, would you keep your eyes and ears open? If you should happen to stumble across any mischief that might connect to him, would you find a way to let me know?"

She did not know quite what she would do if such information came to her, but still it was a place to start.

Taylor looked at her consideringly. "You sweet on him?"

It was a good question, one she couldn't really answer. "I suppose it is something like that," was her best reply.

To use Taylor's slang, she *was* sweet upon the marquess, Mariah decided the following day. Only total infatuation or insanity could explain the web of lies she continued to create to cover her activities! She had told so many plumpers already, and yet here she was again, concocting an elaborate ruse so that she might be able to call on him this afternoon. The old Mariah would never have attempted a plan so bold, and she did not quite know where this new Mariah had sprung from.

There had been no way to contact Harry this time without raising suspicion, so at least for once her scheme did not implicate anyone else. She only hoped that no one in her family would run into Harry in the course of the afternoon rounds. Mariah had claimed that she and Harry planned to spend the afternoon perusing books at Dangerfield's in Berkley Square. By allowing her family's coachman to drop her there, she was able to escape without her maid and saved herself a much longer walk to Grosvenor Square from somewhere else. She was grateful that no one had paid her enough notice to ask her about the large basket she carried with her.

She had stepped inside Dangerfield's only long enough to see the coachman drive away. As soon as she thought he was safely out of sight, she slipped out again and scurried toward the north end of the square, hoping not to see anyone she knew. In the narrow alley that led to Bourden Street, she changed her bonnet for the brown one and slipped the gray cloak on over her pelisse.

It was already half past one o'clock by the time she had accomplished this much. Concern that she might arrive at Lord Milbourne's too late to catch Taylor's visit hurried her feet, as did her nervousness at walking the streets unaccompanied. Dressed as a maid and alone, she knew she could command no respect from any ungentlemanly fellows she chanced to meet.

Keeping her head down as she hastened along, she suffered no worse indignities than a few suggestive comments that made her cheeks burn. In Mount Street and again after she reached Grosvenor Square, she passed people she knew; she drew hardly a glance from any of them as she scurried by. Her mother was right—what a difference proper clothing and posture made in the world!

Unfortunately, the butler who answered the door at Milbourne House would not admit her. A top-lofty fellow with snow white hair, a puffy face, and bloodshot eyes, he looked down his nose at her and suggested that the servants' entrance was the only way she would gain access to *this* house! She had not counted on her disguise being quite so effective but she did not dare entrust her name to the discretion of such a servant.

She was still standing there debating what further argument she could make when she heard another voice in the entryway behind the butler.

"Frothwick?"

"Just an uppity and ill-mannered servant girl, Hajee."

Behind the butler she saw the little man who had brought tea to the marquess's study on the evening she had climbed in the window.

"This man knows I am a friend of Lord Milbourne," she said eagerly, wondering if he could possibly recognize her in such different clothes and under such different circumstances. "Please, it is imperative that I speak with the marquess."

Hajee came forward, eyeing her curiously. Frothwick appeared to be having some doubts after considering her style of speech.

"Do you recognize me, Mr. Hajee?" she said, wondering if that was the correct way to address him. "My last visit was a little out of the ordinary. I am here to see the marquess. I have something to return to him."

Hajee exchanged a look with the butler and then turned back to her with a little bow. His dark eyes looked as if they contained all the wisdom in the world. "Memsahib, please to follow me," he said.

That was all. As she moved after him, she heard Frothwick close the front door behind her, muttering.

Hajee led her to the room across the passage from Lord Milbourne's study, a room that had not been finished when she received her tour. The marquess had told her it was to be his music room, and as Hajee opened the door Mariah heard the exotic notes of some sort of stringed instrument.

Draperies had been drawn across the windows, making the room quite dim. Instead of sunlight, many candles illumined the space, casting shadows that danced in the draft from the door. Imagine burning candles in daytime! It was extravagant beyond words.

By their soft light she could see that the room was beautiful, but strange and exotic like the music she heard. As elsewhere in the house, overlapping layers of richly patterned carpets covered the floor. Painted silk hangings and panels of carved fretwork ornamented the walls. The only piece of furniture she could see was a low rectangular table, which appeared to be set up for chess. Instead of chairs there were large cushions in the deep colors of jewels placed around the room—on one of these reclined the marquess's cheetah, Ranee, looking lazy and contented.

Sitting cross-legged near her on a mat on the floor was Lord Milbourne, playing an instrument that looked to Mariah like a strangely proportioned, overgrown lute. The candlelight gave a golden glow to his white clothing; it glimmered in his hair and made interesting shadows of the angles of his face and the open front of his shirt. The polished, decorated body of his instrument rested on the floor to the right of him and a large, golden bulb supporting the fingerboard was positioned on his left knee. The neck of the instrument was extremely long. She had never seen or heard anything like it.

"Oh," she said softly, feeling as if an enchanter's spell had stolen over her in that instant.

The marquess ceased playing and looked up at the intrusion. "Miss Parbury!" he exclaimed in surprise. "Good Lord, what are you doing here?" He took in her clothing in one rapid glance that swept her from head to toe, then sighed, setting aside his instrument. He got up with a graceful ease she could not help admiring. "Never mind," he said. "I have a suspicion. Thank you, Hajee."

Dismissed, the little man behind her made his exit. Mariah advanced a single step into the room, suddenly very unsure of herself. "I am so sorry to have interrupted. It is my turn to apologize to you."

"Let me guess," Lord Milbourne said dryly. "You thought Taylor would be here, and you would just happen to come by. Only you know very well you should not be here—not at all, and most particularly not alone."

Had she made a huge mistake? Oh Lord. He did not sound the least bit pleased to see her. Moreover, it seemed quite obvious that Taylor was not here. She raised her chin a notch.

"I have brought back the sketchbook you loaned me," she said bravely. "My sister Cassie very nearly stumbled across it in my room yesterday. I have enjoyed looking at it." It sounded stilted and inadequate, but what else was there to say? *I have studied it and thought of you every night. I have filled my dreams with you and the life I imagined you living.*

"I am supposed to believe that this was the only way you could think of to return it to me?"

She clutched the basket handle in a death grip. This was not going at all the way she had expected.

"I suspect by the way you are dressed that no one but Miss Pritchard knows that you are here."

"Actually, not even Harry," she said in a small voice. "There was no chance to contact her."

"How did you . . . ? No, never mind. I do not want to know.

She did not expect a lecture on propriety from him. He was going to simply dismiss her, perhaps with his next words. She could not leave, not yet. "Did Taylor . . . ?"

"Yes, he came. And went. You are too late." For a moment he just stared at her. Would he be so cruel as to say nothing more? He seemed to be considering it. Then with a shrug, he relented. "You will be happy to know, he passed my test."

She let out a breath she did not know she had been holding. "I knew he would," she said. "But will you not tell me what the test was? I could not begin to imagine how you might prove such a thing as you proposed."

"I knew that if he had never seen the inside of this house before, he would not be able to hide or counterfeit his first response to it. It is too far removed from anything he was likely to have ever encountered. He was suitably astounded—his eyes nearly popped right out of his head. I had the uncomfortable notion that he was memorizing every detail of the place—I sincerely hope not for future reference! But the best part of the test was Ranee. I knew I could judge by her response to him whether or not she had ever seen him before, as much as by his response to meeting her."

"Oh, dear. Was he terrified?"

"Miss Parbury, this is Taylor we are talking about."

"He is only a boy."

"All right. He was frightened at first, then cautious, although he tried to hide it. I believe by the time he left here, he and Ranee had become friends. It was clear to me that they had not met before today."

Mariah transferred the gaze she had locked onto Lord Milbourne to the big cat for a moment. Ranee had not stirred from her cushion, although she had assumed a more dignified, upright position upon Mariah's entrance into the room. She was a beautiful creature with her splendid spotted coat and long, lean body. The black lines on her face were very distinctive. She surveyed Mariah with a calm, steady regard.

"Do you think Ranee remembers me? We met so briefly."

"Why not try her and see?"

It was a dare. She knew it, even though the sound of his voice was perfectly ordinary. This man was a master of control, over himself, and over others. He dared her to experiment, to push boundaries.

God knew, she had pushed more boundaries since meeting him than she had ever done in her life. But even more, he was daring her to trust him. He thought her coming meant that she had not trusted him with Taylor, and now he was testing her as surely as he had tested the boy. She knew, in the deepest part of her heart, that he would never dare her to do anything that might bring her harm. With an almost steady step, she walked over to the cat and held out her hand.

"Show it to her palm up, first," he directed, "so she can smell it and see it is empty, as you would with a dog. Then you might try scratching her behind the ear."

The cheetah's ears were rounded and set far apart. Mariah scratched behind one, then the other. Then she tried stroking the cat's head. She had not guessed the fur would feel so soft. Ranee began a low, soft rumbling. "She is purring!" Mariah said in astonishment.

Lord Milbourne chuckled. "Ranee is shy of strangers, but she has a good memory for people. It rather compensates for her lack of aggression as a hunter. She was given to me as a cub when she would not accept the hood and did not train well for the kill. I tell her she is too sociable, although most of the time I am her only company."

The tension between them was easing, although the marquess had yet to move from the spot where he stood. Mariah was encouraged enough to ask questions. She asked about Ranee's age and history, and then moved on to ask about the instrument the marques had been playing. As she got him talking, he seemed to forget that she should not be there. By the time Hajee reappeared a few minutes later bearing a tray with tea and refreshments, she had removed her cloak and both she and the marquess were sitting on the floor cushions. Lord Milbourne merely nodded at Hajee and went on telling Mariah about the forms of Indian music, apparently quite forgetting that he had never asked for tea.

"I knew you liked music," Mariah said. "I remember that you asked my mother if we might not have music instead of playing whist that night you came for dinner."

"You have a remarkable memory, Miss Parbury."

"You do not know it, but you were spared—my sister Aurora does not sing very well."

"Do you?"

"Tolerably, I am told. But please, won't you play something for me? I interrupted you when I first arrived, and it sounded so different, somehow magical."

He played for a few minutes, mesmerizing her as his fingers flew along the long neck of the instrument. The rippling notes seemed to find an answering rhythm inside her body. She let the sound wash over her. Then he stopped. "Would you like to try it?"

"Oh, yes, more than anything!"

"More than *anything*?" A teasing glint sparkled in his eyes.

She blushed, embarrassed by her own enthusiasm.

"To begin, you need to sit this way," he said, indicating his crossed legs with a wave of his hand. She stood up and unfastened her pelisse, laying it aside on the cushion next to her. Without it the skirt of her blue day dress afforded her more freedom to move. She shed gloves and bonnet, too. When she had resettled herself, he got up and brought her the sitar, placing it across her body. Squatting beside her, he began to show her where to position her hands.

His extreme closeness kindled a growing warmth inside Mariah. She nodded, trying hard to pay attention to his instructions when her mind seemed to focus only on his touch.

"The fingers of this hand create the notes," he said, "each one separately, pressing down on the strings." Very gently, he separated her fingers and placed them, his own large ones sliding along hers. A wave of heat passed through Mariah and she caught her breath sharply, hoping he did not notice.

Golden amber eyes flicked a quick glance at her, but he said nothing. Taking up her other hand, he raised her arm over the instrument. "One arm above and one beneath, you see? The fingers on this hand sound the strings. Like this."

Under his guidance, she actually played a few notes. "Heavens!" she said, laughing. "I can hardly imagine having enough skill to get beyond the notes themselves to create a—what did you call it? A *rasa*? A specific kind of mood."

"When you play the pianoforte, do you think about each individual note? No, you perform the piece. This is no different, except that you create more of the music yourself, improvising. The musician draws on his own store of emotions—love, anger, courage, surprise—even desire."

She looked down at her hands and swallowed, not daring to look at him. Did he know what she was feeling?

"The skill comes with practice," he said softly. Then he rose abruptly and went to the tea tray. "Would you like tea?"

After he had served them both, she held her warm cup between her hands, finding the round, firm shape somewhat steadying. She listened to him, thinking of how much she enjoyed the sound of his voice as he identified the Indian sweets they were eating and entertained her with stories of the trials of Syed, his Mohammedan cook.

When she asked him about the game set up on his table, he challenged her to play *chatur-angam,* the ancient Indian form of chess. The set had elephants instead of castles, and chariots where the bishops should be.

"It is a game of military strategy. That is why we have a minister or commander-in-chief instead of a queen. How many queens do you find on a field of battle? Or bishops, for that matter?" He laughed. "This makes much more sense than our version. I found much of life in India to be that way."

"Is that why you try to recreate it here?"

"I would not try to recreate it entirely. What was healthy and suitable to the climate in the Hindustan does not necessarily yield the same result here—in fact it could be as ludicrous as maintaining the English customs there. Since I am forced into a life not of my own choosing, however, I am determined to imprint it with my own style and preferences. In general, I preferred my former life. Thus my attempt to bring this new life as much into line with my previous one as possible."

She nodded, admiring his courage. She thought most people were forced into roles they did not choose, but how meekly many accepted their lot! Even she had always done so, at least until recently. Perhaps Harry was right—perhaps the dutiful daughter had the heart of a rebel, after all. She did not know.

Their game proved to be a poor contest. Her awareness of him distracted her, and he was constantly reaching over to her side to advise her or point out the consequences of moves she thought to make. His large, strong hands moved among the pieces with graceful precision. Whenever she glanced up at him, his gaze was always upon her. She asked for more tea, hoping that would settle her, but watching him go through the motions of getting it for her only stirred her senses more.

Finally, her king was captured and the game was over. She drained the last drop from her cup and set it on the rug beside her. "I must go. I never meant to stay so long."

He gave her a long, disturbing look. "I never meant for you to stay at all." He stood up and came to where she sat, his hand extended. "You are not used to sitting on floors— allow me to assist you."

He was quite correct—her legs were stiff and did not obey her when she tried to rise. She took his hand and found herself inches from his chest when he pulled her to her feet.

"Oh!" she squeaked in surprise.

"This is something else I have wanted to try with you," he said, lowering his head.

"Oh," she started to say again, but her lips had barely opened before his claimed them.

This kiss was nothing like the light brush of lips the day of the picnic. This kiss was drugging, like too much wine gone straight to her head. Nothing existed outside of the gentle sensation of his lips on hers, as if all the universe slowly, slowly spun around them, joined at their kiss. As he eased her body against his and increased the pressure of his kiss, the point of concentration widened, until not merely lips but touching bodies became the center of all existence and feeling.

She pressed closer to him, hardly aware that she did so. When his tongue teased hers she responded, seeking more of his velvet softness, following his invitation to explore. Molten heat poured through her veins and pooled in places that craved relief. In that instant she pushed far beyond any boundaries of experience she had previously known.

He cradled her against him, holding her tight with one hand at her back, while his other hand began gentle, sliding explorations of its own. Her arms had gone around his neck and her hands found his hair, reveling in its silky feel.

And then he stopped. He went completely still, then slowly released her, as if he were making sure she would not fall. She stared up at him and saw what looked like anguish come in to replace the passion that had glazed his eyes seconds before.

"I think perhaps that is what you really came here for, Miss Parbury," he said stiffly, "but we must stop before you get more than you bargained for."

Was he right? Quick thoughts of Taylor and the borrowed sketchbook flashed through her mind, but she knew those had only been excuses. She *had* wanted to know what a real kiss would be like with him. And now that she knew, it still was not enough, God help her. Her cheeks flamed.

"I came to return your book, and it is still in my basket," she said. Her emotions were in turmoil. A huge lump rose into her throat, threatening to trigger tears, but she would not, could not allow herself to cry. How could he kiss her with such warmth and passion, and then speak so severely to her? She started to turn away to fetch the book, but just as she did so, a knock came at the open door.

"William Parbury is here to see you, my lord," Frothwick intoned ceremoniously.

There was no time to worry whether the butler had seen them kissing. Mariah looked at Lord Milbourne in utter panic. What could they do? William must not discover her here.

"Give us a moment, Frothwick," the marquess said, wav-

ing the fellow away. He was already gathering up Mariah's
bonnet and pelisse.

"Quick, behind the drapery," he said tersely, nodding toward the left window enclave and thrusting the armful at
her. She had already grabbed up her basket and cloak and
now piled the other items on top of them. Lord Milbourne
was right—if she tried to leave the room, she ran the risk of
meeting William in the passageway. She headed for the
window and nearly tripped over Ranee, who had risen from
her cushion with the sudden rush of activity.

The draperies were old, heavy velvet, full of dust—obviously the marquess had not replaced them. Mariah tried not
to breathe as he arranged the material around her. There was
no way this drape would match its partner on the other window, but thank God there was at least a small recess, or the
bulge would have been bigger. They would have to hope
that in the shadows away from the candles, it was not noticeable.

I must not sneeze, Mariah chanted to herself in a silent refrain. *I must not sneeze.*

Ren surveyed the room quickly. He could not help that
there were two cups and two plates with the tea things, but
he could always allow that he had been entertaining company earlier in the afternoon. He picked up the sitar and settled himself back on a floor cushion, calling to Ranee, who
was sniffing about the curtain, exhibiting an unfortunate curiosity about Miss Parbury's presence there. A moment later
William bustled in.

"Hope I'm not disturbing you, old man. You've been so
scarce the last few days, just thought I'd pop in and see if
things were as they should be. Not planning to set up as a
recluse, are you?"

"Ha-ha. Far from it," Ren responded heartily. "Just gird-
ing myself for the social whirl to come in the days ahead."

He kept his smile plastered in place, but his heart sank as
he realized that across from him, between the cushions
where Miss Parbury had been sitting, lay one of her gloves.
He set aside the sitar as if he had just finished playing and
began to get up.

"No, no, do not stop on my account," William said, gesturing at him to remain as he had been. "I've a mind to hear you play that thing. What d'you call it?"

"A sitar," he said, standing up anyway. "Truly, my friend, we should be much more comfortable to remove to my study—real chairs to sit in, you know."

Ren was in agony. He did not want to offer tea, for that would only call attention to the cups already used, and he did not want to speak to Ranee again, for although she was still sniffing the drape where Miss Parbury was hidden, calling her away would only bring attention to what she was doing. Definitely, abandoning the room was the best possible move.

"Is this how your house was furnished in Lampur? All mats and cushions on top of the rugs? I suppose one can get accustomed to anything," William said, turning around in wonderment. His eyes lit on the tea tray. "I say, you've had company before me. Has it been a busy afternoon?"

Ren could honestly say that it had been. "Let me send for a freshly made pot, and we'll have it in the other room," he offered, feeling doom in his bones. William, like his sister, was far too observant.

"What is your overgrown cat up to over there in the corner?" he said.

"Oh, you know cats, They're ever-curious, no matter what size they come in. Anything different, such as the draperies closed instead of open . . . Come here, Ranee."

At least Ranee turned her head this time at the sound of her name, but she still did not come. And then a moment later it hardly mattered, anyway. William pounced upon his sister's glove.

"Oho, you sly devil! You did not say it was a lady friend," he said, retrieving the trophy. He opened his mouth to say more, then closed it again. Ren could just see the wheels turning in his friend's mind, putting together what he had seen.

"Rather say, a lady *bird,* I think, eh? And not yet flown!"

There was still a chance William would have the good grace to leave, now that he knew he had interrupted a tryst.

But it was not to be. At the very moment when he might have made such a choice, Miss Parbury sneezed behind the drape.

" 'How now? A rat?'" William said, quoting from *Hamlet*. "I think not. Oh, let us just have a look at her, and then I promise I'll go. Poor dear! How could you make her hide behind a dusty curtain!"

Suiting action to words, William stepped over to the drape and pulled it aside while Ren watched in horror.

Chapter Twelve

There stood Miss Parbury looking extremely indignant, her basket and outerwear still clutched in her arms.

"William," she said, raising her chin. "Both you and that oversized cat are far too nosy for anyone's good. How could you be so rude? A-choo!"

All the color had drained from William's face. "Mariah! What on God's earth are you doing here? This cannot be what I . . . I know you would never . . . How did you . . . ?" His hands curled into fists as he tried to get himself in hand. His face went from colorless to beet red. "Would one or the other of you please explain to me what is going on here? I want desperately to know that it is not the way it looks."

I must be insane, Ren thought. *How did I let this happen?* He looked from William's face to Miss Parbury's and felt as if he were sinking in a great morass of quicksand. In the momentary turmoil of his emotions, the question of whether he had been deliberately trapped crossed his mind—he knew better, he was certain, yet the Parburys could not have done a better job if they had purposely set out to ensnare him.

To do the right thing was impossible—they had no idea how much so. And yet what choice was there? Miss Parbury was compromised. William stood before him, outrage beginning to show on his face as Ren delayed his answer. He would be lucky if William did not call him out in defense of his sister's honor.

"We had some business to conduct, William," Miss Parbury said. "This is all perfectly legitimate. It just seemed so much easier to avoid questions or any appearance of impropriety by doing it in secret. Oh please! Promise that you'll not say anything!"

"What business?" William asked suspiciously.

Ah, now what would she say to that? Their "business" today derived directly from trying to keep secret the last time she had visited Ren's house. It would not fadge. This time they had gone too far beyond the rules.

"No one knows that she is here, William," Ren began, hoping they could reason with his irate friend.

"How can you say that no one knows? Can you say no one saw her come here? What of all your servants? Who answered the door? Who showed her in? Who made the tea? Who served the tea? God, dozens of people probably know she is here. Milbourne, as we are friends, I have to assume you would not touch her. But that is not the point at all."

William looked very much like a man who needed to sit down. That he had called Ren by his title name showed how angry he was. However, Ren doubted that even the most expertly cut doeskin could stretch enough to allow his friend to sit on the floor in such fashionably tight pantaloons.

"Let us adjourn to my study, so we may sit down in a civilized fashion," he suggested, gesturing toward the door. With her arms still full of her belongings, Miss Parbury moved to his side and managed to slip an arm through his.

"That is an excellent notion," she said. He could feel her trembling.

He called to Ranee to follow them and the cheetah reluctantly complied. They crossed the passage into his study, where Ren poured brandy for William and himself. "Miss Parbury? No, I suppose not, although it might help you."

He set his own glass on the desk and took the basket and clothing from her arms, placing them on the carpet. He could not resign himself to fate without at least a good battle. "William, your sister was wearing these when she arrived," he said, holding up the cloak and the brown poke bonnet. "Would you recognize her in them?"

William only moaned.

"Miss Parbury, did you give your name to my butler when you arrived here?" He hoped fervently that she had not, for

Frothwick's fondness for the bottle made his discretion at times unreliable.

"Of course I did not." She sounded indignant. "And I will add that he was so taken in by my appearance that he did not wish to admit me. It was your man called Hajee who brought me in."

Ren put back the clothing and took up his drink. "Unless you gave it to him, Hajee, I know, does not know your name. Beyond that, his English is limited, and his discretion is unquestionable."

He had almost praised Hajee's wisdom along with his discretion, but after today's disaster he was no longer so confident of the former. Hajee had brought Miss Parbury in without so much as asking his master—he had brought the tea unbidden, as well, Ren realized belatedly. There was such a thing as too much independence. He resolved to speak with Hajee later.

"Hajee made and brought the tea, William," he said, "so you see, only two servants in my house have so much as seen her here, and neither one has any idea who she is."

William took a long pull from his brandy glass and looked at his sister, frowning. "Mariah, how *did* you manage to get yourself here? Why are you not at home, or making calls with Mama? For God's sake, where does she think you are?"

Mariah straightened herself up in her chair. "There is no call to keep swearing, William," she said primly. Ren could not help admiring her pluck. She proceeded to explain the ruse she had devised to get there.

"So you see," she finished, "no one so much as noticed me. It was all so I could return Lord Milbourne's sketchbook. Knowing how precious it is to him, I did not dare to entrust the errand to a servant. You just happened to arrive at the most perfectly wrong time, William."

Apparently steadier now than she had been after the initial shock of being discovered, she got up and went to the basket. "You see?" She withdrew Ren's book and held it up. He wondered if she really knew how precious it was to him.

William's eyes narrowed. "It seems to me, dear sister,

that returning a book is a matter that takes no more than a
few seconds of time, even if it is an errand that cannot be en-
trusted to a servant. It does not, to my mind, require the
serving of tea, or for that matter the removal of one's pelisse
and bonnet." He glanced accusingly at the small heap on the
floor, then back at her.

"Let me see this book," he said, holding out his hand im-
periously. "Exactly when did you receive this from Lord
Milbourne, in the first place, or arrange for its loan? There
is still something havey cavey about this whole matter." He
began to examine the pages, looking at the sketches.

"I am not aware of any impropriety in a gentleman loan-
ing a book on a subject of mutual interest to a young lady,"
Ren said quietly. "Your sister's interest in the Hindustan
was apparent to me the night I dined at your home. I later
saw her at Marshall's Lending Library, where we shared a
further discussion of the subject."

"And I suppose that was your subject of discussion at the
Sibbinghams' ball, and at Carrisforte's picnic, and over tea
today? I am not as great a fool as you both take me for. If
you are going to pay court to my sister, Milbourne, I insist
that you shall do so openly, instead of sneaking around behind everyone's back. If my sister has miraculously changed
your attitude about marriage, then I am glad of it. Until this
hour, there is no one whom I would rather have had as a
brother-in-law. But at the moment I feel our friendship has
been sorely abused."

"I am sorry," Ren said with deep conviction. "Sorry" did
not begin to cover how he felt.

"I will expect you to ask my parents' permission to call
on Mariah," William said, adding ominously, "I will make
certain that they give it."

How can I? Ren thought in despair. *I will have to explain
myself.*

"Oh, William, give over," Mariah broke in. "Mama
would be in transports of joy if Lord Milbourne asked to
come calling, and you know it. But you cannot be thinking
of telling them about this."

"I won't say anything if Ren agrees to my terms. There are to be no more stolen moments or secret meetings."

She turned then to Ren and the distress in her eyes appeared to be very genuine. "You cannot know how very sorry I am over this."

"No sorrier than I am, Miss Parbury." He locked his hands behind his back and glanced beyond her to the table where the figure of Ganesha was watching over their gathering. At this moment the carving seemed nothing more than a mockery of human endeavors—god of good fortune and wisdom, indeed! Ren took a deep breath.

"I'm afraid you do not understand. I have to tell you both that I cannot, in good conscience, do what William is asking. My attitude towards marriage has not miraculously changed, but also I believe that by courting Miss Parbury publicly I might do her far more harm than good."

"Would you refuse? I cannot credit this! What of the harm to her reputation? I'm not saying you have to marry her, man!" William exclaimed. "There's plenty of courtships that don't end in betrothal—happens all the time that a couple find they simply don't suit. There's no disgrace in that. It would simply lend countenance to what has happened."

Ren shook his head. He could not face them both sitting there. He strode over to the window and stared out, feeling all the old pain of past losses come flooding back. The true problem was that he had begun to care about her.

"I am afraid that she might come to harm—that something might happen to her. I cannot explain it. Everyone I've ever loved, and anyone who has ever had an important role in my personal life, has died or suffered grievously for it. Whether I am accursed or not, only God knows. But I would not put Miss Parbury to such a risk." He turned back to them, wondering if his face reflected the bleakness in his soul. "That is also why I shall never marry. I believe that serious involvement with me is tantamount to a death sentence."

William snorted. "I never took you for the superstitious sort! What a uniquely original excuse! Are you going to give us some Hindu mumbo jumbo about predestiny or curses and the evil eye? We are in England, man. If you are starting to believe in all that rot, it is a blessing you came back to civilization when you did. It is utter nonsense."

"Is it?" William's callous dismissal stirred Ren's anger. "I was betrothed to the woman who drew those sketches. She was maimed in a terrible accident and later on she died." There was unfathomable pain behind those words. He felt a tiny twinge of bitter satisfaction as he saw William close the book and rather gingerly set it aside.

"There was a woman after her, another woman I thought I loved—she died, too, tragically, unexpectedly. Do you see my loving family anywhere? My father, my mother, my sister? Gone. What of all my grandfather's heirs—my uncle, my two cousins? Call this coincidence if you like—I call it my own personal hell. Why risk it?"

Miss Parbury stood up, her expression unreadable, and his gut twisted with sudden disgust at himself. He had never meant to speak so in front of her.

She moved toward him. "Why risk it? Perhaps to prove it isn't so."

"Yes, just so!" agreed William. "I never thought to see the Lion of Lampur afraid of anything!"

"Do you think I am more than human? No one is immune from having fears. Only fools will not admit them." Ren's anger still simmered. In an effort to cool it, he looked at Mariah Parbury's face and wondered if he could keep himself from caring too much. Or was it already too late?

"In any case, I insist upon this," William said. "It can be a temporary courtship, Ren—for the sake of appearance. It needn't be anything more."

"All right," Ren heard himself agree. He was appalled by the prospect—to pretend to an empty courtship while having to bury his true feelings sounded like its own kind of hell. Despite what she had said, Miss Parbury could not want this any more than he did; he believed she had spoken out of pity for him. The only consolation was that it need not last long—a few weeks at most. So much for his hopes of avoiding her! In the meantime, all he had to do was fool himself and fate as well.

*   *   *

Lord Milbourne arrived at the Parburys' in pouring rain the next day to take care of the expected formalities. The baron and baroness expressed their surprise at his completely unsuspected interest but were perfectly happy to grant permission for him to pay addresses to Mariah.

After a brief and awkward visit in the drawing room with her and her family, the marquess returned home, and Mariah's mother took charge of her with dismaying enthusiasm. As rain continued to batter the windows and flood the sidewalks of London for the next several days, new dresses were ordered, strategies planned, manners reviewed.

"Your mother would have made a great general," Lord Parbury told Mariah with sympathy as she stared out at the grayness in a mood that matched it. "She manages things even more precisely than Wellington and she sees everything as a campaign of one sort or another."

Mariah could only think of how devastated her mother would be when it all came to nothing.

Her sisters responded to the new situation in ways true to their characters. Rorie was at first resentful at the turn of events and then resigned as she fell from the center of her mother's attention. Used to being the daughter least noticed, Mariah felt overwhelmed and would have gladly given back that privileged position. Georgie, privy to somewhat more of the truth behind the circumstances, watched over Mariah with genuine concern. Cassie was ever dubious about the whole thing, yet full of enthusiasm for the new status their family had gained.

Harriet Pritchard, of course, took an optimistic view when Mariah confessed the state of affairs to her. On an afternoon visit in the sanctuary of Mariah's bedchamber she immediately picked up on the thread of Mariah's argument to the marquess.

"You might very well get Lord Milbourne to care for you, Mariah! You could yet prove to him that he need not always lose those he loves, just as you told him! It would be so romantic!"

Mariah thought that was expecting a bit much. She was

not foolish enough to think that one passionate kiss meant anything beyond the one moment it had lasted. Best to take things a step at a time, something she seemed to have forgotten lately.

She would never forget the tortured look on Lord Milbourne's face when he had recited the bitter litany of losses he had suffered. What a sad life he had lived, for all his outward trappings of success! And how completely different from her own. Now she, who could barely begin to understand the pain he must feel everyday, had made herself a nuisance in his life. It was her fault he had been trapped into giving up his privacy to act out yet another lie, a courtship that was only a sham.

She would try to make his time with her as painless as possible. If she could also help to solve his other problems, might that not help somehow to make up for this new burden? The request she had made to Taylor was a weak stab in the dark at best, but something might come of it.

When the rain finally ceased, Lord Milbourne invited Mariah for their first public appearance together, a drive in the park. When he arrived, Mariah was sitting in the chair by her bedroom window, staring out at rooftops and chimney stacks, wondering how everything had gone so wrong. The way Mama had fluttered around her, supervising her choice of clothing and fussing about her hair, one might think the marquess had planned to propose marriage! Mariah knew better, but she was still unaccountably nervous.

A quick knock sounded on the door. Not bothering to wait for an answer, Cassie slipped into the room like a conspirator, closing the door behind her. "He's here," she announced. "Bennett will come creaking up the stairs to announce him any moment." Bennett wore stays.

She crossed the room to where Mariah was sitting, scarcely pausing for breath between words. "He is driving the most splendid rig, and wait until you see his cattle! High-stepping, beautifully matched, black as coal. I was peeking out the drawing room windows. I could almost envy you, Mariah, but then I remember that you have to be polite and listen to him talk."

Mariah laughed. "Oh, Cassie, he is really not so bad. You have hardly seen him except the one night he dined with us and then last week at the picnic."

"Well, I admit he did seem better at the picnic. And God knows, he is handsome!"

"Do not let Mama hear you swear like that! Have you been spending time with William?"

Bennett knocked, effectively ending the conversation. Mariah gathered her gloves and her reticule and stood up, hesitating for only a moment after the butler entered and made his announcement.

"Cassie, do I look all right? Mama fussed me to distraction!" That she asked the one person least likely to give the answer she needed to hear was a testimony to the state of her nerves.

Cassie frowned at her critically. "In truth, you look better than usual. That pelisse is a good color, even if it is the same shade of rose as your new ball gown. If you smile instead of looking so nervous, you'll do. Go and enjoy all the envious stares you will surely draw while you are with him. Go on! I want to watch from the drawing room as you drive away."

Lord Milbourne was waiting in the narrow entry hall as Mariah came down the last turn of the stairs. He seemed to fill the entire space, much as he had done in the hackney to Queen Square. He was not built for ordinary houses or vehicles, she thought—his head was too high, his shoulders too broad. But as he stood there resplendent in a burgundy coat with his gold brocade waistcoat reflecting the tawny gold of his hair, it was perfectly obvious that that was only as it should be, for he was not at all an ordinary man.

Her mother appeared before she could say a word.

"You are so kind to take our Mariah for a drive, Lord Milbourne," Lady Parbury burbled. "Here she is, all ready to go, no waiting at all. I do hope you have a splendid time of it."

Mariah did not like the way her mother said, *here she is, no waiting*. It made her feel like merchandise in a shop window. As she rolled her eyes at the marquess in a mixture of exasperation and apology, however, her glance met his amused one and softened. Her mother meant well. She always did. She was just overeager. *All the time.*

"Now be sure to watch for your sisters in the park, Mariah!" was the baroness's parting comment.

When they stepped outside, Mariah saw that Cassie had been right about Lord Milbourne's equipage. The handsome pair of matched blacks were almost as glossy as the curricle's paint, which gleamed in the pale sunlight like a dark green mirror. Mariah caught a flash of her own rose-colored reflection beside the marquess as he handed her up and then climbed in beside her. A dark-skinned boy wearing a white turban stood stiffly on the back platform of the carriage looking handsome but uncomfortable in formal dark green livery boasting lots of gold buttons and braid.

"What a splendid turnout, Lord Milbourne. And is that Selim on the back?" she asked as they settled themselves on a squab upholstered in fine Moroccan leather.

"Yes, in his favorite occupation. He has a little trouble with the livery—he is very proud to wear it, but he is used to lighter, looser clothing."

She tried unsuccessfully to establish a space of a few safe inches between herself and Lord Milbourne, and tried not to think about clothing. Somehow, the sight of his muscled thigh sheathed in snug, flawlessly fitted doeskin so close to her kept drawing her eyes. As if she had never seen a man beside her before now! She was thankful that the necessity of dealing with traffic prevented him from looking at her, lest he notice her stares. At least they were not actually *touching*. She was having trouble enough settling her nerves as it was.

"I must apologize for my mother," she said once the carriage had left the curb. "Sometimes she has such absurd ambitions, but she does not mean any harm. I hate deceiving her—she has such high hopes for us!"

"She may be just as happy to be rid of me by the time our courtship is over," he said with a wry smile. "But she is only acting as her nature dictates. I remember my own mother fussing over my sister and myself when we were small. Do you not think that is how they are meant to behave?"

"My father likens my mother to Wellington. She can be annoying, but I suppose you are right." She wanted to ask him about his own family, but did not know if she should. "Do you have many happy memories of your childhood? I mean to say—that is—how old were you when you lost your mother? Do you mind my asking?"

"I do not mind," he said, managing to flick a quick glance at her. A trace of the smile still lingered in his eyes. "I was ten—I had been here in England, at Harrow, for six months when my mother died of fever at home in India. She was a strong, proud Austrian, a baron's daughter—I had always thought she was indestructible. I think my father thought so, too."

"Did you worship her?"

"Most definitely. She was beautiful and intelligent. I don't think my father ever quite believed he was worthy of her—he never understood why she was willing to marry him, when he was only a younger son."

"She must have loved him."

"Yes." He was silent for a moment, and she thought he had moved thousands of miles away from London and the traffic around them. Then he added, "My sister was much like her. That was a consolation to my father, until we lost her, too."

"Did she die of fever, like your mother?"

"No. We never did learn quite what took her. Are you certain you wish to hear this? They were sharing a meal—my father said they ate the same foods. But she began to feel unwell. He said she broke out in a sweat as if she was feverish, but she was pale and cold. She lost consciousness. Within two hours she was dead, before the doctor ever arrived."

"How awful! I am sorry. I am sorry to have brought up a topic that brings you pain." In her sincerity, she put her gloved hand on his arm.

It was such a natural, momentary gesture, she did not think about it at all, until she felt the hardness of his muscle under the layers of his coat and shirt, and she sensed his whole body stiffen beside her. She snatched her hand away instantly and put it to her lips as she blushed in embarrassment—she had not meant to offend him! But that second motion was a mistake in itself, for her fingertips tingled from the contact with his arm and now, even through the kidskin covering them, they made her lips burn. She had offended him by her familiar touch, yet now all she could think of was the kiss they had shared in his music room! Underneath her responsible, dutiful self surely lurked the soul of a wanton as well as a rebel.

He spoke as if nothing had occurred, although he did not look at her. "I suppose you are curious about the rest of the people on my list. I owe you an apology for my outburst that day. I never meant to speak so in front of you."

"My brother William can be an insensitive clod—I didn't blame you for feeling angry."

The marquess laughed. "Oh, if William only knew how his name is being taken in vain! I have heard him called a number of things in the past—quite distant past, too—but never that. Still, it does not excuse my lack of control."

She thought she had never met a man so collected and under control. The brief show of anger and pain she had witnessed that day had proved to her what his kiss had suggested—that this was a man who felt deeply. His control was a protection, an armor against the world. She suspected that his determined individualism, his eccentric behavior and devil-may-care attitude were part of his armor, too. But his armor had chinks. She had already discovered that.

As they halted for a tangle of carriages in front of them, he took up his narrative again. He told her about his father's death trying to help a neighbor during a monsoon storm. He told a little of the first woman he had wanted to marry—a beautiful girl of Portuguese and French ancestry, the daughter of a wealthy merchant in Calcutta, the woman who had made the sketchbook. But he would not talk about her death.

"You still miss her."

"Yes."

"One of the sketches is her self-portrait, isn't it?" she

asked with sudden intuition. The white woman in the picture had indeed been lovely.

"Yes." He would not say more.

"Who was the other woman, the second one?"

"She was a native woman—Shanti. She taught me to play the sitar. She lived and traveled with me." He did send a sideways glance at her then. "Does that shock you?"

"I think you want it to. I think you like the idea that sometimes you shock people. I think you do it quite deliberately." *To keep us away.* She smiled at him, to make sure there was no sting of condemnation in her words.

He looked relieved to have the conversation return to the present. He even smiled back at her. "I suppose now you will refuse to be shocked if I smoke my water pipe in public or have one of my ears pierced, as I had been planning to do. By Jove, my secret is found out!"

She let her other questions go, happy that he could so quickly return to good humor and perfectly willing to join in. "I have heard that you are having a *swimming bath* installed in your house!" she said in a voice of mock outrage.

He chuckled. "That one happens to be true. You must promise not to give me away."

"We seem to have accumulated quite a collection of secrets between us," she pointed out, feeling much in accord with him. Did not the sharing of confidences mean they were friends? "I will protect yours, as long as you will protect mine."

Chapter Thirteen

Ren risked another glance at Mariah Parbury's face. Despite his best efforts to fight it, he was much too aware of her sitting primly beside him on the seat of the curricle. Whenever he turned his head toward her for a moment her faint scent of jasmine came through to him over the stench of the city streets. That scent brought back the way she had felt in his arms, and the extraordinary kiss they had shared in secret.

He had hoped that handling the ribbons himself today would prove a sufficient distraction from her presence. Instead, he caught himself wondering if she felt the movement of the carriage as acutely as he did—if the rattle of vehicles and cry of voices that eternally accompanied life in the city seemed as loud to her. It did not help him at all when she touched his arm, or now spoke in such a heartwarming tone of voice. He took a deep breath.

"The latitude I am allowed in my transgressions against the *ton* quite amazes me," he said, turning the horses into the entrance to Hyde Park at last. After all the rain, the park looked vibrantly green.

"I suppose it is the hypocrisy which amuses me. I think it is one reason I am so inclined to push the boundaries—I wonder how far I can go before the Beau Monde closes rank against me. I recognize that no one is immune from that."

He clucked to his blacks, encouraging them to pick up their pace to match the flow of vehicles circling through the park. The splendid creatures tossed their heads and stepped up to an easy trot in response.

"No one could possibly find fault with you today," Miss

Parbury said in an admiring tone. "You and your equipage are turned out to perfection, and we are driving in the park at precisely the fashionable time of day, observing a time-honored and unexceptional ritual."

"One can always find fault, Miss Parbury. If I allowed my cattle their heads, we could be faulted for overrunning another's carriage or driving at a reprehensible speed. I have no doubt that there are those who, if they dared, would fault me for choosing you to take out today and others to fault you for agreeing to be with me. But I believe life is too short for such nonsense."

"I can understand why you would think that," she murmured. "I must say that you have been remarkably well-behaved in the last week or two. I have heard no more of your leaving hostesses in the lurch, racing your cheetah in Green Park, or parading your latest paramour . . . Oh!" She clapped a hand over her mouth in distress. "I should not be speaking of such a thing!"

"Your mother's instructions, no doubt," he said wryly. "Frankly, Miss Parbury, you and I seem to have unconventional conversations, and I am glad of it—how dull in a town full of so many people to confine oneself to discussing only 'proper' topics of the weather, the opera, and the most recent ball. To tell the truth, I've been reconsidering the notion of allowing people to see my house when it is done—if I held a reception, it would give them something new to talk about for weeks. The idea has been rolling around in the back of my mind ever since you claimed the lack of such opportunity made you desperate enough to break into my house like a thief."

She moaned—a little low moan of protest against his mentioning her folly. "Please do not remind me of that night!"

Her innocent moan sent a wave of physical response through his body—worse than when she touched his arm. If they had been elsewhere, if his hands had not been fully occupied with guiding his cattle, he would have liked to pull her into his arms and try kissing her until she moaned from pleasure instead.

Dear God, how was he going to get through a week or two of false courting, walking a fine balance between propriety, appearances, and trying to deny his desire for her? He had been right—it was going to be a special kind of hell. It occurred to him that making plans for a grand unveiling of his refurbishments would provide welcome distraction.

"I thought perhaps to hold a public breakfast—I am impressed by the wisdom of feeding the multitudes at three in the afternoon instead of in the evening when they would consume twice as much food and require twice as many candles to see it."

"On the other hand, since the usual intent behind such entertainments is to impress everyone, it argues that you might prefer to have your opening in the evening, lest someone accuse you of practicing economy."

"Oh, God forbid!" he said, and they both laughed.

At that moment they were hailed and looked up to see a lone rider astride a beautiful gray. It was Carrisforte, dressed to the nines and looking the perfect picture of fashion.

"Good day to you, Milbourne, Miss Parbury! A fine afternoon to be out after all that rain, is it not? All the horses are frisky." He gave Ren a knowing wink and quirked an eyebrow that seemed to suggest that the horses were not the only ones.

Ren found he was not amused, even though it was just the sort of harmless double entendre that Carris might normally make. Perhaps the implication hit too close to home, or Ren simply resented the hint that his interest in Miss Parbury derived from his baser needs.

"That is a fine animal you have there, Carris," he replied, steering the conversation away from such personal matters. "New purchase?"

Carrisforte reached down to stroke his mount's neck. "She's a beauty—used to belong to Lord Gellingston. Heard he was up the River Tick and selling his stable at Tattersall's—picked her up for a song at the sale."

Ren thought Carris must have struck a fine bargain indeed; his friend's purse seldom stretched far enough to cover the kind of impression on others that the man valued.

"She does you proud. Sorry I missed it!" Ren realized that there was a time when he would have accompanied his friend to such a sale. Many things were changing in his life.

"Lots of beauty in the park today," Carris answered, nodding to Miss Parbury and making her blush.

She did look particularly fine today. Ren liked the deep rose-colored pelisse she was wearing, and the short-brimmed straw bonnet she wore seemed to make her gray eyes look huge. The feather on the side nodded in the breeze flirtatiously. But irrationally, he did not like having Carris be the one to make compliments.

"I am thinking about opening up my house for a public 'At Home' when the work is finished, Carris. What do you think of that idea?"

"Ho, ho. Are you not already the subject of enough gossip? You wish for more? I can think of no surer way to achieve it."

"Oh, the tabbies need something to occupy their tongues. Why should we not oblige them, at least until a new scandal comes along?"

"There is always that. Well, I never turn down an invitation—be glad to help you out of a few helpings of veal or prawns. You're likely to have to issue tickets—the curiosity you've aroused around town is tremendous."

The thought of having some five hundred people parade through his house gave Ren pause, but then as he began to think about who he would invite, and the diversity of intense reactions there would be to what he had done to Milbourne House, he nodded his head. He might even enjoy measuring his standing by seeing who came and who stayed away.

"Miss Parbury, do you suppose your estimable mother would be willing to assist in this campaign? There is a great deal of planning to be done!"

Lady Parbury, of course, was only too happy to be asked for her help, and immersed herself and all her daughters in the project. Lists flowed from her Chippendale writing desk like water from a fountain and correspondence flew back and forth between the houses. The Opening of Milbourne

House superseded all topics of conversation at Great Marlborough Street save one, Mariah's courtship by the marquess.

"Mariah, you are fortunate that his taste runs to the unconventional," Rorie said to her as the four sisters gathered one evening in preparation for a ball at Lord and Lady Westby's in Piccadilly. The elder three were having their hair dressed, while Cassie watched. "Still, you must try to make the best of your looks, if you hope to snare him. There seem to be many besides you who are willing to overlook his eccentricities. Ouch, Jennie! Do not pull so."

Mariah was not offended by her sister's offhanded comment. It only pointed to one of several obstacles she could see to any successful result of the courtship, not the least of these being the marquess himself. He had made no secret of his disinclination to marry, and in the past week of attending functions and being seen in each other's company, there had been no more lapses like the kiss in his music room, or even any hints that he remembered what had passed between them there. Indeed, he had been the perfect model of gentlemanly deportment—all that was courteous, solicitous, and kind, quite like an elderly uncle rather than the passionate man she knew lurked somewhere inside him.

He had been forced to become a regular fixture in the Parburys' drawing room on the days when they were "at home," making his appearance among the other young gentlemen who came calling on the sisters and the gossiping matrons who called on their mother. Mariah wondered if she was the only one who could see how these visits pained him—how the other young men variously aped him or resented him, and how the women fawned and fluttered their fans. She constantly felt as though she should be apologizing to him.

She peered critically now at her reflection in the cheval glass standing in the dressing room. "I think we must not allow Mama to get her hopes too high in regards to my success with Lord Milbourne," she said cautiously. She could not reveal that the courtship was a sham, but she did find the strain of remaining silent every time someone dropped hints about her future with him very wearing on her nerves.

That knowledge also ate away at her pleasure in his company, which was all too precious to her. She knew that when the time came for the courtship to discontinue, she would be heartsick. But she was determined to enjoy the time she had while it lasted. She knew that it would not end before the grand opening of his house. And in the deepest recess of her heart, she caught herself hoping that their friendship, such as it was, would in some small measure ease the pain and loneliness she sensed in him.

Tonight she would wear the new ball gown of rose-colored satin, and she hoped the deep color would bring some life to her face. She did want to look her best, even if it was not for the same reason that Rorie supposed. But if the dress did not do the trick, she had a weapon of last resort. Tucked away in her reticule was a small pot of rouge she had purchased while on an outing with Harry. Applied with a very light hand, the cosmetic ought to help her achieve a little equality with the rest of her competition.

Lord Milbourne had not yet arrived when the Parburys greeted their host and hostess at the ball. Mariah peeked through the open doorway into the grand saloon, radiant from the dozens of tapers in the huge crystal chandeliers and filled from wall to wall with the rainbow-hued assemblage of elegant guests. She begged Georgie to accompany her to the ladies' retiring room.

"Beating a retreat already?" asked her quiet sister. "We have not so much as entered the main saloon!"

"I need to make repairs," Mariah whispered urgently.

In the retiring room Georgie protested when she saw what Mariah intended. "You do not need that paint on your face in the least, Mariah Parbury! What would Mama say?"

"I don't doubt that Mama would think it's a good idea! She would probably be amazed that she did not think of it herself. After all, she wants me to drag poor Lord Milbourne to the altar. I believe she'd support anything at all that might help to achieve that outcome."

"Then why did you not put this on at home?"

"Well, I suppose I feared Mama might rather overdo it . . ."

Whether or not the small amount of rouge helped her looks, it certainly helped her confidence, Mariah thought. She emerged from the retiring room feeling far more ready to face the evening—competitors, Lord Milbourne and all.

Several young gentleman soon asked to put their names on her dance card, and she smiled her way through several dances while she kept an eye out for the marquess. The marked favor he had been showing her lately had unquestionably increased her consequence, she noted. Certain men sought dances with her now who never previously had paid her the slightest attention. Perhaps, if she was fortunate, that trend would continue after the marquess supposedly lost interest in her.

She saw him just as the last dance in a set ended—he approached as her partner returned her to her place. The younger fellow relinquished her arm with a quick nod of greeting and fled.

"Good evening to you, Miss Parbury," Lord Milbourne said in his lovely deep voice. "What is this? You look as if you were running a fever." He touched her cheek with a finger which he then inspected.

Before she could utter a word he said, "Yes, yes, a bit warm in here, I agree. Too much dancing? Let us step away from this crowd for some air."

With a firm grip on her elbow he steered her through the chattering crowd of nondancers into a shadowy corner behind a marble column. Without another word he brought out his handkerchief and after a quick glance around, wiped the rogue from her cheeks.

Mortified, she felt genuine color flame into her face. "How dare you?"

"How dare *you*? Painting your face makes you look like a trollop. What sort of man do you think that will attract? I doubt your brother would appreciate seeing you send out that kind of a message."

"So you feel entitled to act in his place?"

"Yes." He gave her a penetrating stare that she found very unsettling.

It seemed to go on for the longest time, until he said, "Well, not exactly," his voice suddenly husky. The look in his eyes changed so subtly, she might have missed it if she had not been staring into them, but all of a sudden she felt the full heat of passion replace the spark of indignation between them. She was as shocked by the suddenness of the change as she was by its force.

They stared at one another for what must have been at least a full minute, neither speaking or making a move. Would he try to kiss her? She knew men sometimes stole such moments in the corners of ballrooms.

Instead he shook himself, as if awakening from a spell. "You do not need the assistance of cosmetics, Miss Parbury. The dance brings a sparkle to your eye and a handsome flush to your cheeks that is natural and appealing. You need not hide behind false colors."

"And besides, you are going to tell me this is not a battle," she added.

He chuckled. "Well, perhaps it is, but I did think honor had something to do with it."

She took his proffered arm and they returned into the main part of the room, where he put his name down for two dances and made certain that one was the supper dance, so that they could share the break together. But the heightened state of her senses did not settle down. She knew, now, that the strong attraction between them was mutual and more than the whim of a passing moment. It lurked hidden below a dangerously thin veneer of polite behavior. The realization that there was in him so much as a faint echo of her own yearnings made her spirits soar. But at the same time she knew that such an attraction was just the thing to ensure that he would never allow himself to take a serious interest in her.

The weeks leading up to Lord Milbourne's opening were busy with preparations. Constructing the guest list and writing cards of invitation took countless hours of effort, even with the help of all the Parbury ladies. The marquess quite intentionally issued his invitations to five hundred of the most powerful and acceptable people in England in two separate batches sent out days apart, leaving many of the second two hundred and fifty in an agony of doubt about their inclusion and greatly enhancing the appearance of exclusivity surrounding the event.

"Only playing by their own rules," he said innocently while chuckling with evil glee.

Huge quantities of food, flowers, candles, ribbons, and decorations were ordered, musicians hired, and extra staff begged and borrowed. Bennett was to assist Frothwick in the butlers' duties, and all of the Parburys' footmen and grooms were added to those employed by the marquess, along with more servants borrowed from friends.

In the meantime, the endless round of routs, dinners, card parties, balls, breakfasts, and other social events continued, as did the supposed courtship between Mariah and Lord Milbourne.

"I can feel the barbs and arrows in my back even now as we walk across the room together," the marquess whispered to her as they attended a musicale one evening. Their shared love of music made these events the sort they often enjoyed the most. "The Duke of Chadwell's daughter is wondering how I can possibly continue to prefer your company to hers, and Lord Drayton's daughter is deciding that I am a much greater sapskull than she had previously imagined. Wild horses could not keep them away from my opening! Then I suspect they will all congratulate you on your narrow escape from me when our courtship is seen to falter and fail in the coming days."

"And as quick as may be they will all begin to vie for your attention once again," Mariah added, hiding the stab of dismay she felt whenever he mentioned the inevitable end of their time together.

"By Jove, I trust not. I wish I were not such a target of interest. You will see—the gossip about me will begin to be more vicious. Jealousy is like a contagion in this town. I am sorry you must be subjected to some of it. I do not think your brother was considering that when he insisted we play this game. All I can say is that they had better have the manners not to indulge in any of it in your hearing!"

"That sounds like a threat against the tabbies!"

"It is. I'll not stand for any discourtesy shown toward you. It is one reason I have been so well-behaved these recent weeks—no new outrages to fire them up. But once they have seen what I've done to Milbourne House, all bets are off."

"I know many people will find it as fascinating and marvelous as I did," she replied with confidence. She could not say more for it was time to take their seats before the music should begin. But she could not help wondering if the marquess was planning further attempts to disgrace himself once his opening and their courtship were over.

Chapter Fourteen

Lord Milbourne looked about helplessly on the day of the great reception. "Remind me again why I wanted to invite all these people to come and shake their heads over the way I have replaced my grandfather's cherubs and velvet swags?"

The appointed hour for the opening was only a few minutes away, and the house looked suitably magnificent, ablaze with light in every room and every polished surface gleaming.

The Parburys had arrived early to lend their support and help oversee the last-minute placement of details. Mariah was standing beside the marquess in the East Drawing Room, where he had stationed himself for the grueling task of greeting his guests.

"You very altruistically decided to give these poor, bored people something different to see and talk about" she said, unable to resist teasing him a little. "I have no doubt that they will thank you from the bottom of their hearts."

"Or from the bottom of their feet as they trample the name of Milbourne in the dust of their scorn."

Mariah looked at him in surprise. His tone conveyed sincere regret. Not once had she ever before heard him express uncertainty or any concern over other people's opinions, nor had she ever sensed any feeling other than resentment toward his family's exalted title.

It was as if he had momentarily opened another window on the hidden man inside himself. He had said once that he was only human and not immune to having fears. Appar-

ently he was also not as immune to connecting with other
people as he thought.

She smiled. "You are not suffering a sudden attack of
doubt over your chosen course, are you? The work you have
had done here is a masterpiece—an astonishing achievement that deserves to be seen. The more enlightened among
the crowd will hail it as such. As for the others, do you care
what they think? I believe you had in mind flaunting all this
in their faces in hopes of proving that you are every bit as
much of an odd fish as they suspect you to be, even though
it is not so."

"Are you calling me a fraud, young lady?"

She laughed. "Yes, most certainly. But never mind. I do
not doubt that Prinny himself will make an appearance here,
to admire what you have done. Do not be surprised if he
steals some ideas to put into use for his own projects!"

"These days having the Prince Regent's admiration is not
necessarily something to brag about," he said, but at least he
smiled.

"You know that no one will be here at the beginning.
They will all be competing with each other to see who can
be the latest. But we are ready for them. I must go down-
stairs now and join my mother."

Impulsively, she touched his arm in a small gesture of
comfort. "It will be all right, you know." She suspected now
that he did not know himself whether he hoped the event
would put him beyond the pale or would merely add another
peg to the crown of social adoration that already weighed
heavily on him.

The small trickle of guests began a short while later and
grew into a veritable human flood by the end of the first
hour. All of London's upper crust, great and small, appeared
to be in attendance—even the great Wellington himself.

William was kind enough to escort Mariah around the circuit of the open rooms a number of times, so that she could
enjoy the spectacle and catch bits and pieces of people's reactions. She noticed that her sisters did not lack for escorts,
nor did Harry after she arrived with her family, for Mr. Car-

risforte was soon observed steering her toward one of the artfully arranged piles of food in the great dining room.

The entire first two floors of the house were open except for the two rooms upstairs that made up Ranee's suite. To spare the cat the distress of the noise and commotion and to eliminate the chance of any accidental intrusion upon her, the marquess had had her removed to the top floor of the house for the duration of the reception. Mariah thought this was both wise and humane, although a part of her missed the cheetah's presence. Lord, had she become so attached to both the man and his pet? She did wonder who was minding Ranee as she saw Selim bustling about among the battalion of other busy servants, but she did not dwell on the thought.

The perfection of the layout of the house proved itself in accommodating the crush of people who visited the next few hours. Cards and dancing in the anteroom and grand saloon upstairs were almost as great an attraction as the food in the dining room, the music room, and the so-called Little Drawing Room on the ground floor, but the guests appeared to circulate with a minimum of discomfort as the rooms opened into each other or were connected by what Mariah had come to think of as "the great cave temple passage." Chamber music from the library at one end behind the entrance hall could be heard faintly all the way to the other end where Lord Milbourne's study was open with more tables available for cards.

Mariah discovered that behind the carved screen in the corner of that room was the door to his dressing room in the service wing, which he had given over to the installation of the soon-to-be-famous swimming bath. A footman assigned to the room explained how special supports had been installed in the scullery below it to support its weight when filled with water and how special pipes connected it to the cistern on the roof.

Mariah was not the only one both fascinated and impressed. "Can you imagine immersing oneself in such an amount of water without going to the seaside!" exclaimed one turbaned guest who was literally festooned with diamonds. Mariah suspected the lady would soon be studying her own residence to determine if a similar installation might be feasible.

The response Mariah overheard as people exclaimed over the house in general told her a great deal about the former appearance of the place as well as about the people responding.

"Hmph. Took those demmed old statutes of fighting stags off the stair landing," commented one ancient gentleman. "About time some Milbourne had the sense to do it. Only a miracle those antlers never blinded anyone."

"A blessing that they mounted that tiger's pelt on the wall—I could just see tripping over its head," his companion answered. "Did you ever see such huge fangs?"

Mariah smiled, thinking of her own reaction the first time she had seen the tigerskin run on the landing. It had been her mother's suggestion that it be hung up to preserve it from the trampling of so many feet at one time.

Members of the *ton* who had recently refitted their own great houses with lavish amounts of gilding and velvet or who aped the French styles to the exclusion of all else took a predictably dim view of Lord Milbourne's achievement.

"'Tis a travesty, a tragedy!" Lady Greenwood was heard to comment with a sad shake of her head. "He has ruined his grandfather's perfectly beautiful house, replacing all that fine gilding and damask with images of heathen idols, monstrous columns and statues of elephants! Barbaric!"

On the other hand, Mariah also glimpsed Lord Milbourne receiving hearty congratulations from numbers of people, including the Earl of Egremont and several other former commissioners and high officials of the East India Company's board.

"'Tis a masterpiece, a triumph! He has captured the look and feeling of the Hindustan right within these walls. Makes me feel as if I were back there again, only without the accursed heat!" she heard an elderly fellow exclaim.

"Fine enough if you *want* to feel you are back there," grumbled a younger man behind him.

Many comments likened the marquess's own designs to Repton's designs for the Pavilion at Brighton and to Samuel

Cockerell's work on Sezincote, his brother's house in the Cotswolds.

As the end of the evening drew nearer, a great commotion and fanfare announced the arrival of the portly Prince Regent. The crowds miraculously parted like the Red Sea for him and Mariah thought he probably obtained a far better view of the house than most people had received. He made the circuit of the rooms escorted by Lord Milbourne, stopping here and there to make a comment or pose a question. He greeted people as he went around; some were as eager as ever to be recognized, but Mariah was surprised at the number who edged themselves discreetly out of his way to avoid the encounter. Truly, the regent's popularity was at a low ebb.

"Crowd seems to be thinning a bit," William said a short time after the prince's departure.

"Thank heavens." Mariah was just beginning to realize that she was exhausted, and she had not even had the duty of greeting all these people. She supposed Lord Milbourne's stamina must be greater than her own, but she still imagined that he would be thoroughly tired by the time the last guest left.

She saw the Pritchards making their way toward the hall, and realized that she had hardly had a chance to speak with Harry all evening.

"William, may I ask you something?" she said, drawing him aside next to the grand staircase. "When I see Mr. Carrisforte with Harry, I wonder why you and he are not closer friends, as he and Lord Milbourne are. You were all at Harrow together."

"Well, it is no oddity, I think. He and Milbourne both went to Hailey Bury, when I went off to Cambridge, and then they both worked for the Company in Bengal. They have a great many more experiences in common than I."

"Is that all?"

"You want to know if he is good company for Harry, is that it? Aside from the fact that he ought to be looking out for someone with a greater fortune than she has, I see no objection. He is a bit of a fribble—I've always thought of him as a looking glass, always reflecting other people, with no real substance of his own. But that describes half the fellows in this town, I would say! No crime in that."

"I just hope Harry will not be hurt if his intentions toward her are not serious."

"You worry too much. Do you honestly think Harry's interest in *him* is serious at this point? She's still in the midst of her first Season—the plumes are barely out of her hair from her presentation at court. Give over."

Perhaps William was right. Did she worry too much? Perhaps it was just easier to worry about Harry's fragile heart than her own. Reassured, Mariah took her brother's arm and strolled up the staircase to check on the progress of departures from the upper rooms. Lord Milbourne, returned to his post in the East Drawing Room, was still surrounded by well-wishers.

"Never cared much for naked Greeks cavorting with figures from mythology, m'self," Mariah heard someone say as she and William passed by them. She smiled, yet she wished they would all go home. It had been hours since she had been able to exchange a single word with the marquess.

The reception had been an outstanding success, she felt, regardless of whether or not public perception eventually decided so. Despite his current unpopularity, the Prince Regent's attendance at the affair still gave it tremendous consequence. However, it was the interest and support shown by so many in the course of the evening that pleased Mariah most. She hoped that it would prove to Lord Milbourne that there were more sincere and worthwhile people among the *ton* than he supposed.

Finally, eventually, all the guests were gone except for Mr. Carrisforte and the Parburys. Servants busy with the cleanup bustled about the rooms, and the musicians in the alcove off the Grand Saloon were still packing up their music and instruments. Mariah dropped gratefully into a chair at the nearest end of that room and was talking quietly with William and Mr. Carrisforte when Lord Milbourne found them. He pulled up another chair and bid the other two gentlemen to do likewise.

"If I ever get a notion to do something like this again, I am depending upon you all to stop me," he said ruefully. "I never imagined that five hundred people could seem so close to a thousand!"

He did indeed look tired now, Mariah thought as an urge to hold him overtook her. For a moment the fantastic notion of what it might be like to be married to him danced through her brain—a dangerous notion indeed! Before she managed to banish the image she pictured them retiring for the night hand in hand, seeking comfort in each other's arms in the final bliss of privacy after such a long and busy evening.

"People will be talking about this event for weeks to come," Carrisforte said. "Your success is unequaled—there was no one of consequence who was not here!"

"Did you ever see so many craned necks and quizzing glasses in a crowd all at once?" William chuckled.

Mariah glanced furtively at the marquess, wondering what sort of thoughts were going through his tired mind. As he so often did, he caught her looking and answered her with a smile that left her wondering even more.

"You have surpassed even yourself this time, old friend," Carrisforte continued, apparently quite oblivious to the silent exchange taking place between the marquess and Mariah.

"Gentlemen," Lord Milbourne said finally, still looking at her, "we have survived to see another day. William, it is time to take your weary sister home. I have no idea what has become of the rest of your family—they have probably dropped in their tracks in some other part of the house. We should go and seek them out. And, Carris, I do not believe there is a single prawn left to be had in the house. It is time this evening came to a close."

Long after everyone had left or retired, Ren lay awake in his bed reviewing the evening. Although it was no easy task to sort through five hundred guests, Ren knew Carris was wrong—there were a few people of consequence who had not come. Colonel Agworth was one, although Ren had not in the least expected the man to turn up.

A friend of Ren's uncle, Agworth had been Ren's sponsor at Hailey Bury and his mentor when he'd first arrived in Calcutta. The fellow had never understood Ren's reasons for leaving the East India Company or his subsequent conduct as an agent and advisor for the Raja of Lampur. The loss of the friendship hurt, but like others of his ilk, the colonel possessed strong opinions about the native populations in India and the proper role of the Company that differed radically from Ren's. No doubt he and his cronies saw Ren's transformation of Milbourne House as yet more evidence that to his own shame he had "gone native" and embraced the "barbaric" culture they abhorred. There was no use in trying to make them understand, although Ren had sent several of them invitations all the same.

All in all, the reception had exceeded his wildest expectations. Oh, to be sure, he had heard snatches of jealous sniping behind his back as people entertained themselves at his expense, but he was vastly surprised that there had not been more of it. He had to admit he was somewhat heartened by the number of seemingly sincere compliments he'd received and the amount of genuine interest people had shown.

He was also pleased that his arrangements for Ranee had seemed to work out well. Selim had come to him with the suggestion that he hire young Taylor to keep company with the cheetah during the event, and when Ren had gone up to check on them and bring Ranee back down to her rooms at the end of the evening, he had found both of them curled up asleep on Selim's bed.

Ren had been doing what he could to help the boy. Taylor had been given a place in one of the charity schools, where he might have prospered by studying, but within a week the lad had been dismissed again for his frequent truancy. He had been sent back to the workhouse, his precious freedom regained only temporarily, for now there was talk of sending him north to work in the cotton mills. Ren had sent gifts of food and new clothing—he had stopped short of sending funds, for he thought the workhouse overseers might only pocket those for themselves. He had also left standing instructions in the Milbourne House kitchen that

Taylor might be fed any time he happened to come round for a visit, which as Ren heard it was happening quite often of late. Somehow the lad managed to turn meals in the kitchen into visits with Selim and Ranee—it was amazing how quickly the boy had won over the hearts of at least half of Ren's staff.

Unfortunately, Ren had made no similar progress with his investigations into the thefts of small items from his house, even though Frothwick had dismissed at least one footman under suspicion. That Taylor was often in the house combined with the fact that the disappearances were still continuing made Ren uneasy, although he wanted to trust the boy. The most recent casualty was a small box made of camel bone, decorated with brass fittings and inlays of precious stones, including a large ruby set into the lid. He remembered that Taylor had particularly admired it.

Taylor's inability to read or write certainly absolved him from any involvement with Ren's peculiar mail. The most recent nuisance to arrive had been not a blank note but a new twist on the theme. This time the note had actually borne a message, the four words "you will be sorry" in a crudely printed hand. Ren had balled up the note and thrown it in the fire, but the damage was done—all the actions he suspected he would regret in the days ahead stirred in his mind and kept company with the ghostly regrets that haunted his past.

He knew it was foolish to allow four such little words to work on him so—it was precisely the effect the anonymous letter sender no doubt desired. But at times like this night when his brain was too stimulated to sleep and too tired to be reasonable he was the perfect target, and knowing so did nothing to help him.

Was he sorry he had given the reception? No. But would he be? Who knew? Most definitely he was sorry he had formed an attachment to Miss Parbury—and that he had done so he could no longer deny. The strain of hiding his feelings was beginning to tell on him, and he knew he would have to break off their so-called courtship very soon. He would be sorry then, too, although not as sorry as he would be if he did not do it.

This evening he had actually caught himself wishing she were by his side as his hostess—his wife. And then, at the end of the evening, she had looked at him with such a warm and tender expression in her gentle gray eyes. . . . Perhaps that explained why just before she left he had impulsively asked her to join him tomorrow to visit Lord and Lady Buxton, who had invited him during the reception to see their collection of Indian arts.

Why had he done that? It was just the opposite of what he needed to do. He obviously lost all reason when he was with her, and certainly that could be dangerous. Pah! Thinking of her was another form of torment. That he could not stop doing so was a very bad sign, indeed.

Chapter Fifteen

"It is not such a great distance from here to Golden Square, just straight down Carnaby Street," Miss Parbury said when Ren came to fetch her the following afternoon. "The day is so beautiful—may we not walk there? Would it make us terribly late?"

Ren smiled, charmed as always by her bright enthusiasm and courtesy. The idea of taking her on his arm and strolling beside her down the length of the commercial street with all its little shops was very appealing. "I think our host will forgive us if we are not perfectly punctual. I will tell Ahmed to pick us up at the Buxtons' at four."

With matters so arranged, he and Miss Parbury set off to view Lord and Lady Buxton's collection, feeling in great charity with one another and the world in general. It was only natural that they should pursue the topic of the previous evening's reception.

"You seem quite recovered today from the exertion of your triumph last night," Miss Parbury said. "Are you happy with the way it all turned out?"

Ren thought he was recovered from the event, if not from the hours of sleeplessness that had followed. He had convinced himself to simply enjoy the present for this one day, undaunted by the past or the future.

"I must confess to being pleasantly surprised," he said, tucking her arm more snugly under his. He shortened his stride to accommodate her slower pace. "I expected a good deal more condemnation—questions about what I've done with all the pier glasses and family portraits and how I could dare to strip away those marvelous carved urns and fruit gar-lands from over the doorways."

She giggled. "I am quite certain I overheard someone ask-ing just those things!"

"I will not apologize for preferring waterfalls and pic-turesque ruins to winged cherubs raising mischief among a bunch of clouds. It surprised me that I was not made to feel I should."

"And indeed you should not. Although I must confess I could not resist pointing out to Lady Byngley that the splen-did mural wallpaper in the Little Drawing Room was French. The thought seemed to reassure her greatly, even if the scenes were still depictions of the Hindustan."

"Depictions based on the Daniells' work, but I must say, mixed together like a great stew! The overall effect is pleas-ing, however. I find the random juxtapositions amusing. On gloomy days Hajee or Nuseer and I go in and stare at the wallpaper, laughing to see Ganges fishermen working their nets in the shadow of a South Indian mountain temple. It makes a good tonic!"

Being with her was a good tonic for him, too. He was feeling immensely contented walking along with her, proud to have her on his arm and enjoying the closeness.

"Speaking of such designs, look in here." She pulled him over to the display of blue-and-white pottery in the window of a small shop they were passing. Among the platters and bowls stood a large pitcher boldly sporting palm trees and a rendition of a Hindu temple that Ren realized was composed of parts from three different places. He laughed.

"I had not realized that interest in the Hindustan had reached all the way to Staffordshire!"

They moved on, looking in other shop windows and en-joying the pleasure of each other's company. The street was busy, for it ran along one edge of the Carnaby Market, and vendors and buyers alike seemed to spill over into the nearby thoroughfares bustling with wagons and carts. Ahead of them a crowd had gathered on the sidewalk; as they came up to it they saw that an apple cart had tipped onto the sidewalk, creating an obstruction to the pedestrian traffic.

"Hm, I think we might do best to go around," Ren said, frowning. He released Miss Parbury's arm and took her hand instead, for they could not hope to pass through the congested area except in single file. Thinking they might cross over to the other side, he steered her around the edge of the crowd of onlookers and looked out for approaching vehicles.

What came next happened so quickly that afterward Ren could not quite get it straight in his mind. He blamed himself that he and Miss Parbury were poised at the edge of the street curb, for she must have been jostled by the crowd. In exactly the moment his own eyes were upon the large dray that was approaching, she slipped—someone's shout of alarm still echoed in his head.

Thank God her hand was still in his. He only managed to pull her back a split second before it would have been too late. The sad sight of her reticule lying in the muddy street afterward underscored how very near a thing it had been; the purse had been caught in the too-close brush with the passing vehicle, ripped by the strings from her wrist and crushed under the rear wheels. He thanked God the only casualty was that bit of beaded silk and velvet—looking at it filled him with such horror and relief that he nearly crushed Miss Parbury himself as he held her wrapped in his arms.

"My God! Miss Parbury!" He was thoroughly shaken, perhaps more than she. So he had thought he could ignore the past and forget the future, even for one day? More the fool he.

He had saved her—this time. Barely. He had nearly lost her in those precious seconds. What about the next time? Sooner or later the Lion would fail. It was obvious to him now that he had allowed their courtship to go on too long.

In his distress he continued to cradle her close against him, oblivious to the crowd, to propriety, even to her beyond the solid feel of her safe in his arms. He did not want to let her go, out of his arms or out of his life. He knew he must.

"Ahem. Lord Milbourne?"

Slowly he came back to the moment.

"Lord Milbourne, I am all right. You may release me."

It was the note of embarrassment in her voice that finally reached him. "Yes, yes, my apologies." He stood her back on her feet and surveyed her anxiously. "You are certain you are not harmed?"

"Frightened and shaken, that is all. It was just a mishap—you reacted so quickly! Without you I might have been crushed or injured badly. Truly you are the hero of the moment."

Impulsively she kissed his cheek, and the crowd around them cheered. Worse and worse!

"I hope my quick action did not wrench your arm, Miss Parbury. It was only lucky that I had hold of your hand! A most unfortunate accident," he said, shaking his head. "Shall I rescue the reticule?" Two more vehicles had run over it since the dray.

"Thank you, no. There was little in it—a few pence, a handkerchief. I do not generally carry a vinaigrette, and had not thought I would need a fan this afternoon. There is not enough there to be worth risking yourself in the traffic, not to mention the mud. We should go on—we shall be later than we thought. I am all right, truly. My nerves will be settled by the time we reach Lord and Lady Buxton's. The walking will help to calm me."

The crowd variously turned back to the matter of righting the apple cart or getting past, and some went off shouting after a street urchin who apparently had seized the opportunity to snatch a share of the apples. A narrow stream of movement opened up between the stationary bodies. Ren and Miss Parbury made their way through to the other side and breathed a shared sigh of relief. After a few more minutes of walking they reached the Buxton town house in Golden Square.

Mariah could guess what was going through Lord Milbourne's mind. He was very quiet, and the relaxed congeniality they had shared before the mishap had entirely disappeared in its wake. She dreaded the conclusion he was likely to draw from the incident and was almost grateful for his silence. As long as he said nothing she could pretend nothing had changed.

She had been pushed. She was quite certain of that—she could still feel the sudden pressure behind her, forcing her off the curb. She had not realized how close she was to the dray until she had turned her head—Lord Milbourne was already hauling her out of harm's way by the time she recognized her danger. It had all happened in seconds; the push, the agonizing realization, the brush of the vehicle, and the snagging of her reticule. But so many people had been crowded on the sidewalk, she was certain it had been an accident—whoever had pushed her had not meant to and perhaps never even realized what happened.

Nevertheless, she was not about to tell Lord Milbourne. She needed to make as little of what had happened as possible.

Neither of them mentioned the event to Lord or Lady Buxton. They sat politely in the Buxtons' drawing room while the viscount trotted out the various prizes in his collection, and indeed some of them were lovely beyond words. Mariah particularly admired a priceless set of cups carved from jade, crystal, and agate, incised with designs and inlaid with precious stones. The items in the collection ranged from the smallest boxes made from shell or ebony to the jewel-studded, gold-embroidered trappings worn by an elephant. Mariah did not think the Buxtons could tell that their guests were both more than a little preoccupied.

Finally, the visit was over. Lord Milbourne's carriage was waiting at the door, and Mariah and the marquess took their leave. There was an awkward silence as they settled themselves inside the coach; Mariah avoided looking at Lord Milbourne and gazed out the window at the old houses of the square with an interest she did not feel in the least. Perhaps he would not say anything—by carriage it was a very short distance indeed between here and her house.

"Miss Parbury, look at me."

Oh, dear.

"You know that we indulged in this sham courtship of

ours to oblige your brother and protect your honor if any question had arisen after your secret visits to me. I would not be truthful if I said I did not enjoy your company in these past few weeks. But you saw what almost happened today. I must withdraw from the courtship—I am convinced that to continue now would be injurious to you."

How wooden he sounded, as if he had been rehearsing what to say all during their visit to the Buxtons. She closed her eyes, trying to reach beyond her own pain at his words to feel what he must be feeling, and to find some way to fight it.

"No," she said bluntly. "I do not agree to it." She could see that her refusal surprised him.

"What happened today was the simplest of accidents, which could have happened to anyone on that crowded sidewalk. Quite contrary to putting me at risk, you were the one who saved me—just think if you had not been there! I think it far more logical to draw the opposite conclusion—that to part company could be far more harmful to me!"

She would not mention the harm she feared would be done to her heart—she had only now begun to realize the true depth of her feelings for him, now that she faced the actual prospect of separation. *Oh, William! I could blame this on you.* Only she had a strong sense that she had been falling in love with the marquess from the very first night she had met him.

"If I had not asked you to come with me to the Buxtons', you would not have been on that sidewalk at all, Miss Parbury," he said softly. "I cannot risk it. Have you ever had to watch someone you loved suffer and die? If you knew what I have been through in the past you would understand."

She understood that she could not let this happen. "I know that you think something bad will overtake anyone you care about, and that somehow you hold yourself responsible, as if somehow you could or should be able to prevent this. To spare yourself the risk of pain, you would cut yourself off from others forever! Never to love or be loved seems a heavy price to pay. I cannot imagine any pain that great."

He was looking at her intently. "I hope you shall never have to experience it."

She shook her head. "I would do so willingly, to feel so great a love for someone! What I do not understand is how you, having been blessed with such love twice, can wish to live the rest of your life without the chance of ever knowing such a thing again."

"Perhaps I do not have the soul of a gambler, Miss Parbury."

She was losing this battle. In desperation she said, "It is as if you were punishing yourself. Did you think you should be able to control Death?"

"No. But since he seems to haunt me, I thought I should at least not spread him like a contagion."

Damn him, he was smiling at her. Sadly, but still smiling, while she felt near to choking on her swallowed tears. How could he sit across from her, so cool and controlled? Perhaps she had been mistaken, after all, in what she'd thought he felt for her. Perhaps he saw what had happened as an opportunity to end their charade. . . .

Well, if she could not win, she would negotiate terms. "Will you at least agree not to end our courtship so abruptly? It is bound to cause talk. And think of my poor mother! She would feel sorely abused, undoubtedly, after all the help she has just given you."

"I might be branded a heartless cad, indeed, but you would gain much sympathy for escaping me. And I doubt any would still view me as quite the marriage prize they previously thought me."

"Not only will my mother's sensibilities be crushed, my brother's will, as well." *Not to mention mine,* she thought. *I refuse to mention mine.* "Does your friendship with William mean less to you than your desire to blacken your reputation?"

Ah. She had hit a chink in his armor at last—she could see it in his face. "Would it not be more seemly to taper off? You would appear less the blackguard, but my family would be spared the scandal."

"All right," he said, capitulating at last. "Let us agree,

then, that we will gradually increase the intervals between times when we are seen together, until finally it is ended."

The look of pain in his eyes went straight to her heart. Did he feel so trapped? They sat regarding one another warily until the carriage stopped in front of Mariah's house. She could not help feeling that neither of them had been fully truthful with the other. But at least it was not yet over between them.

Mariah did not see him for several days, but he did agree to dance with her at Almack's on the following Wednesday night. She knew he likely would have preferred to put himself in a pit of poison snakes than show himself in that exclusive bastion of the marriage-minded *haut ton,* but her mother had insisted. If he had refused to appear, it would have been the same as a declaration that the courtship was over, and it was still too soon for that.

There were good reasons for attending. The Season was half over, yet Mariah and her sisters had been seen there very little, a sinful waste of their costly and highly prized subscription. Lady Parbury was determined that this Season would be Rorie's last, and Mariah knew that she and Georgie also must begin to give serious attention to finding husbands. To add yet more reason, Harry had particularly begged Mariah to be there, to lend her some support.

"The patronesses make me so nervous," she had confessed to Mariah several days after Mariah's argument with the marquess. "I am always afraid I will say or do just the wrong thing and be banished in disgrace! I know they cannot be watching every moment, but I always feel as if they are, which amounts to the same thing. Everyone knows that they scrutinize those of us just making our come-out much harder than the rest of you who have survived from previous years!"

"Lord, Harry, you make me feel ancient!" Mariah had replied.

But now as she stood beside her mother watching the dancers in the assembly room, she felt decidedly peculiar, as if despite their veteran status she and her sisters were under great scrutiny indeed. Her dance card was not filled, and while no one had given a noticeable cut to any of the Parburys, people seemed uneasy talking to them. Eyes shifted and hands fidgeted, excuses were made to escape to conversations with other people. She could not imagine what was wrong. And there was no sign of Lord Milbourne anywhere, so far.

She scanned the room for him anxiously, certain that he would not break his word, no matter how unpleasant he might find the duty.

"Is it my imagination, or are people acting very strangely toward us this evening?" asked Lady Parbury. "I do not understand it."

The buzz of voices around the room seemed no louder than usual, and yet Mariah could not shake the impression that heads were shaking, fans fluttering, and eyebrows lifting to a greater extent than was normal. And several times she felt certain that she caught surreptitious glances directed toward her own little family group.

"I have not yet seen Harry," she announced. "I am going to find her. If anything has happened, she will know, and she would not be afraid to tell us."

"You will go nowhere without an escort, young lady," her mother chided.

"Georgie will walk with me, will you not, Georgie?"

Chin up, Mariah tried to locate her friend, who was not to be found among the dancers. As she and her sister made a circuit of the ballroom, she continued to watch hopefully for the marquess as well. Finally she saw Harry, lemonade in hand, sitting sedately with Lady Pritchard and Juliana.

It was not permissible to wave from across the room, but surely Harry would be keeping an eye out for her. With Georgie in tow, Mariah hurried toward her friend and tipped her head inquiringly when she could tell that Harry had finally spotted her.

"Harry! I need a word with you," she said in a hushed but urgent tone as she came up to where Harry was sitting. Harry set aside her cup and after excusing herself, withdrew a little ways with Mariah and Georgie.

"What is wrong with everyone tonight?" Mariah asked. "Did something happen before we arrived? No one has said anything to us yet, but the atmosphere feels so strained! Is there some new scandal? And have you seen Lord Milbourne here yet tonight? I have been looking for him."

"You must have only just arrived," Harry said, casting a quick look around them. "Oh, Mariah, it is too awful. I will tell you, but I think we had better find you a seat."

Mariah knew in that instant it was something about the marquess. Her heart felt as if a giant hand had suddenly clenched tight around it. "Just tell me, Harry. Right now."

"Lord Milbourne was here, Mariah, but he left. They are saying it is all around town that he *murdered* someone in India, but was never brought to trial. Can you believe it? A woman, too! It is too shocking!"

"It is shocking to think that anyone actually believes it! It is outrageous, ridiculous. You say the marquess left?"

Harry nodded. "He was here, but as soon as someone told him what was going around, he left. Just turned on his heel and walked out, without another word to anyone."

Chapter Sixteen

The notes from Lord Milbourne arrived the next morning. Mariah's was sealed and enclosed inside a formal one addressed to her parents withdrawing his suit "for obvious reasons."

"Thank God," said Lord Parbury.

"Who would have thought?" wailed Lady Parbury. She had marched her daughters out of Almack's with great dignity upon receiving a report of the gossip, but once at home she had lapsed into a state of semimourning.

Mariah took her note up to her room but it was some time before she opened it. So many questions were troubling her, and she doubted that he would address any of them in the note. She had lost, after all. She felt numb and empty inside.

She wished she knew how he was feeling, how the scandal was affecting him. Was he devastated? He had already suffered so much in the past! How could he be untouched by this? Yet she could not shake off the idea that he had achieved just what he wanted—the notoriety of having his name connected with such a heinous rumor, even though untrue, would be enough to drive away all but the most desperate fortune-seekers. It would drive away most of society in general! Surely she did not think that he had started the rumor himself?

He had said he had enemies, and had mentioned the troubles he was having at his home. But who would risk a lawsuit to circulate such a cruel story about him? Defaming a peer was a punishable crime. What would they hope to gain? Did they not realize that his social ruin was something he would only embrace? Suddenly she remembered that he had predicted that the gossip about him would get worse.

She still had not opened his note when Georgina slipped into her room a little while later.

"Are you going to sit in that chair staring into space without opening it all day? I cannot see much point in that." Georgie's tone sounded unsympathetic. Mariah knew that was meant to be for her own good.

"What is there for him to say? If he is in agony, he will not reveal it." *If he did this to be rid of me, I cannot bear it.*

"You will only know by reading his note." Georgie plopped herself onto Mariah's bed.

With a resigned sigh, Mariah broke the seal and opened the letter. His hand was familiar enough to her by now that simply seeing it on the page caused a lump in her throat.

Dear Miss Parbury, I wanted you to know how sincerely I regret that things have turned out exactly as you did not wish them—a sudden end in the midst of scandal. As you no doubt are aware, I have written to your parents to withdraw my suit. No other course was possible under these circumstances. You must not feel obliged to accept my apologies, nor to have any further contact. Please rest assured that I will always wish you the very best.—Milbourne"

It said so little, yet stabbed to the heart. Mariah tried to choke back the single sob that threatened to slip out, but somehow she missed it. And once that sob had sounded in the room, more followed—loud, wrenching sobs that seemed to well up out of her very bones. Finally the tears spilled down in earnest and Georgie came and held her until the crying eased.

"You have come to care for him a great deal, haven't you?" Georgie asked.

Mariah nodded as she tried to dry her eyes with a soggy handkerchief.

"He did not say very much. He did not even deny the rumors!"

"He did not need to. He knows I would not believe them."

"An explanation would have been nice."

"Yes." Yet she had not expected one.

"He seemed to care about you, too, Mariah. I don't understand," Georgie added. "It sounds as if you and he had talked about an ending—just not like this."

"Oh, Georgie." Mariah looked at her sister, wondering how she could possibly explain. And suddenly she wanted to, needed to. She had been hiding the truth from everyone for so long. How good it would feel to confide in someone! But she could not explain a part of the story without telling Georgie nearly everything. . . .

The story poured out of her as if she were purging her soul—the trip to see Taylor, the second secret visit she had made, William's insistence on the courtship. She even mentioned the near-accident in Carnaby Street and the discussion that had followed. "So as you see," she finished a few minutes later, "there never was any question of our courtship ending in a betrothal. It was all a sham."

"Unless he loved you enough to change his mind. Oh, Mariah." Georgie hugged her again, her eyes moist. "If only you had thought to protect your own heart! But it is too late, I can see that. I wonder if there ever is a way to do that, in any circumstance."

"I do not know if I am grieving for myself, for him, or for the death of hopes I hardly knew I was carrying." Mariah closed her eyes to hold back a fresh bout of tears.

"I do not doubt it is for all of those things, poor sister. But in time your heart will mend. It does rather sound as if his never has. It is so unfair, so cruel! To what purpose? What do you suppose is the real truth behind it all?"

"He has never told me what really happened to the two women he loved in India. And now I suppose I shall never know."

"Take heart, love. William has gone charging off to his club to do what he can to fight the rumors. I have seldom seen him so angry."

"It is good of him to try, although I wonder how one person can prevail in a town that thrives on gossip." *And*

William does not know any more than I do what really happened in India.

Mariah hated herself for having any doubts. All she had to do was picture the pain in Lord Milbourne's eyes when he spoke of his past or recall his gentleness when he was teaching her to play the sitar to reassure herself that he could never have killed his own lover in India. Yet the rumors persisted, and other memories played upon her mind. Not knowing the truth undermined her confidence in him. Even William had warned her that the man had a dark side, although Lord Milbourne had kept it well hidden from her, if that was so.

This time, she could not go to him, although that was the one thing she most wanted to do. If she could have confronted him—looked into his eyes! Armed with the truth, she would have been willing to face the entire town by his side. But during the days following the start of the scandal, her mother was keeping close company with her, almost as if Lady Parbury suspected the broken yet rebellious state of Mariah's heart.

Almost exactly a week after the episode in Almack's, a package arrived at Great Marlborough Street for Mariah. She was reading in her father's bookroom when Bennett brought it in to her. The outer wrappings gave no indication of the sender. Mystified, she began to open it just as Cassie came in, full of curiosity.

"Who could have sent it? Do you think you have a new secret admirer? Maybe it is a sympathy gift!"

"Cassie, hush! I expect there will be a card inside."

Nested within the layers of paper was a long, shallow box of the sort that usually contained handkerchiefs, and indeed, that proved to be what lay inside. They were beautiful—the finest white cambric with elegant lace edges.

"Ooh," said Cassie, peeking over Mariah's shoulder.

"They are so soft," Mariah said, taking one out. There was no card underneath. She searched among the others in the box, but found no clue to the sender.

"It almost seems a mockery—handkerchiefs on which to

dry your tears! Do you think Lord Milbourne could have sent them?" Cassie ran her fingers over one in the box. "They are beautiful. Perhaps it is his idea of an apology."

But Mariah did not answer. A tingling had started in her fingers almost as soon as she had picked up the first hand-kerchief. The burning sensation had spread and now numbness was seizing her tongue and her throat. Her skin prickled and her blood felt like ice in her veins. She dropped the handkerchief she was holding with a kind of choking sound, and knocked Cassie's hands away from the box. "Cassie!" she gasped. But by then it was clear that Cassie had begun to feel similar effects.

"What *is* it?" Cassie cried, shaking her hands like a dog shedding water. "Mama! Bennett! Help! Poison!"

Mariah saw Bennett come into the room, although her vision was becoming blurry. She had never seen him react to anything before.

"Dear Lord! Oh, dear!" cried the distraught man. He rushed from the room, shouting, "My lady!" and "We need a doctor!"

The horrible sensations continued to advance through Mariah's system, causing pain in her chest and difficulty breathing, as if someone heavy was sitting on her. Perhaps worst of all, given the numbness now in her throat and face, she began to feel giddy and nauseous and suddenly began to retch. A detached part of her brain wondered curiously if she was going to die.

Chaos reigned over the Parbury household for the next several hours. A doctor was sent for, and William and Lord Parbury were fetched home. Remedies were sought from the nearest apothecary, to no avail. Mariah and Cassie were put in their beds, where they remained very ill.

All this activity did not pass unnoticed by watchful eyes outside the house. Within two hours Lord Milbourne had a visitor.

Ren was in his study going over some accounts with Hajee when a discreet knock sounded on the door. At his biding, Selim entered, bowing in respect to both men.

"Sahib, young Taylor waits in the kitchen," he said. "Very upset he is. He says he must talk with you—right now, very important."

"Send him up, then." Ren did not dismiss Hajee, for if something "important" indeed was going on, he wanted the man to know about it. He could not imagine what might have set the boy off, unless some change in his status at the workhouse was imminent.

The young fellow wasted not a second after he walked through the study door.

"Sir, somethin' terrible has happened to your lady," he said with ghastly simplicity. "Miss Parbury is took very sick—the help are sayin' that she's poisoned!"

"What the devil?" Ren was on his feet in an instant. All the familiar dread poured into his heart, confirming both his feelings about Miss Parbury and his certainty that his caring about her had doomed her. "And just how would you happen to know this?"

Taylor looked down at his feet and then glanced at the doorway, where Ren discovered Selim was still lurking. "We been keepin' watch, me and Selim, since that day the dray almost ran her down. Till then I was only keepin' watch on you, but when I seen the fellow push her that day, we figured we'd better split the job. I been watchin' over Miss Parbury since then."

"You've been. . . You say someone . . . ? Never mind." Ren could not believe his ears. No wonder the boy had lost his place at the charity school! But now was not the time to discuss or deal with boys playing spy. Or the idea that someone might have deliberately pushed Miss Parbury into the path of the dray on that dreadful day.

"Get my horse ready!" Scandal and rumor-mongers be damned, he was not going to stay away from the Parburys at such a time of crisis.

He earned a few curses as he urged his mount through the streets at an unneighborly speed, but he reached Great Marlborough Street in record time. Tossing a coin to the lad who ran up offering to watch his horse, he took the steps in a bound and pounded the knocker without ceremony.

Bennett did not respond with his usual alacrity, and when he did open the door, his face blanched.

"I've been told Miss Mariah is very ill," Ren said, surprised when the butler did not immediately admit him. Things were worse than he thought. Could the Parburys possibly have believed the rumors?

"I will tell his lordship that you are here," Bennett said icily, and made to close the door again.

Ren put his foot out to stop it, not believing that the butler was about to shut it in his face. "Bennett, do you mean to leave me standing on the step?" He could not keep the indignation out of his voice.

"Yes, my lord."

Further altercation between them was cut off by Lady Parbury's voice in the hall behind the butler. "Who is it, Bennett?"

"Lord Milbourne, my lady."

Ren heard a shriek. "He is by no means to be admitted! Has he not done enough harm already? Does he want to poison us all? How dare he?"

Bennett's hand came through the opening of the door and gave Ren a push so unexpected that it rocked him backward, causing his foot to lose its advantage. A moment later the door slammed shut.

Devastated, Ren stared at it. *Now what?* They were not going to let him see or try to save her. He remounted and rode home slowly, sick at heart and puzzling over the baroness's strange comment. Did they think that he had poisoned Miss Parbury, just because of some damned foolish rumors? How could he possibly, when he had not been near her? What could have happened?

In the back of his mind a damning voice said he might as well have poisoned her, for he had known all along he must not fall in love with her. He might have fooled her, and he had succeeded in fooling himself for a while, but the plain truth was that he had failed. He did love her, and now he would pay the crushing price for loving yet again. He had killed her. How many times could a man face this pain and still survive?

At home he called for the brandy bottle and locked himself alone in his study. Even Ranee's company could not give him solace. But the soothing effects of the amber narcotic took time to shut off his brain.

He knew a good deal about poisons, for their use was still commonplace in the Hindustan. The more he thought about the danger to Miss Parbury, the more he felt the need to see her and to know what exactly had happened. What if he could help? He had not even learned how ill she was, or if she might live. Or why *they* thought he was to blame. He should go back. But slowly, as the level of liquid in the bottle sank lower and lower, Ren found relief from his misery and slept, collapsed on his desk.

He was in his own bed when he opened his eyes again. A sliver of bright daylight gleamed through the crack of the draperies, hurting his eyes and raising a moan of agony that further hurt his aching head. He could call for Nuseer, but the thought of making any sound that loud himself was horrifying. He pulled his pillow over his face, blocking out the light. It did not help much. He was now fully awake, and with wakefulness came awareness and remembrance. He thought of Miss Parbury, and moaned again.

She could be dead by now, for all he knew. He didn't even know what time of day it was, or what day it was. The amount of prickly stubble on his jaws reassured him that not more than one had passed. As his brain slowly processed these facts, Nuseer came into the room with a tray which held a plate of toast and a glass of liquid Ren eyed with abhorrence. Nuseer's hangover remedy tasted like the foul dredgings of a river bottom.

"What time is it?" he asked in Hindustani.

"Just past the hour of one, sahib."

"In the afternoon?" Ren groaned and sat up. "I must go to the Parburys' again. This time I *will* gain admittance. You and Ahmed are to come with me."

"Drink this, sahib. And you must be made presentable."

Ren made a horrible face and then, steeling himself, drank down the herbal remedy in a steady series of gulps. He shook his head as if to rid himself of the aftertaste, then swung his feet out of the bed. "No bath, no shave. Just get me some clothes, man. She could be dead or dying. I have to go now."

This time Ren had Ahmed stop the carriage further down the block from the Parburys' residence, and he sent Nuseer to the door. As soon as Bennett opened it the tall Mohammedan forced his way in and Ahmed and Ren hurried in after him. It was the first time Ren had ever seen Bennett's composure completely shattered.

"Here now, you can't do this!" the fellow spluttered, but Ren had no patience now. He seized the butler by his neck-cloth, nearly lifting the smaller man off the floor.

"Is Miss Mariah alive or dead?" he demanded.

The butler made a great show of pressing his lips together and shaking his head in a brave refusal to answer.

Ren set him down. "Fine. I will find out for myself!" Without another word he bounded up the stairs, while behind him the butler protested and began to call for his master and mistress. Ahmed and Nuseer moved in on him and indicated clearly that he should be silent.

Ren went up two floors and then had to stop, for he had no way of knowing where Mariah's room might be. The butler's cries had alerted the household, however, and there was commotion on the floors below him. A maid came out of one room with a pile of linens on her arm, and he grabbed her by the elbow.

"You will take me to Miss Mariah's room," he said in a low voice that carried every ounce of threatening authority he could muster. Eyes wide with fear, the maid complied, leading him up one more flight and to a room at the back. When she stopped at the door, he saw that tears were coursing down her cheeks.

"Dear God, I am not a monster," he said softly. "You can tell them all I mean her no harm."

She scuttled away, and he paused in the doorway a moment, taking in the room. It was like her, plain and straightforward. There was a chair by the window, where he could well imagine her dreaming away the hours. At this moment, however, she lay between the covers of the bed, her soft hair loose beneath her cap and spread on the pillow. Her eyes were closed, and her skin had such a pallor that for a moment he thought the worst. Staring, he moved closer and was reassured by the slight rise and fall of the bedclothes.

Quietly, he picked up the chair and brought it to the bedside, sitting and preparing himself to keep vigil there as long as necessary. He needed to know that she would be all right. He needed to know what had happened. Once he knew that, he would take himself out of her life forever and hope that such a sacrifice would be sufficient. He studied her face in repose as if he would engrave the image on his heart to last a lifetime. He did not know how many minutes he would have before they would be interrupted. He would fight anyone who tried to make him leave.

Angry voices in the passageway outside the room distracted him, and when he turned back to her, her eyes were open.

"You are here!" she said, the softness of sleep still in her voice, and puzzlement, too. She put out her hand to him. "Lord Milbourne," she said dreamily.

He clasped her precious hand between both of his. "Yes, love, I am here." She was not fully awake, and he thought sleep would reclaim her.

Instead, she stiffened as she became more awake. "Lord Milbourne! Oh, lord, what are you doing here?" She started to sit up, and he raised one hand.

"Do not be alarmed. Rest. I only came to see if you were all right." He smiled at her reassuringly. "You will never guess how I learned you were ill. Taylor."

She settled back against the pillows. "Taylor?"

"He has been spying upon you—I believe he thought he was guarding you against danger. The commotion in the house alerted him." He paused for a moment, ashamed of the lapse of time he had allowed since his first attempt to see her. "I tried to come yesterday, but they would not let me in."

"And today they did?"

"No." He looked toward the door, beyond which the arguing voices could still be heard. "Today I did not let them stop me."

"You did not send the handkerchiefs, did you." It was a statement, faint but definite, although he did not know what she meant.

He raised his eyebrows questioningly. "Handkerchiefs?"

"That is what made me ill. Cassie, too. We were exposed when we handled them . . ."

So it had been poison. Taylor was right. And Ren could see that Miss Parbury was still very weak. "I can find out what happened from the others. You must save your strength. But I had to come. I had to know that you would be all right."

He still held her small hand in his, savoring that brief contact. He knew he must let go. As he went to place it gently back on the covers, she turned it and grasped his wrist.

"I knew it was not you. But do you not see what this means? This was someone else's doing, what has happened to me. Someone real, not Fate, or a curse, or unlucky stars. Someone with a mind, a purpose." She spoke with some urgency, but the effort was clearly exhausting her.

"We can speak of this some other time." *If there ever is another time.* "Your first business must be to get well."

She would not release his hand. "Perhaps those other times it was not Fate, as well. Have you thought . . ."

"Sh-h. Not now." He stood up, and was trying to extricate his hand when the door opened and William came in.

"Here, what are you doing?"

"William, I want him to stay," Miss Parbury said, but Ren shook his head.

"Mariah. He and I must talk," William said gently. "Father is asking for him, and I have promised Mother that I would bring him out this instant. This is all the time I could give you."

Chapter Seventeen

Ren listened carefully in the baron's bookroom as William and his father described the horror they had been through. The anguish of the past day and night showed clearly on William's ravaged face, and Lord Parbury looked as if he had aged a decade in that short space of time. Ren was aware that he looked as bad or worse himself.

"I have never felt so helpless," admitted Lord Parbury. "To see my daughters suffering so! The twenty-four hours we have just been through were the longest I have ever spent in my life, waiting out the time the doctor said the poison would take to run its course. But now both Cassie and Mariah are recovering quickly."

"Aconite, or monkshood," Ren said, shaking his head and then heartily regretting it. "It is an ancient poison, found in most parts of the world. In India it is often used to kill tigers; they sell it openly in the bazaars in Calcutta."

"The doctor told us it was the only poison he knew of that could be absorbed through the skin, but he had no antidote," William said, his voice hoarse from exhaustion. "He did not even dare to give Mariah or Cassie laudanum until the first twelve hours were past. We did not know if they would live or die."

"They must have been exposed to only a slight amount," Ren said. "Thank God. It is very lethal."

He looked hard at the two men across from him. "Did you truly believe that I could have sent the handkerchiefs?"

He had his answer in the fractional moment of hesitation before they answered. It hurt to know that William had doubted him, yet Ren could not say for certain that he would not have felt the same way in his place.

"My wife did," said the baron, clearing the sudden congestion in his throat. "The rumors, you know. It seemed to bear them out."

"I could not credit such a thing," William said. "But *someone* sent them."

"Yes. Handkerchiefs are not soaked in or powdered with aconite by accident," Ren said dryly. "But I think whoever did this knew exactly how strong to make the application. That should help me to narrow down the possible suspects. I do not believe she was meant to suffer any greater harm than she has—I think the strike against her was indirectly aimed at me."

He looked around the room. "You said she was here when she received the package? What has become of it?"

The baron nodded toward the hearth. "Burned the damn thing."

"The box gave no indication of its source, and such handkerchiefs could have been purchased in any linen shop," William pointed out. "We were very afraid that someone else might be afflicted from touching any of it." He paused, looking at Ren with what almost appeared to be regret. "How did you know she was taken ill?"

Ah, so he still had some unresolved doubts. "Word reached me, after the amount of commotion that was stirred up in your house." Ren could not blame William for asking, but neither could he expose Taylor. "Servants talk. I do not think you will be able to keep people from knowing about this."

He stood up, maintaining an outer calmness he was far from feeling. "I will get to the bottom of this, you may rest assured. And I give you my pledge that I will have no further contact with Miss Mariah. I only had to know that she would be all right."

Mariah was frustrated by the interference of her family and the brief time she had spent with Lord Milbourne. Seeing him had lifted her spirits remarkably, but there was so much she needed to discuss with him! Sure of him now and unaware of the promise he had given her father and brother, she awaited his next visit impatiently. She was determined that together they should root out the true villain behind everything that had happened.

She was enough improved to be sitting up in the drawing room on the following afternoon when she had a caller, but it was not the marquess.

"Miss Parbury! I heard at my club about your illness. I had to come," Hayden Carrisforte assured her, bowing over her hand. "What a terrible thing! I hope you are feeling better? I cannot begin to imagine a more frightening experience."

She was appalled to think the clubs were full of talk about what had happened to her. He was kind to have come, although she could not help wondering if he had hoped Harry might be here, too.

"It was indeed horrifying," she said, "although I am recovering very quickly, thank you. Why or how such a thing could happen is quite the mystery!"

"To say the least!" He looked about for a seat and selected a rosewood armchair across from her. "Although with the rumors that are going around, one wonders what the world is coming to. You could not believe that Lord Milbourne had anything to do with it, of course," he continued loyally. "In view of those rumors it seems to me more likely that someone wanted to purposely give an appearance that he might be involved."

"Yes, that is my thought, too." She was pleased to hear him voice the same suspicion that had occurred to her. She was also reassured to hear him defend the marquess. If Mr. Carrisforte was truly as appearance-conscious as William suggested, she had wondered if he might strive to separate himself from his slandered friend. Perhaps here was an ally.

Bennett had sent Jennie in to chaperon the visit, but Mariah wanted privacy to talk with her visitor. She asked the maid to go check on the progress of tea in the kitchen.

"Can you think of anyone who would hold so great a grudge against Lord Milbourne that they would go to such lengths to disgrace him?" she asked once Jennie had left the room. "He had been having some trouble at his home even before this."

"That is true. He discussed it with me. We tried a few schemes to trap the culprit, but to no avail. Do not suppose for a minute that I have not been wracking my brain over it."

"Also to no avail?"

He looked uncomfortable. "Miss Parbury, I hate to point fingers when there is no evidence. Look at the damage that is being done to him! There are a few people who will never forgive him for leaving the Company, I know that much. I was not still in India when he earned his reputation in Lampur, but I gather he earned some enmity as well as a great deal of respect during those years. Then, of course, there are his Indian servants, who have been with him through everything. He is too devoted to them to be willing to take a hard look at them. One of them could be harboring a grudge and he would never know it."

Could it be one of his servants? That thought was frightening indeed. How would one go about uncovering such a secret? She leaned forward in her chair.

"Mr. Carrisforte, Lord Milbourne has never been willing to talk about what happened to his fiancées in India. It would help me so much to know the truth. Would you tell me?"

"To have suffered two such tragedies in so close a time would have shattered a weaker man, Miss Parbury. It is small wonder that he retreated into the mountains of Lampur. But the circumstances are not at all what I would care to relate to a gently bred woman such as yourself."

"Please. I need to know."

"Your state of health is especially delicate right now. Do you think it would be wise? The story is not pretty—I am not at all surprised he would not tell you."

"I am stronger than people think," she said with some exasperation. "I promise I will not faint, nor suffer a relapse of poison!"

At her insistence, Mr. Carrisforte proceeded to relate the details of Reinhart Maycott's three years with the East India

Company, based in Calcutta. Mariah heard how he met his first fiancée, the beautiful woman who had made the sketchbook, and heard of the appalling way she had died—by her own hand after weeks of agonized suffering from injuries sustained in a carriage accident. When Mariah thought of how the woman's young fiancé, Lord Milbourne, must have suffered every moment alongside her, ever hoping for improvement, she could not help the tears that ran down her face.

"Oh, dear," exclaimed Mr. Carrisforte. "You see? I knew it would upset you."

"Please go on," Mariah said, determined to hear it all.

Dubiously, he related how Maycott had met Shanti, the native woman who had begun to travel and live with him.

"She was brutally murdered one night and left in a hut set on fire to destroy the evidence, if you must know. But her body was discovered before it was too late. To make matters even more unbearable, Maycott was accused of killing her, and then of course questions were asked about the death of his first fiancée," Mr. Carrisforte said. "Nothing was ever proven against him, however. I am certain the rumors now are based on that old history. I am sure they must open up old wounds."

Mariah was certain that the marquess had loved these women—she had heard it in his voice and seen it in his eyes the few times he had ever mentioned them. For all his passion, she did not believe he could have killed them. How much pain he must hold locked away inside his heart! Yet the tragedies were a part of him, and she was glad that she knew now. She marveled that he had withstood the pain at all.

"You are right—it is unspeakably horrible," she said, wiping away tears. The story showed the present rumors were all the more cruel! "But why did they ever think he would murder his own fiancée?"

Mr. Carrisforte took a sudden interest in the chimney mantel and cleared his throat. "Well, um, er. There really is no delicate way to put this. She was not his fiancée, exactly. She was a prostitute, Miss Parbury. He wanted to marry her—to do the honorable thing, and also I suppose to have her strictly for himself. I think he wanted children. She apparently was less enthused about giving up her calling."

That same afternoon Reinhart sat in his library making lists. Now that he knew Miss Parbury would recover from the poison, leaving London as soon as possible had become his new goal. He took his responsibilities seriously and could visit his estates—maybe he would even force himself to go to the one in Derbyshire. If he stayed here, he would see her constantly—at events, passing on a sidewalk, in his mind and in the flesh. She would be always there, just close enough to keep his new pain fresh and persistent, at least until the Season ended. He had given his word there would be no further contact between them, and that was the end of it. But he could not leave until he had uncovered his enemy. He wanted no risk that Miss Parbury could ever again be endangered in a move against him.

He had decided to put on paper every theory and scrap of information of any kind that had to do with his mail, the thefts from his house, the canceled order, the rumor campaign, and now the poisoned handkerchiefs. Somewhere in all of that activity, there had to be a common thread—a clue that would help him begin to unravel it. He had covered the library table with sheets of paper by late afternoon, when he had an early dinner served to him there.

"All right, Ranee, I know five pounds of horsemeat every day is unutterably boring. I should not, but I will give you a little reward for being such a good companion."

The cheetah posed on the carpet beside him, her chin on her paws. Owing in part to the "tear lines" that marked her face, she could look particularly soulful at times, and she was using every ounce of feline charm on him just now.

"There, half the roast beef from my plate—will that make you happy?"

Ren thought he could almost envy her, with her wants so simple. But except for him and his servants, she was essentially alone in a foreign place, and he felt a great kinship with her. "At least we have each other, royal lady."

In the aftermath of his hangover the previous day he had banished the brandy from his study, but Hajee had served him an excellent claret with his present meal. He was reaching for his glass when Selim knocked at the open door.

"I am sorry to disturb you, sahib," the boy said respectfully in Hindustani, "but Taylor is here. He has something to tell you again."

"Twice in three days? Is this becoming a habit? I am already sharing my dinner with Ranee," Ren said with mock irritation.

Not fooled in the slightest, Selim grinned and Ren nodded. "All right. Bring him up."

"Did they feed you in the kitchen?" was the first thing Ren said to Taylor when he arrived.

"They will, sir. I needed to spill this to you first. I seen that box with the ruby on it turned up in a fence's shop in St. Martin's Lane. Between keepin' an eye out for Miss Parbury, I been scoutin' the fences regularlike, you know?"

Taylor's speech patterns made Ren wince, but the news he delivered set off a flood of hope. Ren had tortured himself all day going over his notes to find some kind of lead, and here was Taylor delivering one to him on a silver platter. If they could manage to buy, trick, or pry information from the fence, he might have a suspect at last.

"Excellent, excellent, my boy! I'll ask Syed to make *saundesh* for you—it tastes as sweet as a piece of heaven. We will have to pay a visit to this 'fence' of yours, but it is rather too late in the day to go now—I'd like to come back alive and with my shirt still on my back. Will you show me the place in the morning?"

Thinking about Taylor traveling between Grosvenor Square and the workhouse in Holborn, Ren suggested, "Perhaps I should come for you at the workhouse, instead of having you make the trip back here again. I can well imagine the means of transportation you have been using to get about the city—it is a dangerous practice to be hitching rides on the backs of moving wagons and carriages, lad."

"Naw, there ain't nothin' to it," Taylor said, "S'long as

you don't let a jervey nip you with his whip. But if I sleep in your stables tonight, I'll be on hand whenever you like to go in the mornin', guv'nor, so that's all right."

Cheeky—there was no other word for the boy. Yet he was fascinating in his own independent, streetwise fashion. Ren knew that Taylor would be insulted if Ren offered him the use of a bed. "Have it your way," he said with a shrug. "I suspect you would in any case!"

Mariah missed the marquess more than she had dreamed was possible. She knew her heartache and leaden limbs were not an aftereffect of the poison but her response to waiting each day for a visit from him which never came. When she finally spoke of his absence to her parents and learned of the promise he had made, she was devastated. How could they have agreed to it, and how not have told her, too? Had they not realized how much she wanted to see him? She had not expected her own family to turn their backs on him completely as had the rest of the town, all when he had done nothing to deserve it!

He was not as cut off from the world as he had been living in remote Lampur, but she could see that his aim had been the same. Between his own efforts and those of his unknown enemy, he had achieved a good measure of success.

"William, you have been his friend for all these years," she reminded her brother. "How could you simply turn your back? You should be helping him to discover the perpetrator of all the things that have happened. Someone who is desperate enough to use poison is capable of any kind of nefarious deed!"

"I would like nothing better than to find the villain who sent you that package, Mariah," William answered. "But your safety is more important than even that, and cutting all family connection to Milbourne appears to be the best way to insure it. If the poison was sent as a warning, we would be foolhardy to ignore it. Do not imagine that I feel nothing—I have lost a valued friendship in the process, you know."

Mariah believed that was a coward's way out of the

coil—she was convinced that her family and the marquess should stand and fight. The idea that the same villain who was causing trouble now might also have been connected with the deaths of Lord Milbourne's first loves haunted her, as did the thought that his betrayer might be living right under his own roof. She confided her doubts and fears to Harry, who began to make daily visits as soon as Mariah was sufficiently recovered to receive her.

On Harry's fourth such visit, Mariah outlined a new plan. She was feeling more than ready to be out and about again, and had spent her confinement thinking.

"Harry, we must find a way to meet and talk with some of Lord Milbourne's former colleagues in the East India Company. Do you suppose the Asiatic Society ever holds any receptions? It should not be difficult to lead them into discussing the marquess, and I feel certain we should be able to judge if any of them harbored particularly bitter resentment or hatred. Such strong feelings would be difficult to hide."

"If Mr. Carrisforte were to attend some function of that kind, Mariah, perhaps we could be invited as guests. He is taking me to the British Museum tomorrow and asked me if I thought you might like to join us. If you come, perhaps we could talk over this new idea of yours! Are you not dying from staying in all these days? The outing should do you good."

"Shall I actually visit the inside of the museum this time?" Mariah asked with a chuckle. Getting out of the house sounded splendid, but she hesitated. "You will not mind my company?"

Harry laughed. "Oh, heavens, it is not like that between Mr. Carrisforte and myself, Mariah. At least, not at present. I find him an amiable friend, that is all. Please do come."

"Be careful not to break his heart, Harry. I think you might do so easily!" How recently she had been worried about Harry's heart! But many things had changed since then. "Perhaps he has been to see Lord Milbourne and could give me some tidings of how the marquess is faring."

Mariah's thoughts did not stray far from Grosvenor Square these days.

"Indeed! And if you will walk over, we can have a coze before he arrives to pick us up. I will send word to him that you've agreed to come along."

Chapter Eighteen

By the time Mariah was to leave for Harry's the following afternoon, her patience with her mother had worn thin. How grateful she was to be going out!

"I do realize that you cannot stay inside this house forever, Mariah, but I would simply feel safer if you took John or James with you when you go out, instead of Jennie," Lady Parbury said. "After all . . ."

"Yes, Mama, I know, 'we cannot guess who is a threat to us these days.' I will agree to take one of the footmen, but I will not agree to stop living! If I should have to be so cautious every minute of every day, the poison might just as well have done its work!"

"My dear! That is not a matter to make light of."

"I apologize. However, it is but a short walk to Harry's—you need not worry. I shan't become overtired. And I am looking forward to getting out in the air and going to the museum."

"Museum, museum. Again! You are entirely too caught up in your scholarly pursuits, Mariah. How will you expect to interest another young man?"

I do not want any other young man, Mariah thought. *I want Lord Milbourne, with all my heart.*

Perhaps if she knew for certain that he did not return her feelings, she could eventually come to some acceptance of their separation. But when he had been sitting at her bedside disheveled and unshaven, holding her hand, she had received a very different impression of the state of his heart. Unless they cleared away all the obstacles standing in their way, how would she ever truly know?

"Mama, please. I must finish getting ready to go."

Only a few minutes later, Mariah set off up Argyle Street heading toward Henrietta Street in Cavendish Square, where the Pritchards had leased a house for the Season. James followed silently a respectful pace behind her, unlike Jennie, with whom Mariah would sometimes exchange a comment or two as they walked along. There was a carriage stopped in Little Argyle Street; Mariah noticed it as she turned the corner into the narrow way, but she thought nothing of it even when a man approached her politely, hat in hands.

"Excuse me, miss," he said, and she lifted an eyebrow questioningly, expecting that he was probably lost and seeking some direction.

She turned back to have James speak to the man and only then discovered that a second man had already accosted her servant. The alarm that sounded in her head then came too late—the first man took her arm like a gentleman friend and told her in a very quiet voice that he had a pistol under his hat that was aimed at her heart.

What did they want? For an instant she thought to resist—it was broad daylight and not two blocks away from the Westminster police court on her own street. How could this be happening? But apparently the fellow sensed her hesitation.

"Come into the carriage, dearie—my friend's got 'is pistol aimed at yer sarvant, hand don't mind iffen 'e uses it." Tightening his grip on his arm, he nodded and smiled politely at a man and a woman who passed by just then. "Now me, I might mind, but t'wouldn't stop me."

Mariah wanted to scream, or push the man down, or call out to the couple to run for help. But she did not dare. Even if she managed to push away his gun and make it discharge, she could not prevent the second man from shooting James. A woman and child were passing along the narrow sidewalk now. It was too dangerous. Some other opportunity would have to present itself.

She climbed into the shabby coach, followed closely by her unwelcome companion. He had clapped his hat back on his head as he climbed in, revealing the naked pistol clutched in his hand. James and the second man climbed in behind them. The two ruffians sat impassively across from her and James. Who were these men? Without taking his eyes off Mariah the first man banged a fist against the wall of the coach. The vehicle lurched once and began to move in response.

Just as the carriage turned the street corner, Mariah felt a thump against her back, as if something large had been thrown or lodged at the back of the coach. Could there have been a third blackguard standing watch? She hoped not, for the odds then were even more against her.

There was no indication of anything amiss at the house in Great Marlborough Street until nearly an hour later, when Harriet Pritchard and Mr. Carrisforte arrived there inquiring after Mariah. Harry had waited for her friend without too much alarm until Mr. Carrisforte had come at the appointed time and Mariah still had not appeared. Thinking perhaps that she had merely been detained, they had waited a little longer, and then had driven to Great Marlborough Street by a roundabout route covering all of the nearby streets in case Mariah was walking along one of them *en route*.

Lady Parbury fell into near hysteria as soon as she heard that her daughter had not reached Henrietta Street. Cassie unhelpfully burst into tears. Georgina and Rorie had just returned from a shopping expedition and it was left to them to question the pair standing before them. When they learned that Harry and Hayden Carrisforte had already searched the neighborhood streets and found no sign of Mariah or their footman, they were at a loss as to what to do.

"Send for your father! Send for your father!" wailed Lady Parbury, waving her vinaigrette in front of her face. Lord Parbury was attending the usual late afternoon session of Parliament.

"That is a sound idea," said Mr. Carrisforte. "And where is your brother William at this hour?"

Told that William was at his club, Mr. Carrisforte offered to deliver the bad news and fetch him home. "I will be praying that in the meantime Miss Mariah appears or that you receive some word from her."

However, no word came in the interval between the time he left and the time he and William arrived back at the house. A kind of silent anguish settled over the house while the women were waiting, punctuated by occasional outbursts.

"I should never have let her out of the house!" Lady Parbury moaned from the sofa where her remaining daughters had made her lie down.

"It is all my fault!" wailed Harry, nearly beside herself with guilt and worry. "I should never have suggested that she walk to my house!"

"Nonsense, Harry," Georgina interposed. "It is the fault of whoever did this—whatever it is that has happened!"

When William arrived, he bid them all to calm themselves. "I fancy that I may know where she is, but the fewer who know of it the better. Let me assure you, I believe that she is perfectly safe, and you have upset yourselves beyond call."

This announcement created its own hubbub of reaction.

"Why, whatever can you mean, William?" Lady Parbury asked in the midst of it. "Where is she?"

"I suspect she may be at Milbourne House. We shall soon find out, as I intend to call there immediately!"

"Milbourne House!" The first two words were almost a unified chorus, which then broke down into disharmonious babble. Lady Parbury's shrill voice was most audible above the others.

"The marquess gave his word that he would have no more contact with her. You think he would be so dishonorable?"

"No, Mother. I think Mariah has gone to him."

"Our Mariah would never do such a disreputable thing!"

"She does have James with her, Mama. Perhaps it is not so bad?"

"Cassie, that is not sufficient to lend countenance to her visiting a bachelor's home! William, why would you think she might go there? Especially after all that has happened between them."

William sighed. "You do not know the half of it. That is exactly why I suspect that she *has* gone there. It will not be the first time."

There was an ominous silence in the room as soon as the words left his mouth. William paled, but his error could not be undone.

Mr. Carrisforte stepped into the breach. "Perhaps it would be best if I took Miss Pritchard home? This is clearly a family matter. I know I can assure you that neither of us would dream of mentioning a word of what has happened. Please, be sure to let me know if there is anything at all I can do."

The marquess and Taylor had gone quietly to St. Martin's Lane in a common hackney the morning after the boy reported seeing the stolen box. They had concocted a plan as they went, and surveyed the pawnbroker's shop from the entrance of an alley across the way once they arrived. On Taylor's advice Reinhart had first purchased and donned rather disreputable-looking clothing; the boy had then further convinced him that confronting the "fence" himself would gain nothing but trouble. The man was a notorious dealer of stolen goods, and would never stay in business if he was to "snitch" on a client.

Somewhat amused by the irony of taking orders from a gutter-born lad, Ren followed Taylor's instructions to go into the shop, purchase the box, and speak as little as possible, if he did not want to give away his high station. Their plan was to return the box to its place in Ren's house and hope that this mysterious happening would trigger a reaction in some guilty member of his staff. Ren theorized that the culprit, seeing the box, would go hurrying back to St. Martin's Lane to ascertain how the reappearance had come about and whether or not he was at risk. A police constable was hired to keep a watch on Milbourne House and to track any servants engaged in unauthorized errands.

After following one footman to a secret tryst with his lady and another on a visit to his sister, the constable finally followed a furtive soul who made his way to St. Martin's Lane on the third day of watching. He was a white-haired longshanks who had the look of a fellow too fond of the bottle, the constable later reported to Ren. Frothwick, without a doubt.

Ren guessed that Frothwick had debts or was paying blackmail money to someone, as his salary as a butler at Milbourne House was more than adequate to keep him in drinks. He would have to be sacked. However, Ren had said and done nothing about it yet, saddened that the old fellow had not been able to make something better of his later years with the chance that he had been given.

In one way Ren felt reassured—he was now convinced that the thefts were not related to the other, more serious problems that had occurred. But that conviction also left him back in his library staring at his lists on the afternoon that William arrived, angrily demanding to see his sister.

Neither Frothwick nor Hajee had a chance to intervene or even announce William before he came barging into the library, which was unfortunately the first room to be encountered beyond the entrance hall. The door stood open and William charged right in as Ren rose to his feet to meet the onslaught.

"All right, where is she? Hiding behind curtains again this time, Milbourne?"

Ren moved toward his friend, staring. William was so angry he barely stopped for breath.

"I never doubted your word when you said you'd have nothing more to do with her, and I still trust that this was not your doing. But you are still to blame for not packing her off home the instant she appeared here!" As he spoke he made a thorough inspection of the library, looking under the table and checking the corner alcoves. He returned to glare at Ren as his search revealed nothing.

Ren stood still as William's words sank into his brain and a feeling of utter desolation began to take shape there.

"William, calm down and talk to me," he said with the sharp, cold clarity he reserved for addressing exceedingly difficult people. If he did not remain calm himself, he would have no hope of getting any sense out of William. "What has happened? Tell me. Your sister is not here."

William looked at him then, clearly focusing his attention upon Ren for the first time. The fury went out of him almost as visibly as if Ren had punched him in the belly and let out all of his air. "She is not here?"

"If you do not trust my word, you are welcome to search my entire house, but I am telling you she is not here, nor has she been. I have not seen her at all since I forced my way into *your* house six days ago." *Except in my dreams and half of my waking thoughts.*

"I ask again, what has happened?" Ren restrained the urge to shake the answer out of his friend.

"All right, I believe you," William said. "I think I'd have preferred it if she was here. Now I do not know what to think, except the worst—Mariah has disappeared! Apparently she left our house to walk to Cavendish Square, with our footman James. They did not arrive when they were expected, nor anytime after that, nor can they be found."

The worst. Ren sat down again as anguish filled his heart. "How long ago?"

"I would say at least one and a half hours ago. I was not at home at the time she set out."

"You trust the footman?"

"He is young, but he has served our family faithfully for several years. Yes, I trust him. I hope he does not do anything rash."

"At least she is not alone." Ren stared at his papers, willing them to yield up the clues he needed. There was no more time for investigation—he needed answers now! Too much time had already passed. Who knew what could have happened? *She could be dead. She could be dead.* The evil refrain echoed in his mind, tormenting him. He would not say the words in front of William, however. He would not allow the agonizing pain searing through him to cripple him. He must think.

He picked up a page from the table with hands that shook. "I have been trying to wrestle it all out, William. The worst enemy is an unknown one. I wish to God whoever it is would just confront me. But I will say one thing. Whoever it is could have killed Mariah when he sent the poison, and he did not. I think he is just using her to get at me and will not harm her."

"But we cannot just sit here and wait to see, man! We must do something!" William stood there, almost as pale as the papers.

"Yes, I agree." If only he knew what! Ren balled up the paper in his hand violently and threw it into the far corner of the room. "Bah!" he said wrathfully, getting up from his seat. "I will shake this city upside down from one end to the other until we find her. If she is not in this city, I will over-turn every blade of grass and dig out every foxhole outside it. I will post a reward so huge babes in arms would turn in their mothers and our poor, mad King will want to inspect his own cellar. Enough!!"

It was a declaration of war. What good was all the fortune at his command if he could not protect the woman he loved? "I will offer five hundred thousand pounds for her safe re-turn and the culprit who has taken her."

William's mouth opened. It was ten times the sum of a huge lottery prize, six times a rich duke's annual income. "My God, man. You will bankrupt yourself."

"I will start with my own servants." Not bothering to ring, Ren stalked to the door of the library and bellowed. "Hajee! I want all staff in the dining room, *now!*" The fierce sound reverberated through the house and set feet running.

Within minutes, the small army of servants who bore the responsibility of running Milbourne House were assembled in the dining room with their master before them. Frothwick was not among them. Ren sent Nuseer to find the fellow and then explained to the rest what had happened, and what he was planning to do.

"There has been mischief aplenty going on in this house, as all of you are aware," Ren told them. "But this time a young woman's life is at stake. If any of you know or so much as think you might know something, anything, that could help, for God's sake, I am begging you to step forward and promising you more than ample reward."

Frothwick's absence among them was glaring. Where

was he? Why had he disappeared? Did he know something, after all? Ren feared he had made a terrible mistake.

As he stood in front of the others studying their faces, another set of running feet could be heard on the service stairs and then in the passageway behind the room. A voice called out "Halloo?" and "Where is everyone?". It was not Nuseer or Frothwick. Puzzled faces turned to the door. A moment later, Taylor burst into the room.

"Oh, sir! They've nabbed Miss Parbury! They've took her into the heart of St. Giles, but I know where she is." He was breathless and spent—he had obviously been running even before he had entered the house. "I 'ad to come back through Seven Dials to see iffen I couldn't 'elp James, her lackey. They knocked the poor cull in the head and dumped 'im out at th' top o' an alley—I figured he'd be stripped naked and dead iffen I didn't stop back there."

The boy's struggle to get himself back to Grosvenor Square in the fastest possible time had no doubt been a major undertaking. Ren wanted to hug him, but instead he bade him sit. "Catch your breath first, then out with it all. Someone fetch the lad something to drink!"

It took only minutes more to hear Taylor's story. He had been lurking about Great Marlborough Street keeping an eye on Miss Parbury's residence, as had become his usual afternoon's occupation. He had picked up a few pence holding horses and such when he saw Miss Parbury leave the house with her footman. Following them, he had witnessed their abduction and had jumped onto the back of the carriage.

"Them's got Miss Parbury in a warehouse near the brewery, in a court off Castle Street," Taylor said, "but I don't know as they'll stay there!"

Ren heard the note of anguish in the boy's voice and realized Taylor was almost as distraught as he was.

"Was she unharmed?"

Taylor nodded. "When I left."

It was a painfully honest answer. Time was more than precious now. "How many of the villains?"

"Two. I didn't see no more coves inside, but I wouldn't say for certain."

Ren began to issue orders right and left. He sent Selim to fetch Ranee and two footmen to fetch hackneys, for he deemed it unwise to take a gleaming, fancy carriage into the most criminal part of the city. "Ahmed, I want you and Nuseer with me. One of you can ride on the box. Taylor must show us the place, and Selim can mind the cat. Good luck to anyone who tries to flee! William, I imagine you will want to squeeze in with us—the boys can take the floor. As many of the rest of you who will—follow us in the second coach. Make certain your driver does not lose sight of us!"

As the servants scrambled to their tasks, Nuseer returned clutching Frothwick by a handful of the coat on his back. In Hindustani Nuseer informed Ren that he had found the old butler packing his belongings into a bag in his room.

Furious, Ren grabbed the fellow by his cravat. "What do you know about this, old man?" He guessed that William's outburst upon arriving had frightened the butler into a panic. "Speak now or you'll wish the law had got hold of you instead of me."

Chapter Nineteen

In the back room of a warehouse deep in St. Giles, Mariah tipped her head back against the wall and closed her eyes, willing her mind to rest. The fear, the heightened awareness of every muscle in her body that hurt, and the constant wariness of watching for a chance to help herself were taking their toll on her.

She had already schooled herself not to think about what might become of James, dumped out of the coach unconscious in the worst part of London. She knew she must not think of Lord Milbourne, either, lest despair overwhelm her. Stopping those thoughts was hardest of all.

She was not certain what her part was in someone's evil plan, but she was convinced that whatever it was had to do with hurting the marquess. Was she meant to join the other dead souls who haunted his heart? For his sake even more than her own, she must continue to think of how to escape and watch for a chance. She must not become fully exhausted. She would need to have the energy to act if and when an opportunity to escape arose. There was no one else who could help her.

Her abductors had not seriously harmed her—she hurt from their rough handling, the ropes that bound her, and the hardness of the wood beneath and behind her. She was still waiting for them to leave her alone so that she might test her bonds. She had flexed her arms and expanded her chest with as big a breath as she could hold when they had bound her, hoping to create some slack when she drew herself in. If she could wriggle free, she would thank God till her dying day for granting her the small hands and thin arms she had often bemoaned.

"Look, our pretty dell is stealin' a snooze on us," she heard one of the men say. "I didn't think we'd left 'er so comfortable as all that."

She heard his chair scrape, but forced herself to keep her eyes closed, praying that he wouldn't touch her.

"Leave 'er be," said the other man. "My guts think my throat's cut—let's go get our grub. We should be lookin' out fer the swell, too."

Mariah thought "swell" meant a gentleman. Had they set a trap for the marquess? She *must* get loose! She heard the second villain get up and both men go clumping out of the room. The instant the door shut, she began to work at wriggling her hands and arms into some position even remotely useful. If she could move enough to reach any of the knots in the rope, she could do this.

Little by little, Mariah worked herself free. Her ears strained for sounds from the outer room as she did so, and she prayed the men would not return too soon. Just what her next step would be, she did not yet know.

When she finally got one arm free, it was a matter of seconds to loosen the rest and drop the rope quietly to the floor. She got up from her knees and stepped cautiously across the room to the door, praying that neither floor nor door would squeak and give her away. She peeked out into the next room, a cavernous part of the warehouse with piles of boxes that would give her some shelter. Did she dare to open the door enough to dash through? She could not see the men, which made her extremely uneasy. But did she have any choice?

As silently as she could manage, she pushed the door wider and slipped through, hiding behind the first pile of crates. She moved from one pile to the next, advancing through the room, until she could see the men eating at a small table in the open center of the storeroom. God, she was hungry, too! The smell of their cheese reawakened another discomfort she had managed to quiet for a while. She wondered how much time had passed since they had snatched her and James in Little Argyle Street.

Beyond them Mariah recognized the door that led to the stairway. If she was lucky, both men would go back to check on her when they finished their meal, and her path to freedom would be clear. Outside, she could hide again and stop Lord Milbourne before he entered their trap. If only they would eat faster! They were talking as much about getting the balance of their pay as they were chewing their food. She had sensed from the start that this was only a job to them—that her Fate meant nothing. Whoever was behind this cared deeply, to go to so much trouble and expense. The thought made her shiver.

So far luck was with her. She did not even wait for them to reach the other room when they finally finished and headed back in that direction. Moving quickly but on tiptoe, she had almost reached the door when it opened.

Fear leaped into her throat. But as soon as she saw who was there a flood of relief washed it away. "Oh, thank heavens! Mr. Carrisforte," she whispered, unable to stop herself from hugging him. She put a finger to her lips and nodded her head in the direction of the other room. "There are men in the back. Hurry!" she added, taking in his look of surprise. "Is Lord Milbourne with you? It is a trap!"

His look of surprise had changed to one of horror, but still he stood blocking the way. "Miss Parbury," he said, "this was not part of the plan at all."

She only began to understand when he gripped her arm and turned her around to face back into the room.

"No, I'm afraid that Lord Milbourne is not here, nor do I expect him—at least not until I have things arranged for him," he said, pushing her toward the center space. "Cully, Robbins! Where the devil are you? Your bird almost flew. I've got her here."

"Ho!" they answered.

"You're hurting me," she said as his grip on her arm tightened.

"Please accept my apologies," he answered. He did not relax his hand, and Mariah realized then that his apology was meant to cover more—much more. "Let me assure you that this is nothing personal."

The two men appeared, looking slightly embarrassed, if such a thing were possible. "We figured she was hiding in them piles, so we was looking for 'er quietlike."

Bone-deep fear made Mariah desperate. "Listen to me!" she blurted out. "The man he wants to harm has far more money than he does—Lord Milbourne will pay you any sum you name if you will help me!"

An instant later Mr. Carrisforte's hand cracked her across the face. Pain seared through her jaw and stars danced before her eyes. She almost swooned.

"She's lying to you," he told the other men. "Let's get on with this. Cully, clean up any evidence we've left in the other room. Robbins, watch the door."

Dragging her with him, he moved to a box that sat open near the table where the men had eaten. She put her free hand to her mouth and felt blood there.

"This should do nicely," Carrisforte said, bending slightly to take something from the box.

She tried to break free, but he straightened up and pulled her against him. " 'Tis a shame, I always liked you," he said. "I never intended for us to meet face-to-face here. You should not have tried to escape!"

She looked up into his face and the glitter she saw in his eyes struck more fear and alarm into her heart than anything she had ever felt. Was this the same man she had thought she knew?

It was then she saw the dagger in his hand and recognized it as the same one Lord Milbourne had shown her on the night of her tour. How long ago that seemed now! Like a dream, except that what was happening at this moment felt even more unreal. In the box she saw other articles that she recognized from Milbourne House. She simply could not understand.

"Why are you doing this? I thought you were his friend!"

"We do have a long history," he said. "And we *were* friends, in the beginning."

He pushed her down into one of the chairs. "You made a

mistake to fall in love with him, although you are not the first. Even Shakespeare knew, 'The hind that would be mated by the lion/must die for love.' So true!" He laughed.

She stared at him, horrified. "*You* killed Shanti."

He withdrew the dagger from its jeweled sheath. "Yes, I learned my lesson the first time. Accidents leave too much to chance—too messy."

Dear Lord. So he had even been behind the death of the marquess's first fiancée.

"Was the poison a mistake?" Perhaps if she could distract him enough with talking she could find a moment in which to bolt. Thank God he had not tied her!

"Oh, no, not at all. You might have taken that as a warning, but no—you clove to him even more! It will prove just as useful to let it appear as his first attempt to kill you. Even with the rumors that was not quite enough to convince people, but that was my intention. This time, however, he will have succeeded, and they will all believe it."

"What makes you think you will get away with this?"

He laughed again. "It worked the last time. And this will be exactly the same, only this time he will be found in the fire, too."

Tears pooled in her eyes, but they did not lessen her anger. "Why would you kill him now, after all that you have done to make him suffer?"

"He is too protected here, the high-and-mighty marquess. And you are a baron's daughter. There would be a thorough investigation, not just a cursory one. His denials might be believed. There is more risk to me here than in India."

He glanced down at the blade of the dagger, perhaps taking note of its odd form. Mariah threw herself out of the chair and tried to run, but he grabbed her by the arm and yanked her back, shoving her into the chair. It rocked with the force of his push and nearly tipped over.

"Don't make this harder than it already is," he shouted at her. She had made him very angry.

"Why do it? Why do you hate him so much?" she asked quietly. The tears were running down her face now, and she did not try to stop them.

"He has had everything handed to him. Look at what he has! He won all the prizes in school. His skills were so superior at Hailey Bury they did not have him bother to finish! He spent only months as a clerk-writer in Calcutta before he was promoted to a position translating for the surveying teams. Most men spend years—sometimes half their career—as lowly writers before they can advance in the company! Wealth, prestige, women—everything came easily to him.

"Even after I robbed him of his women and made him suffer, look what became of him! He ran away to Lampur and became the raja's darling—loaded with treasure and wealth beyond dreaming! Anything a man could want! Small wonder he resented having to come home to lowly England and condescend to become a marquess. How could I *not* hate him, standing in his shadow? We started out together and we became farther and farther apart."

Clearly, Carrisforte had suffered his own kind of anguish for many years. His jealousy had hardened into a consuming hatred.

"I guess she weren't lyin'," said Robbins, the man who was supposed to be guarding the door. He had left his post and now stood halfway between it and where Mariah and her nemesis were in the center of the open space. Apparently he had taken in every word of Carrisforte's confession and was rethinking his position.

His interruption distracted Carrisforte, and Mariah made one more desperate attempt to save herself. She leaped up but instead of running she seized the wooden chair and swung it at Carrisforte, hoping to knock him down.

He dodged quickly and the chair glanced off his shoulder. Knocking it out of her hands, he lunged at her. As she tried to fend him off, he got a grip on her wrist. He waved the knife in his other hand.

"No, no, Miss Parbury. There will be no escape."

"Help me!" she called to the other man standing by watching. She made a grab for Carrisforte's hand with the knife and managed to lock onto his wrist. Speed and an element of surprise were what she needed, for she had not the advantage of strength. His wrist was so much larger than hers! She could not hold on for long.

They engaged in a desperate dance at arm's length, he trying to overcome her, she resisting. As Carrisforte pressed his advantage she retreated, allowing him to back her toward the nearest pile of crates. If she could just hold out long enough! At the moment her back touched against it, she suddenly relaxed her arm.

The dagger in his hand slammed against the wood. Triggered by the blow, the multiple blades sprang out. In the same instant, Mariah ducked down and sideways under his other arm, wrenching her wrist free. She heard him cry out as she went. Caught by surprise and carried by his own momentum, Carrisforte had fallen on the knife.

With a moan he slid to the floor, and suddenly there was a great deal of blood. Mariah covered her face with her hands. He had left her no choice, but that fact did not lessen the horror. She was appalled and sickened.

"Nice move, dearie!" said Robbins admiringly. "Pluck to the bone! I can see why your marquess sets a store by you. But I can't let you go—Cully an' me's got to get our pay someway. Bet he'll pay plenty to get you back."

However, as he spoke there was noise on the stairs and the door opened behind him. Mariah looked up and saw Lord Milbourne rushing in.

"I would pay gladly, but not to the likes of you!" he told Robbins. "Seize him," he called to the small army who poured in behind him.

"Mariah, are you all right?" It was William. "Dear God," he added in a whisper when he saw Carrisforte lying on the floor with his blood pooling around him.

Nuseer and the boys had come in, with Ranee on her leash. Several more footmen and assorted persons were still coming in behind them.

"There's another man in the back room, or by now he may be hiding among the crates," Mariah said. "I don't know what has become of him."

"Flush him out, fellows," directed the marquess, waving

an arm at the warehouse in general. "Selim, use Ranee. If he tries to run, let her have him."

This was too much for Robbins, who was now sweating profusely. "Cully! Them's got a tiger!"

Taylor walked up to the man and kicked him in the shin. "That's a *cheetah,* you hulking piece of hung beef!"

In the meantime, Lord Milbourne approached Mariah. Just seeing him caused a new freshet of tears to spill down her cheeks. How could he look at her so tenderly when she was dirty, bloodied, and tearstained? Love swelled in her heart. But the mixed terror and relief of what she had just been through and the revulsion and aching sadness she felt when she looked at Carrisforte combined to overwhelm her. She began to tremble.

"Carrisforte—"

"I know. It is all over—it is all right now." He enfolded her in his arms and just held her there against him. She felt safe and protected. "You are a wonder," he murmured into her hair.

He continued to hold her as his servants returned with Cully, who apparently had surrendered meekly rather than face a race with Ranee.

William squatted beside Carrisforte and examined his wounds. "I'm afraid there's nothing to be done for him," he said, shaking his head.

The marquess lifted his own head to look at his fallen friend, but he did not release Mariah. "Why, Carris, why? That is what I do not understand." Even as he looked, Carrisforte shuddered and lay still.

Mariah buried her face against Lord Milbourne's shoulder. "He was going to kill me. You, too. We struggled, and he was struck by the knife." She was still for a moment, trying to overcome the horror of it. "He was jealous of you. He told it all to me. Do you want to know?"

"No. Well, yes, someday, but not today, not now. There will be days ahead of us when you can tell me."

"He was not expecting you—he said he was not ready for you. How did you know to come, and where?"

The marquess tightened his protective arms around her

and smiled, although it was a smile tinged with sadness for the loss of his friend. "Your shadow, yet again. Taylor was following you and saw the abduction. He hopped onto the back of the carriage that took you and rode it all the way here. Then he made his way back to Grosvenor Square to summon us."

He sighed. "It was Frothwick who told me Carris was behind it all—he sent the mystery mail and was paying the old fool to steal from me and to create aggravation in whatever ways he could. I never suspected. Most especially I never suspected Carris."

He held her close and rested his head against the top of hers, as if he drew some comfort from her. "If Frothwick had not decided to sell a few of the stolen items on the side, I still would not have known. I cannot begin to guess how much the sight that greeted us here would have shocked me. By God, I am so glad you are safe. But you are not unharmed."

He pulled back enough to look down into her face again and gently traced the path of her tears along one cheek. His finger stopped at her lip. "He struck you, the bloody bastard. And inflicted a nightmare upon you that only time will erase." There was a tremor of dangerous anger in his voice. "I think it is just as well for him that he is already dead."

She put her hand up to touch his and their fingers met and entwined. He brushed his lips across the back of her hand, ever so briefly. Then, abruptly, he released her.

"This is no place for you to be. And your family are waiting, worrying. William, take your sister home."

On the way to Great Marlborough Street, William warned Mariah that there had been no time to send word to their parents.

"They knew I went off to seek you at Milbourne House, and have heard nothing more since then. They will be shocked when they see you in such a state, and may jump to wrong conclusions before we can explain."

He paused awkwardly and cleared his throat. "I'm afraid I let the cat out of the bag about your having visited there before. And now with this, I do not know what they are going to think."

"I think we must do whatever is necessary to get the marquess to marry me," she answered, speaking as much to herself as to William. She knew now that Lord Milbourne loved her, even if he had never spoken the words. The message had been clear there in the warehouse, in his arms and in his eyes. With Carrisforte gone, could he bring himself to reopen his heart? Could she make him?

Mariah's mother burst into tears the moment she saw her. The Parburys had all gathered anxiously in their drawing room, and when William and Mariah walked through the door, they were instantly surrounded by a circle of loving, albeit sometimes misguided, parents and sisters. Mariah could not help thinking of the marquess. Here was more family than she could sometimes cope with, all his for the sharing if she could only convince him to marry her.

Explanations were offered and questions asked, reassurances given. William told them that James was safe and would be returned, discreetly withholding the information that Taylor had put him into the care of a group of ladies in the nearest bawdy house to where the poor footman had been abandoned.

"We owe a tremendous debt to this boy, Taylor, for Mariah's rescue. We must do something for him," Lady Parbury said, finally calmer after her initial reactions. "Although I must say I still do not understand how he came to be involved."

With a sigh, Mariah decided to confess the rest of her misdeeds. There would never be a better time, for how could things possibly get worse? When she finished, she could see that even William was amazed. Georgie, her silent confidante, stepped up and hugged her.

"Mariah, you and I have some things to discuss," her father said. "However, it can wait. What you need at this moment is to be bathed and pampered and put to bed. I will meet with you in my bookroom first thing in the morning."

Chapter Twenty

Mariah was visiting with Harriet Pritchard in her bedroom when Lord Milbourne called at the Parburys' the next day. Carrisforte's duplicity shocked Harry so deeply, there was no room left for any regrets.

"To think he knew exactly where you were and what was happening the whole time he calmly suggested we wait for you at my house! And then! If you could have seen the sympathy and concern he showed to your family! He fetched William for them, and when he took me home he was so reassuring. He must have left me directly to go to you. When I received your message last evening, I couldn't have been more astounded."

Her eyes filled with tears, for the third time. "Oh, Mariah, when I think what almost happened!"

"Ah, but it did not, Harry, and today I am as right as rain, as long as I do not think about what did happen." Mariah gave her a quick reassuring hug just as Bennett appeared in the doorway to announced Lord Milbourne.

No one had the slightest objection to allowing the marquess to take Mariah for a drive.

"I will simply toddle on home," Harry said graciously down in the entry hall where her maid was waiting. She whispered, "Good luck!" and held up crossed fingers as she kissed Mariah good-bye.

"This may be the last time you will see Selim riding as tiger on my curricle," the marquess said as he helped Mariah into the carriage a few minutes later. "He is getting too big for the position, so we will be training his replacement."

"But I thought he loved the job!" Mariah protested. A

twinkle in Lord Milbourne's handsome eyes made her suddenly suspicious. "Who have you . . . Taylor! Have you given the job to him?"

The marquess snapped the reins and started the horses away from the curb. "It seemed the least I could offer, after all that he had done for us."

He paused, his expression serious again. "I only wish there was some way I could undo everything that Carrisforte made you suffer. I fear the memories will stay with you forever."

As the carriage retraced her route of the previous day up Argyle heading for Oxford Street, she knew it was probably true. When they passed the corner of Little Argyle Street, she shuddered.

"I have been trying not to think about it," she admitted. "But I must know what you did after William and I left. What will become of Robbins and Cully? And of Carrisforte?"

"We summoned the authorities, and handed it all over to them. We explained that we had thwarted the men in an attempted crime, and that Carris had been slain in a struggle. I made it clear that discretion was required in the case. I doubt that Robbins or Cully will care to give too many details—it will only make them look worse. The police will have to notify Carrisforte's family."

The sadness in his voice touched her deeply. Intending to comfort him, she said, "What he did to me was nothing compared to what he has made you suffer over the years. At least it is over now."

When she saw the question in his face she knew that he still did not understand the full magnitude of his friend's betrayal. It was best for him to know it all. "It was Mr. Carrisforte who killed Shanti and set the fire that terrible night."

She could hardly bear the look of pain and realization that came into his eyes, but from this day on, she thought he could begin to heal.

"My first love's accident—was he behind that, too?"

She nodded. "I am so sorry."

He shook his head. "I cannot believe it. We were friends

for so many years. How did I not know? I might have saved her and Shanti."

"You must not go on blaming yourself. He fooled everyone! He should have gone for a career on the stage."

"It is a shame he did not apply himself as diligently to his own career—he might have made a success of himself."

"It explains why he was so familiar with the details of your tragic history. It was he who told me the full story, since you would not. I needed to know. And even then, I did not guess! But there was one part I could not believe."

"What part was that?"

"When he said Shanti did not want to marry you. No woman who was that close to you could possibly resist the idea."

"I believe you may be overstating the case. But might I dare to hope from that bold statement that if I asked *you* to marry me, you might not refuse me?"

"Are you asking me?"

"No. For one thing, I may soon be a pauper. I promised to pay a reward of five hundred thousand pounds for your safe return yesterday."

"Good heavens!" She searched his face, hoping he was jesting. She thought the twinkle had returned to his eyes, but she knew she might only be imagining it out of her own hopes.

"I offered it to Taylor, who surely earned it by his vigilance and bravery. And do you know what he said? 'Now what would I do wi' five hundred thou?.' " His perfect imitation of Taylor's speech made her giggle.

"He said I'd best keep it, or else give it to you. He pointed out that to a large degree, you had saved yourself. You do realize, of course, that what you did was very brave, my dear. Perhaps you have discovered at last that you have within you enough spirit and courage for ten ordinary people."

Mariah was smiling. "Now who is overstating the case? However, I might consider accepting the reward. If you give it to me, then perhaps you will ask me to marry you after all, since you'll be needing a wife with a suitable portion. Would you marry me for my fortune?"

"No."

He was silent for a moment, and she bit back her disappointment. If he meant to offer for her, had she not just given him the perfect opportunity?

They were not yet near the park, but suddenly he slowed the horses. He turned them into the narrow entrance to a mews and stopped the carriage there. "Not for a fortune, and not for the sake of the entire city's opinion. But I would marry you if I loved you and found I could not bear to live without you."

He tipped her face up to his and Mariah discovered that she was holding her breath. "Let me see if that could possibly be the case."

He kissed her then, very gently and carefully because of her sore lip, but long—oh, for so very long. Mariah clung to him and could not believe the number and variety of sensations that began to erupt like fireworks inside her. Nor could she believe how greatly those intensified when he trailed kisses along her jaw and down her neck, and when his hand began to massage the tired muscles in her back. She almost cried out when suddenly he stopped.

"Yes, that is it. Marry me, Miss Mariah Parbury. I need you. I love you with all my heart. I love you more than I have ever loved anyone, and I never thought such a thing could be possible. Please, please, say you will marry me."

She laughed in delight, her heart filled with joy. "Of course I will. My only fear was that you would never ask." She hugged him, wishing they could sit where they were for hours longer.

"It will have to be by special license, which I have every intention of applying for tomorrow," he said. "I do not intend to wait through a lengthy period of betrothal. After all, we have already endured a brief courtship. How much more gossip-fodder need we provide?"

He kissed her again, she supposed just in case she needed convincing—which of course she did not.

"You do realize that both Harry and William will think

they can claim credit for bringing us together," she said when they stopped to draw breath.

"Not to mention Taylor. And then there is Hajee. When I look back upon his actions, I think I see that he was working toward this in his own way. I don't doubt now that he was making offerings and praying to his gods about us every day."

"You will be gaining an entire family," she warned.

"And I hope we will soon add to it." As she watched, she saw moisture come into his eyes. "I had given up all hope of a future like this."

"And I had never dared to dream of such a one."

They held each other close, reveling in their love and the happiness they had found in each other. She could barely believe even now that the magnificent marquess would be hers. This time, it was she who initiated their kiss. The park, and the world, could wait for another day.